"K ... ots
an ... kly

"Ms. Kane creates all her chara ... sur-
rounds them with action, great dialogue and strong feelings of love."
—*Rendezvous*

"Kathleen Kane infuses her novels with the wonderful sense of warmth and sweetness that makes you feel toasty right down to your toes."
—*Romantic Times*

Wish Upon a Cowboy

"Kane's remarkable storytelling talents shine once again in this captivating and wonderful tale that showcases love's amazing power to triumph over evil and heal wounded souls. A rare and delicious treat to savor . . . will make you laugh out loud and fill your heart with warmth." —*Romantic Times*

"Ms. Kane tickles your funny bone and waves her magic wand to insure a good time is had by all. Missed spells and thunderstorms whet your imagination. As Ms. Kane reminds us, 'Witchcraft is not important . . . Love is the greatest power in the universe.' Bravo!"
—*Rendezvous*

"Kane blends folk legend and magic into a charming . . . plot."
—*Publishers Weekly*

Catch a Fallen Angel

"Offers . . . readers highly unusual characters and a clever plot, which add up to a surprisingly charming story of redemption."
—*Booklist*

"Once again, Kane gives readers an extraordinary story that will warm your heart with a tear and a smile. She is an expert at playing upon our emotions, and as always, pens a captivating soul-stirring tale."
—*Romantic Times*

"Ms. Kane writes beautiful stories that will live in the heart forever."
—*Bell, Book & Candle*

St. Martin's Paperbacks Titles
by Kathleen Kane

JUST WEST OF HEAVEN

CATCH A FALLEN ANGEL

WISH UPON A COWBOY

SIMPLY MAGIC

DREAMWEAVER

THIS TIME FOR KEEPS

STILL CLOSE TO HEAVEN

THE SOUL COLLECTOR

When The Halo Falls

KATHLEEN KANE

St. Martin's Paperbacks

WHEN THE HALO FALLS

ISBN: 0-312-97842-1

Printed in the United States of America

St. Martin's Paperbacks edition / February 2002

St. Martin's Paperbacks are published by St. Martin's Press, 175 Fifth Avenue, New York, NY 10010.

10 9 8 7 6 5 4 3 2 1

CHAPTER ONE

FORTUNE, NEW MEXICO, 1885

"There's no point in rumbling thunder at me," Patience Goodfellow muttered, throwing a dark look heavenward. "You sent me here and I'll handle the assignment as I please."

Overhead, the night sky shimmered with banked lightning hidden behind a wall of clouds rolling across the star-studded blackness. Wind kicked up out of nowhere, sending dust devils dancing across the wide main street of Fortune.

Deliberately, Patience reached up and gave her halo a defiant tilt. Heaven knew, she'd gone toe to toe with her superiors on more than one occasion over the last couple of centuries. Yet they still sometimes resorted to tawdry displays of power in a futile attempt to intimidate her.

Which was most certainly a waste of their time and hers. Patience was not a woman—er, angel—to back down from any situation in which she thought she was right. And with that thought firmly in mind, she turned her back on the heavenly temper tantrum and moved off down the dark street.

For pity's sake, she thought. One would think one

would have the support of one's superiors when one was confronted with a problem, wouldn't one? She scowled to herself and wondered if perhaps she hadn't thrown one too many "ones" into that thought. Then she dismissed the whole notion along with the still-rumbling heavens. "Ask a simple question and you get enough noise to wake the dead," she murmured.

Rain pattered all around her, but Patience remained as dry and warm as she had for more than two hundred years. She turned her face up and imagined the cool, slick feel of raindrops sliding down her cheeks. Opening her eyes, she frowned slightly, then shrugged. True, she sometimes missed the simple pleasures of being alive. But on the other hand, there were certainly compensations—her dress wasn't soiled, her hair wasn't soaking wet, and she certainly didn't have to worry about stepping into a puddle.

Still, indulging her mind in its attempt to wander wasn't solving her problem. "And you were absolutely no help," she muttered again, shooting one last disgusted glance skyward.

All she'd wanted was a touch of advice. But as expected, she'd only received the usual sorry speech about free will. "What in heaven is the purpose of assigning guardian angels to human beings if we're not allowed to interfere in their best interests?"

And heaven knew, Brady Shaw, gambler, womanizer, and all-around bounder, desperately needed guidance. A flicker of warmth stirred in her heart as she drew the man's image up in her mind. She'd been Brady's guardian angel since he was eleven years old. And by the time she was assigned to him, he'd already worn out three perfectly good angels. Her predecessors had given up on him, but even when he was a child, Patience had seen something noble in Brady. Something that had touched her heart and made her want to do anything in her power to help him. Now that he was a man, though, that streak was buried so deeply inside him, she wasn't sure that even he knew it existed anymore.

"But it does," Patience muttered firmly, refusing to accept the alternative. She'd watched him grow, seen him make poor choices and recover again only to make more of the same. She'd ached to help him. She'd whispered advice in his ear, as guardians often did, but he'd chosen not to listen. And now he was so firmly entrenched in his solitude, she wasn't at all sure she could make him hear her anymore.

"Which is exactly why I asked permission to show myself to him," she snapped, knowing very well that heaven was still listening.

A bolt of lightning scratched the sky and a rumble of thunder shook the wooden buildings around her. "Pestilence!" she muttered and tried to kick at a rock in her path. Naturally, her foot sailed right through the obstacle, which only infuriated her more.

After all, it wasn't as if she would be the first angel in history to be seen. Hadn't there been annunciations and proclamations for untold centuries? And hadn't mankind always benefited from them? For pity's sake, all she wanted to do was show Brady that he wasn't alone.

But even as she thought it, she knew that wasn't the whole truth. Which was, most likely, the problem on high.

She loved Brady Shaw. Always had. And she suspected everyone in heaven knew it. From the moment she first saw him, it was as if their souls had touched. As if they'd been meant to be together. Although, of course, that could never be. It was forbidden for an angel, especially a guardian angel, to fall in love with the mortal in their charge.

But there had been rumors, over the centuries, that some angels had found love where it was least expected. So it wasn't at all surprising that her superiors didn't want Patience revealing herself to Brady. No matter how desperately he might need her. And he did need her, she thought, feeling that ache in her heart again.

Sighing, she continued on down the street, toward the closed and shuttered dress shop. As she did most nights, she glided directly through the wall of the small store and wandered among the stacks of merchandise.

A purely feminine ribbon of want rippled through Patience as she admired all of the finery. When she was alive, she'd worn mostly black with the occasional gray dress—like the one she was wearing now—to liven things up. But then, that was hardly surprising. When she was alive, the Pilgrims, as so many people thought of her people today, were much too busy trying to stay alive in a hostile new country to worry overmuch about their appearance. Besides, as she recalled, the elders of her church had considered "fripperies" to be just a bit decadent.

So much had changed over the last two hundred years, she thought with an inward sigh of regret that she couldn't take advantage of those changes. Today, there were so many lovely colors for women to choose from. So many different types of adornment.

And once again, her imagination took flight. She saw herself as Brady's fiancée, strolling arm in arm with him along the dusty street, nodding to their friends, smiling secretively at each other—happily planning a wedding that would be just lovely. So clear was the dream, she could almost feel his hand on hers, sense the warmth of his touch, the shine in his eyes.

Then her own eyes opened again and she was alone in the darkness, surrounded by fripperies she would never wear. Regrets fluttered through her and Patience sighed heavily, shifting her gaze to the hats lining one wall of the store. In among the straws and velvets, she spied a froth of white lace attached to a crown of artificial pink roses.

"Oh," she said softly, moving toward it. "Isn't it lovely?" A bridal veil. Patience had never been a bride, though she'd attended many weddings over the last two hundred years—never as a guest, of course. Merely an observer. Her gaze moved over the cloth flowers and she had to marvel at the genius behind them. Imagine, being able to have the beauty of spring flowers all year round. And what a delicate touch the milliner had displayed in attaching the lace to those flowers, she thought, already reaching for it.

Her hand, though, slipped right through the delicate material. She frowned thoughtfully and stared down at her empty hand. One more disappointment this night. But perhaps . . . Giving in to temptation, Patience tossed a quick look around the empty, dark shop, as if checking to be assured she was alone.

"Silly," she said, with a guilty chuckle. "Who would be watching?" She turned toward a long, oval mirror and studied her reflection. After all, just because no human was able to see an angel's reflection didn't mean it wasn't there.

A tall woman with long, curly black hair stared back at her. Her long, gray dress was, she supposed, serviceable, though hardly attractive, though she really couldn't blame its effect entirely on the fabric. Her figure was hardly lush, after all. Small breasts, narrow hips, a too long neck—no, even in life, Patience had never been one to stir up feelings of lust in men.

Although she'd once been called a "handsome woman" and had never really been sure if that was a compliment or not. After all, men were handsome, weren't they? But as she studied her own good, but unremarkable features, she wondered what Brady would think of her.

Shaking her head, she reached up and plucked the shimmering golden halo off her head. As soon as she did, she waited, half expecting another lightning bolt to shoot right through the roof and sizzle her on the spot. Halos were never to be removed. Without a halo, an angel was visible—and in trouble. Guiltily, she set it to one side and watched as the glow of heavenly light dimmed, leaving it looking like no more than a tarnished brass circlet. She waited another moment or two and when retribution didn't come crashing out of the sky, Patience determinedly reached for the veil again. This time, her fingers curled around the rose wreath firmly and Patience set it carefully atop her head. The pink flowers stood out in stark relief against her black, curly hair and she smiled to herself, imagining walking down a flower-strewn church aisle toward a grinning Brady.

White lace billowed around her shoulders and bunched up beneath her ears. Patience tried unsuccessfully to smooth it down then gave the excess lace a tug. But it appeared to be stuck beneath the mountain of hatboxes piled on the tabletop. It didn't budge. She tugged again, scowling fiercely at the stubborn bit of lace. How could she possibly get the full effect of how she looked if the confounded material wasn't in place correctly?

Giving one more mighty yank, Patience smiled when the veil flew free, pulling the bottom box on the stack askew at the same time. The lace settled gently around her shoulders, but she had no more than a moment to enjoy her reflection. In the next instant, the dislodged pile of boxes toppled over. She ducked instinctively, but the heaviest of the lot smacked into Patience's head and stars burst in front of her eyes.

She groaned tightly and fell to one side, her elbow tipping the halo off the edge of the table. Patience lay still and quiet on the littered floor and the halo rolled away, off into the shadows.

Brady Shaw picked up his cup of coffee and glanced over the ledger. Profits were up, but the nightly fights in the saloon were cutting into the take. He'd already had to replace the mirror behind the bar twice this week and one of his best bottles of brandy had been used to club Mick Donovan's thick head.

He smiled, remembering how the barrel-chested miner had roared, "*For God's sake, man, don't waste the good stuff,*" just before plowing his hamlike fist into his attacker's face.

"You want me to get another mirror out of the storeroom, boss?" a voice asked from off to his left.

Brady half turned to look at Joe Dawson, the bartender. An ex–prize fighter, the man was always willing to wade into trouble. And for his efforts last night, his left eye was swollen nearly shut.

"Yeah, Joe," Brady said. "Go ahead."

"We're down to our last two, boss."

"I know. You can go over to the Mercantile later and order another half dozen."

"Gettin' mighty expensive keepin' those mirrors up over the bar."

"Yeah," Brady agreed with a smile. "But it gives the place some class."

"If you say so." Joe shrugged and shuffled off to the storeroom, apparently unconvinced of the gentility of the Fortune's Own saloon.

Not that Brady could blame him any. It wasn't class his customers were looking for when they came through those double doors. It was liquor, women, and poker. Not necessarily in that order.

And Brady was pleased to supply all three. Of course, he thought, with a glance at the staircase leading to the half-dozen rooms on the second story, the ladies here just rented rooms from him. What they did with their time was their business. As long as they paid their rent the first of every month, he was happy.

Taking up his coffee cup again, he came out from behind the bar and walked across the room to the front windows. Staring out at Main Street as it slowly came to life, he thought about that for a minute. Happy.

He squinted into the morning sunlight and considered the word. Well, hell, he wasn't *un*happy, so he must be happy. Right?

"Who're you?"

Patience stirred and winced as her body complained about the night spent on the cold, hard wooden floor. Every inch of her ached and there seemed to be a marching band trooping through her head. She lifted one hand to her forehead and found a knot the size of a walnut. For pity's sake. What had happened?

"Lady?" the voice asked again. "You all right?"

She opened one eye and stared up into the face of a boy no more than ten. His too long brown hair fell across his forehead, and from behind that curtain, big brown eyes watched her curiously.

"Davey," she said slowly, then more surely as her mind began to clear. "Davey Howard."

His eyes widened and he stared at her as if she'd grown another head. Well, whatever was wrong with the boy? She squirmed around until she was sitting up, then shoved the fall of lace out of her face. "What am I doing here?" she asked the boy, not really expecting a reply, since he seemed to have been stricken dumb.

"Ma'am," he said and swallowed hard enough that it looked as though he were trying to dislodge a chicken bone from his throat. "If you don't mind me askin', who are you?"

She pulled her head back and stared at him. For one brief, horrifying moment, she wasn't entirely sure she'd be able to answer that question, then her mind righted itself and she blurted, "For pity's sakes Davey, it's me."

"Yes, ma'am," he agreed, "I can see that. But *who* are you?"

What on earth was the child talking about? He knew her every bit as well as she knew him. Davey Howard, ten years old, an orphan, poor child. He survived by doing odd jobs for the storekeepers in town. Which is why he was here at the dress shop so early in the morning. To sweep up and straighten before the store opened for customers. He was an industrious boy with a good heart and a yearning for family, and she'd known him for—well, she frowned thoughtfully, forever, it seemed.

"I'm Patience, of course," she said, reaching up to tug the annoying piece of lace from atop her head. She barely glanced at the bridal veil before tossing it to one side. "Patience Goodfellow."

"Uh-huh." He still looked at her strangely and she could only guess that he'd decided, for whatever reason, to pretend to not know her.

She smiled at him and wagged one finger in his direction. "I'm in no mood for games this morning, Davey. Would you mind helping me up?"

"Yes, ma'am," he said and took her hand in both of his.

The feel of those small, callused hands took her briefly by surprise, but Patience disregarded the notion and concentrated on extricating herself from the pile of boxes. Once on her feet again, she looked around in dismay. "Oh my, Beatrice is not going to be pleased about this."

"No, ma'am," Davey said, "reckon not."

Beatrice Martel was not the kind of woman who would appreciate finding her shop in a state of disarray. A place for everything and everything in its place, that was the motto Beatrice lived by. It made for an organized, if empty life.

"If we work together," Patience offered suddenly, "we can have these boxes restacked neatly before she arrives."

The boy's eyes were wary, but he accepted her offer of help quickly enough. And in just a few minutes, the boxes were neat, the hats replaced on their stands, and the veil once more sitting in a place of honor.

For the life of her, Patience couldn't remember coming to the store last night. Or trying on the bridal veil. It was as if there had been a spill of ink in her mind and those particular events had been blacked out. She rubbed at the spot on her forehead, just between her eyes. No doubt, once the pain in her head eased back, her memory would fit itself back together.

Until then, she would simply go back to her life and carry on as if everything was just as it should be. And as that thought rose up, she suddenly said, "Brady!"

"Ma'am?"

She glanced down into Davey's surprised eyes and said, "Brady must be worried to death about me."

"He must?" The boy shoved his hair back from his face, and Patience, smiling, reached down to scoop that hair back farther.

"We're going to have to get you a haircut, Davey, or soon you'll be stumbling around with your hands stretched out in front of you."

"I don't need no haircut," he grumbled and stepped back from her, despite the sudden urge to stay close. He didn't know who she was and figured she just might be a bit touched in the head. But when she touched him, he felt all *right* inside. Kind of warm and nice. Like nothing he'd ever felt before.

But that was just foolishness, he told himself. She was just some loco woman.

She smiled at him, but he saw the sadness in it and immediately felt bad about thinking such things about her. Durned if he knew why, though.

"It's all right, Davey," she said and her voice sounded real pretty now. Soft and gentle, like he figured his ma must have sounded before she up and died on him when he was a child.

"It is?" he asked, not really sure what they were talking about now.

"It is," she said firmly. "Everything is all right now. You'll see." Then she walked past him toward the front door.

The bell jangled as she opened it and Davey couldn't keep from shouting out, "Ma'am, where you goin' now?"

She glanced back at him over her shoulder and gave him a smile bright enough to make the sun ashamed. "I'm going to see my fiancé, silly."

"Your fiancé?" He'd heard the word. He knew she meant her intended.

"Yes. Brady Shaw." She shook her head and clucked her tongue at him. "Now, you're not going to try to pretend you don't know Brady too, are you?"

"No, ma'am," he whispered, "I sure ain't." Heck, everybody from here to California knew Brady Shaw.

"Am not," she corrected.

"Am not," he parroted right after her.

"Good," she said and gave him one last smile. "I'll see you later, then, Davey," she called as she sailed out of the dress shop headed for the saloon.

The boy watched her go and told himself if he was a bettin' man, which he wasn't, he'd bet he wouldn't be seein' her later at all. Not if she was going to try to tell Brady that she was his fiancée.

Everybody knew Brady didn't take kindly to liars and cheats.

Chapter Two

Everything looked achingly familiar—yet different, at the same time. Patience closed the door of the dressmaker's shop behind her and walked to the edge of the boardwalk. Letting her gaze shift down the length of the main street, she took in the town of Fortune as it slowly came to life.

Apparently, there'd been a rainstorm the night before, though she had no recollection of it. Which was certainly odd. Almost as odd as waking up on the floor of the dress shop. But as soon as that thought fluttered through her mind, her head pounded in response, so she set the thought aside for the moment. After all, it didn't really matter *why* she'd been in the dress shop, did it? All that was important was seeing Brady and assuring him that she was safe.

Blinking at the brilliant sunshine pouring down onto Fortune, Patience smiled to herself. It was a good morning to be alive, she thought, and set off down the boardwalk, grateful that she didn't have to step off into the muddy street.

Behind her, a door opened and shut, then before she could wonder who it was, Davey Howard ran past her. Glancing back at her briefly, he never slowed down. Shirt tail fluttering, bootheels clattering on the wooden walk, he raced down the uneven boardwalk as if the hounds of hell were on his heels.

"Well, now," she wondered aloud, as the boy leapt over Marvin Soames's sleeping dog, "what in heaven is wrong with him?"

In the next instant, though, she dismissed his actions by remembering that children sometimes had no reason at all for peculiar behavior. Besides, her head pounded forcefully and Patience had the oddest feeling that she was somehow forgetting . . . *something*. Frowning to herself, she paused and tried to think what it might be. Nothing came though and trying to probe her memory only made the ache in her head more insistent. Lifting one hand, she rubbed at a spot between her eyes in an effort to ease back the discomfort.

Continuing on toward the saloon, she fought that niggling sensation that she should be doing—something. Whatever it was would come to her no doubt. She seldom forgot even the tiniest detail.

Patience sailed down the boardwalk, running the length of Main Street with purpose in her steps. The walkway rose and fell like ocean waves, but the unevenness of it didn't slow her one bit. Chin lifted, shoulders back, she glanced around as she went. Storefront doors opened as she passed, almost as though someone had sent word that she would be arriving.

"Good morning, Mr. Taylor," she sang out, giving the short, bald-headed barber a winning smile.

"Ma'am," he replied with a nod, a bemused expression flitting across his features.

Odd, Patience told herself, the little man was usually far more talkative. So much so, in fact, that most townspeople crossed the street to avoid having to stop and be drawn into an unending conversation with the friendly but long-winded fellow.

She felt his gaze on her back as she continued on, but thought no more about him. Instead, she smiled at Vonda Shales as the tall, thin woman opened the door of her laundry and waved to Treasure Morgan as she swept the steps of the Mercantile.

Both women smiled, but Patience didn't notice the curious expressions stamped on their features. She was simply too intent on reaching the saloon. And Brady.

"She's comin'!" Davey Howard shouted out his warning, then bent over, hands on his knees and struggled for air.

Brady chuckled, shook his head, and settled into one of the captain's chairs drawn up to an empty card table. Apparently, the kid had run all the way from up the street to deliver his piece of news.

"Slow down, boy," he said, reaching for his second cup of coffee. "Nothin's important enough to get a man to be running first thing in the morning."

Hell, this was the best part of the day as far as Brady was concerned. Most gamblers he knew didn't even bother waking up until late afternoon. But Brady'd always enjoyed the peace and quiet to be found in an empty saloon. A man could think and not have his thoughts rattled by a bunch of noisy drunks or an out-of-tune piano played by a fella with very little enthusiasm and less talent. But then, you couldn't expect to find a good piano player working in a saloon for tips and free beer.

His gaze slid around the main room and he smiled to himself. Maybe there were bigger and better saloons, but this one was his. His business. His home. Hell, the first real home he'd ever had.

And as that thought presented itself, a flicker of guilt crept in and ruined it. Scowling to himself, he shifted in his chair and told himself to forget that night two years ago when he'd won the deed to the place. And though that memory would never really leave him, it did at least fade into the background for now.

The past was done. Nothing could be changed. He'd charted his course long ago and now all he could do was keep moving fast enough that the ghosts trailing after him couldn't keep up.

But for now, he was more interested in what had brought Davey Howard to his door first thing in the morning.

He stretched out his legs and crossed one booted foot atop the other as he stared at the kid opposite him. The boy's shirt was torn, but clean and his hands looked almost blue from the early morning cold. He needed a coat, Brady thought and knew even as he considered getting him one that the boy wouldn't take it.

Kid had more pride than some men twice his age and size. And damned if Brady didn't recall all too well when pride was the only thing he himself had had to call his own. He wouldn't have taken charity and he doubted this boy would feel any different.

"What's goin' on, boss?" Joe asked as he walked back into the main room.

Brady shot him a look. "I'm just about to find out."

Shifting his gaze back to the boy, he asked, "So Davey, you going to tell me what's got you running all wild eyed and breathless?"

"I'm tryin'."

Joe snorted.

Brady ignored him. "Take a breath and go then," he said, hiding the smile he knew the kid wouldn't appreciate.

The boy swung his hair back from his eyes and fixed a stare on him. "A woman. She's comin' for you."

Joe laughed shortly.

And Brady knew why. Well, hell. All this fuss over a female looking for him? He let that grin loose now.

Lifting one eyebrow, Brady took a swallow of his coffee, set the cup back down and said, "Kid, if a woman's comin' for me, that's not bad news."

"Can't have too many women," Joe mused.

"You ain't seen this one yet," Davey insisted.

Curiosity stirred inside Brady. What kind of woman was it, he wondered, that could get this kind of reaction out of the boy? "Pretty, is she?" he asked, more as a matter of course than real interest.

After all, he wasn't exactly looking for a woman. If he wanted company, all he had to do was go upstairs. And any other kind of woman was out of the question. Like everywhere else, the upright, God-fearing females of Fortune usually avoided him like the plague—which was all right with him, since he was pretty sure he wouldn't know what to do with a "good" woman if he got his hands on one anyway.

He liked his women willing and eager and a Bible thumper just didn't spring to mind when he got that old, familiar itch.

The kid eased up from his bent-over position and drew a long breath. "She's kinda tall and skinny," Davey said, then added, "but she's got nice eyes."

"Who is she?" he asked, already halfway dismissing the mystery female because of that description. Tall and skinny didn't exactly churn up notions of lust in a man and "nice eyes" was just that. Nice.

"Don't rightly know," Davey muttered. "Never seen her before." His features screwed up as if he were deep in thought. "But she knew me. Knew my name and talked to me like we was old friends."

"Were," Brady said.

"Were." The boy parroted the correction.

"Interesting," Brady told him, "but not really worth a run like you just made. What else is there? What aren't you telling me?"

"She says she's your—" Davey swallowed hard, glanced around the empty room, and then shifted his gaze back to the man watching him. "*fiancée*."

"Fiancée?" Brady echoed, stunned. He straightened up, looked at the boy for a long minute, and then shaking his head, laughed loud enough to rattle the windows. "She says she's my fiancée?"

Joe laughed, long and hard, and didn't shut up until Brady shot him a look that should have fried the soles of his feet. "Don't you have something to do?" he demanded.

"Nope," Joe said and leaned both beefy forearms on the bartop, obviously getting comfortable.

"Nosy as an old woman," Brady muttered, then turned back to the kid. "You're sure she told you she was my fiancée?"

"Yes sir, she sure did."

He ignored another rumble of laughter from Joe. "Well, hell, boy. She must be crazy."

The kid looked thoughtful for a moment, as if considering that possibility. Then shrugging, he said, "She didn't look crazy at all. Wasn't rollin' her eyes and moanin' or nothing."

"Oh, now that's a shame," Joe mumbled. "That would've been a sight indeed."

Foaming at the mouth or not, the woman was clearly out of her mind, Brady thought. Yet for the first time since Davey had rushed into the room, he felt a flicker of foreboding.

Fiancée?

Outside, the distinct click of high heels against the boardwalk sounded out and Davey turned to watch the double door swing inward.

Brady swiveled his head to stare at the woman silhouetted in the doorway. Just as Davey'd said, she was tall and skinny. But the kid hadn't mentioned her hair, long and curly and black as midnight. He also hadn't said anything about her skin, so pale it looked almost translucent. And those "nice eyes" of hers were also big and such a light brown as to be near golden. She had a stubborn tilt to her chin and she carried herself as straight as though she had a board strapped to her back. The ugly gray dress she wore did nothing for her figure, but somehow, she managed to look damn good despite the lack of frills.

Slowly, Brady came to his feet, unconsciously standing in the presence of a lady. And she was a lady, of that he had no doubt. Hell, even Joe had stopped his snickering.

Her gaze slid around the room, passed over Davey, and Joe, who stood up straight and ran a hand across his hair nervously. Then she turned to Brady. She smiled and he felt the hard punch of it slam into him.

Damn.

That smile of hers was as potent a weapon as a loaded Colt.

"Oh my," Joe whispered, but Brady ignored him, focusing instead on the woman watching him.

"Brady!" she called and stepped into the room. Hurrying to him, she went up on her toes, kissed his cheek, then eased back to give him a close look at that amazing smile. "You're looking well this morning."

"Thanks," he said, his gaze moving over her features. Now that he had the opportunity for a longer look, he had to admit that she wasn't what a man would ordinarily think of as "pretty." But she was one that a man would definitely take a second look at.

Well, most men, anyway.

Not him.

But there was something about her. Something . . . not exactly familiar, because he knew for damn sure he'd never seen her before. If nothing else, he would have remembered that smile. Still, there was a sensation of—

He shook it off and moved back a step or two, just

to keep a safe distance between them. There wouldn't be any more kisses, even though he could still feel the imprint of her lips on his cheek. She was clearly loco and Brady wasn't taking any chances with a woman who was a couple cars short of a train. Besides, she had to have a keeper somewhere and whoever it was, was probably running all over town looking for her.

Hopefully, that keeper would find her real soon.

"Are you feeling all right, ma'am?" he asked and pulled out a chair so she could sit down.

"I'm perfectly fine, Brady," she said and gave him a look that clearly said she thought it was *he* who was a bit under the weather.

Morning sun drifted in through the wide front window and lit the ends of her hair with a soft, golden light. Black eyebrows arched high over those big eyes of hers as she watched him study her. And that fabulous smile slowly faded to be replaced with a stern expression he hadn't seen since he was a boy and his teacher threw a book at his head for talking out of turn.

As if from a distance, he heard the town stirring to life. Wagon wheels creaked as teamsters made their way down the muddy street. A dog barked, Adelaide Stevens shouted for her wayward husband, Tom, and the school bell pealed out over it all. And over in the corner, Joe coughed nervously.

A perfectly ordinary day.

But for the fact that a complete stranger had wandered into his life acting as though she had a claim on him. Which he'd best straighten out right now.

"Ma'am—"

She frowned at him. "Patience."

All right. "Patience," he repeated and kept his voice slow and steady. Wouldn't do to upset a woman clearly on the fine edge of sanity. "Just what is it I can do for you?"

"Do for me?" She drew her head back to stare at him. Slanting a quick look at the boy standing to one side of her, she shifted her gaze to Brady again and said, "I don't know what you mean. I hurried home because I knew you'd be worried about me and—"

"Home?" he interrupted, latching on to that one word as if it were a log being carried down the rapids. Here, he thought. Here he could prove to her that she was mistaken. A woman like her wouldn't be living in a saloon, of all places.

"Home," she said firmly. "Here."

"Uh-oh," Joe whispered and Brady threw a quick frown at him.

Joe shrugged helplessly, then leaned onto the bar again. Obviously, the man wasn't going anywhere. And neither, he thought, was Davey. The kid's eyebrows lifted into an "I told you so" arch, but Brady ignored it. Hell, he had bigger fish to fry. Immediately.

Now, he was as willing as the next man to be kind to crazy folk. And Lord knew there was enough decency in him to never call a lady a liar—at least not to her face. But there was a limit to any man's patience and forbearance. And he'd reached his.

"Now ma'am, if you'll just stop and think for a minute, you'll realize that this saloon isn't really your home."

She laughed shortly and reached up to push a stray black curl out of her face. "Of course this saloon isn't a home," she said.

Brady's tension eased off a bit, but he relaxed too soon.

"It's your business." Shaking her head, she added, "But you must admit we do live here, so at least temporarily, it is home."

"You live here, ma'am?" the bartender blurted, despite the glare Brady threw at him.

"For pity's sake, Joe," she said. "You know that as well as I do." Then she gave him a decisive nod. "Naturally, we live in separate rooms. Then, after we're married, we'll be building a home out on the knoll above Hanging Woman Creek. Although," she added thoughtfully as she turned back to Brady, "I do think it might be easier if we simply lived here most of the week and kept the new house for private getaways."

Something inside Brady stopped dead and he gave her a long look. A cold, hard knot of suspicion settled in the pit of his stomach. Now how in heaven had she known about his plans for the knoll outside town? He'd told no one. He'd shown no one the spot he'd found little more than a year ago on one of his long, solitary rides.

It was perfect. He'd known it from the first minute he laid eyes on it. Acres of scrub brush, juniper, and piñon trees spread out below the gentle rise. And from the top of that knoll, there was a view of the distant mountains that was enough to steal a wandering man's breath away. There were *tinajas,* natural stone tanks to catch rainwater, and a dry creekbed where he'd dig a well until he reached the water he just knew was down there.

He'd never thought to have a home until he saw that spot. Then it was as if the land itself had called to him. Sand and rocks and scrub brush wouldn't sound like much to most people, but the serenity of the place spoke to the heart of him.

But those plans were just that—plans. They existed only in his mind and he damn well wanted to know how this woman had guessed them.

"How do you know about the knoll?" he asked, his voice tight, low.

Her brow furrowed and her eyes narrowed. "Are you sure you're feeling all right?"

"I'm just dandy," he snapped. "How'd you know?"

"You took me there," she said.

"That's a lie," Brady said in a near growl.

She sucked in a gulp of air and reared back so far that if she'd been a rattlesnake, Brady would have pulled out a gun and shot her before she could strike.

"I am *not* a liar, Brady Shaw."

"You damn sure are if you're saying I took you to that knoll," he countered.

"Now boss . . ." Joe's cautious voice spoke up.

Before Brady could tell him to keep quiet though, Patience turned on the man. "Thank you, but I'm quite capable of speaking for myself."

"Yes, ma'am."

She turned back to Brady. "As for you. Don't you swear at *me*," she said and stabbed her index finger in the air just inches short of his chest.

"Lady, I don't know who you are or what your game is, but you'd better start talkin'."

"I am not playing any sort of game and you know very well who I am. I am your fiancée. I've come west to marry you and I truly resent this inquisition."

"You're out of your mind, lady," Brady snapped, his patience long gone. "I've never seen you before in my life!"

"Brady!" Twin spots of color flushed her cheeks as anger swept through her until she nearly shook with it.

Well, fine. Anger he could deal with.

"Why don't you tell me when was the last time I took you out to the knoll?" he asked, knowing full well she couldn't do it. This would put an end to her ploy, whatever it was.

"Very well," she said, sparing another quick look at the boy and Joe as though she wished they would leave.

But Brady didn't care who was here to listen. He wanted this settled now.

"Just last week, we rode out there at sunset," she said and her voice went soft and dreamy. "The sky was a brilliant shade of scarlet and we sat atop the knoll and watched as the first stars came up."

He *had* done all that. *Alone.* So nothing she said was enough to convince him. After all, she could be making this whole thing up. Hell, she *must* be making it up. She hadn't been there. He damn well would have noticed if he'd had a woman sitting beside him on that rocky hill. Particularly *this* woman, since she didn't seem the type to keep quiet for long.

What he had to do was ask her specific questions—to catch her up and force her to admit she was lying. For whatever reason.

"All right," he said tightly, "if you were there, what was the last thing I did before heading back to town?"

She smiled at him, and if he hadn't been so blasted wary, he might have been caught up in the warmth of that smile of hers. Thankfully, he thought, he was tougher than that.

"You walked off the paces for the house," she said, just a little bit smugly as she folded her arms across her chest and watched him. "You even laid down a small square of stones to mark the spot where the fireplace will go."

His back teeth ground together and his hands fisted at his sides. He had done just that, damn it.

But how did she know?

Was somebody following him around? Reaching up, Brady scraped one hand across his jaw and looked at her. Who the hell was she? How had she seen him giving in to an inexplicable urge to plan his future house? There'd been no one around for miles. A ripple of unease spread along his spine and Brady stiffened in response.

"Nothing to say?" she asked brightly.

"Lady," he muttered darkly, "I've got plenty to say, but none of it's fit for mixed company."

"Brady Shaw," she said, planting both hands on those narrow hips, "you should know me well enough by now to know that I am *not* a woman to be cowed by surliness."

He threw his hands wide and let them slap against his thighs. Damn it, where was this crazy woman's keeper? Shouldn't she be locked in someone's attic somewhere? "I don't know you at all."

"Pestilence."

"What?"

"I said pestilence." Shaking her head, she looked up at him, meeting his gaze with a golden glare. "You know me as well as I do you, and I know you very well indeed."

"Is that right?" he asked and straightened up, crossing his arms over his chest.

"It is. And sometimes, I swear I don't know why I ever agreed to marry you."

"I'm wondering that myself," he said and tried to figure out just why a clearly addled woman would set her sights on him as a husband.

And just how soon he'd be able to get her the hell out of his saloon *and* his life.

Chapter Three

This morning had not started out well at all, Patience told herself as she headed for the wide staircase on the far right side of the room. She felt three pairs of eyes follow her every step and for some reason, that attention only irritated her. For pity's sake, they behaved as though they'd never seen her before.

Grasping the hem of her skirt in both hands, she yanked it up several inches and started the long climb to the second story. Her steps were muffled on the nearly threadbare carpet runner and she made a mental note to speak to Brady about appearances. He was a successful businessman—although it was a business Patience certainly didn't approve of—and he should present the best front possible to his customers. She shook her head. Men just didn't seem to understand that it was the small things in life that bore the most scrutiny.

But, she told herself with a small, satisfied smile, with her help, Brady would become the man she knew he was destined to be.

With that fond feeling still wrapped around her heart, she paused at the head of the stairs for a quick glance below. Both the men and the boy were still staring after her. They hadn't moved a muscle. Their features mirrored the same stunned expression she'd seen on them earlier and Patience thought the three of them looked as though they'd been turned into pillars of salt.

Briefly, she studied the face of the man she loved. A strong jaw, high cheekbones, and pale blue eyes that seemed to look inside a person to all their secrets. He stood well over six feet tall and his body was muscled without being overbearingly so. His black hair was too long and his knee-length black frock coat looked perfectly tailored.

Just looking at him was enough to quicken her heartbeat and make her pulse pound. Or it would have been if he—and the others—hadn't been staring at her as though she'd lost her mind.

Impatience flickered to life inside her. What in heaven was wrong with them?

"Is there a problem, gentlemen?" she asked abruptly.

Her voice broke whatever spell had been holding them in place. Instantly, Joe went back to the bar and Davey sprinted for the double doors. Only Brady held his ground. He didn't move. His expression didn't shift. He simply stared at her until, even from a distance, she felt the chill in his gaze and a shiver rippled along her spine in response.

She'd seen that look in his eyes before—many times, in fact. She'd watched him stare down an enemy with one glare from those clear blue eyes. She'd watched dangerous men walk a wide path around Brady Shaw. She knew that over the years, his reputation had grown to the point where the mere mention of his name was enough to bring conversations to a stuttering halt. She'd seen men and women cross the street to avoid making eye contact with him.

And in turn, she'd watched Brady become a man who didn't trust. Didn't love. She'd seen him pull back from the world around him until he was standing alone in the shadows. She'd watched him become a man who would risk his life before he would his heart.

But then, she told herself firmly, that was before he'd had *her*. Wasn't it? She frowned to herself. She couldn't seem to remember when he'd actually proposed to her. Odd, how that thought fluttered through her brain. Still, she shook her head. Her mind might be a little fuzzy about some things, but about this, she was certain. She loved Brady Shaw. And he loved her. And if he thought he could use that steely-eyed glare on Patience Goodfellow, then he had another think coming.

From downstairs somewhere came the sound of a door quietly shutting and she knew that Joe had gone into the back room, leaving the two of them alone. Another moment or two of silence ticked by, though, before she said, "I'm not afraid of you, Brady," and her voice almost seemed to echo in the room.

His gaze narrowed slightly and she thought she saw him flinch at her words, but she might have been mistaken. "And why's that?" he asked.

"Because I know you."

He crossed his arms over his chest, spread his feet wide apart, and lifted his chin. "Lady, if you really knew me, you'd be hightailing it out of here so fast, your skirt would catch fire."

Patience chuckled. Honestly, were other men really cowed by such posturing? "That's what you'd like to think," she said, shaking her head. "But I know better."

Abruptly, he unfolded his arms only to slam both fists on his hips. "Lady, you don't know anything about me. I don't know you from Adam's great-aunt. Now, it's clear to me that you're having some kind of trouble and I—"

"Want to help," she finished for him. Laying both hands on the banister in front of her, she leaned forward and met his gaze squarely. "Do you see, Brady? It's your instinct to help people in need."

He laughed and the booming sound would have been infectious if she hadn't detected the tinge of bitterness coloring it. A pang of sorrow jabbed at her heart then disappeared when he said, "You just proved me right, ma'am. You ask anyone in Fortune. They'll tell you the only person I'm interested in helping is me."

"They don't know you as I do."

He actually scowled at her and Patience was sure some people would have been terrified at the glint of mayhem in his eyes. She, however, was not.

"Look, what I was going to say," he said through gritted teeth, "was that though it's clear you're having some trouble, it's not *my* trouble—and I want you out of here."

"Nonsense," she said.

"What?"

"Nonsense," she repeated and straightened up from the banister. "You don't want me to leave or you never would have asked me to marry you."

"I didn't."

A brief jab of hurt stabbed at her. Why would he even pretend to deny their love? After all they'd been through together, after all they'd seen and felt and said, how could he look her in the eye and make such a wild claim? Was he getting cold feet? Was he beginning to doubt that he would be a good enough husband for her?

The hurt inside ebbed back slightly as warm affection filled her. How like him. To worry about pleasing her so much that he was willing to deny his own happiness.

Brady truly was a good-hearted man.

Still, though, it would be best if she let him know right away that she wouldn't stand for any more of this playacting. They were getting married and that was that!

"Pestilence," she snapped, waving one hand in complete dismissal of his argument. "Of course you proposed, else why would I be here?"

"That's what I'm trying to find out!" he shouted.

One of her black eyebrows lifted into an arch. She felt it and didn't bother to squelch the motion. "That tone of voice doesn't intimidate *me,* Brady. You should understand that right away. When we're married—"

"We're not getting ma—"

"I will not be shouted at," she continued, interrupting him cleanly as if he hadn't tried to get a word in at all.

He threw his hands high in obvious surrender and let them fall to slap against his thighs. Satisfaction pooled in the pit of her stomach, but Patience knew enough not to be smug.

"Well," she said, "now that that's settled, I'll just be going along to my room to freshen up."

"You don't *have* a room," he pointed out, but even his tone told her that he didn't expect her to believe him.

"I'll be down directly," she called, already sailing off down the hall toward the last door on the right. "Then we can talk again."

Frustration mounting, Brady watched her go, reluctantly admiring the stiffness of her spine and the determination in her step. Just as he admired the way she'd faced him down without batting an eyelash. It had been a long time since anyone had stood up to him like that. Hell, he'd known grown men to back up and crawl away rather than make Brady Shaw angry.

But not her. Nope.

Most crazy folks he'd heard tell of spent their days cowering in a corner quietly crying. Disgusted, he told himself that it just figured he'd end up with the only crazy woman in the country who had more sand than most men he knew.

And since it didn't look like she was planning on leaving anytime soon, the question was, just what in the hell was he supposed to do with her? He scraped one hand across the back of his neck and cursed Lady Luck for deserting him. Brady watched Patience open a door and step inside and another question came to him. How did she know which was the only empty room upstairs?

She hadn't had to wander the hall, peeking into rooms. Hadn't had to hunt for it. She'd gone right to it. Like it was hers.

Brady frowned at the thought. Something was happening here, he could feel it. That old sixth sense that had always alerted him to danger was now pinging around inside him like a spent bullet bouncing off rock walls.

But he had no idea what to do about it. Shoving one hand through his hair, Brady turned his back on the crazy woman upstairs and walked across the room to the window overlooking Main Street. His mind raced, searching for a solution, but he kept coming up empty.

And that felt . . . *strange*.

Ever since he was a kid, he'd listened to what he'd long thought of as his "quiet voice." It had been there, inside him, guiding him, telling him what to do or where to go. And when he listened to it, things usually worked out. When he didn't, he'd found himself in piles of trouble.

Now, though, when he could really use that quiet voice, it wasn't there—for the first time in years.

And Brady wasn't sure which worried him more. The woman upstairs or the fact that that voice was gone—leaving him truly alone.

Davey straightened up the last of the mess that woman had left behind at the dressmaker's shop, then glanced at the wall clock hanging opposite him. It was still early enough that he might be able to get some work done down at the livery stable before it was time to head to the barber's to sweep up.

He jammed one hand into his pants pocket and jingled the few coins he'd earned the day before. Once he added them to the rest of his money in the secret box under the loose floorboard in the hotel, he'd count it all up again. Even though he knew to the penny how much he had, it gave him a good feeling to count the coins and make plans. He already had durn near four dollars saved up. And that was more cash money than his pa had ever had. Pretty soon, he'd have fifty whole dollars. And then maybe a hundred, although even the thought of such a huge sum was almost more than he could handle.

But it wasn't the money Davey longed for. It was the warmth and the food and the safety it would bring. One of these ol' days, he told himself, he'd be livin' high off the hog. He'd have him a hotel room with a soft bed and a real feather pillow. And he'd wear nice clothes and he'd eat hot food every night, even if he wasn't hungry. And he'd have him a coat and some gloves and maybe even a fine hat and folks would look at him respectful. And he wouldn't ever have to be alone no more.

Davey sighed and smiled to himself at the wonderful dream. Someday, he thought, and that made the coldness in his hands a little easier to bear.

Swiping one hand under his nose, he set the broom into its corner and called out, "I'm leavin', Miss Bea."

At the back of the store, the droning whir and clank of the treadle sewing machine stopped briefly. "Did you sweep in the corners this time?" Beatrice

Martel asked, her booming voice easily carrying into the main room.

Davey smiled and shook his head. She asked the same question every day and every day he gave her the same answer. "Yes, ma'am, I surely did."

"That's fine then, Davey," she said. "Your money's on the counter and, mind you, take that sandwich with you."

"Yes'm." He'd heard some men call Miss Bea a "harpy," whatever that was, but he figured it was just because they didn't know her good. She had some real strange notions about females and voting and such, but she'd always been good to him. Every morning, she set out a sandwich for him and he'd learned to make that one meal last until he could cadge a meal off the cook at the hotel later in the evening. And that meant he didn't have to spend many of his hard-won coins buying himself food.

Shuffling off toward the counter, he stopped suddenly when a glimmer of something shiny caught the corner of his eye. Frowning, he bent down for a closer look, then reached for the brass circle lying half-hidden behind a tower of empty hatboxes.

"Well, now," he muttered, turning the metal ring over in his hands. "Where'd this come from? And what in tarnation is it?" It was dull and kind of old-looking, so he knew it didn't belong to Miss Bea. That woman was the scrubbingest woman he'd ever come across. If this belonged to her, Davey had no doubt that it would be shining as bright as the Pearly Gates.

Shrugging, he slung the circle over one arm and carried it with him to the counter. There, he pocketed the handful of coins, snatched up the sandwich waiting for him, and headed for the door. If he hurried, he'd be able to finish up at the livery stable in no time at all.

The bell over the door at the Mercantile clanged noisily as Patience stepped inside. She stood just beyond the threshold and let the door swing slowly shut behind her. Smiling to herself, she let her gaze sweep the darkened interior of the well-stocked store.

A counter ran the length of the far wall and on that counter were stacks of Levis and piles of shirts in all possible sizes. On the wall behind that counter hung holsters, suspenders, and anything else the proprietress could think to hook on to the wooden dowels pounded into the plank wall. Beneath those items, boots were lined up in neat ranks, as if waiting to be marched into battle, and alongside those boots were stacked bolts of fabric in eye-catching colors and patterns. Shelves set up in the middle of the store, forming narrow aisles, held cookware, knives, guns, ammunition, spices, and all manner of tonics claiming to cure every illness ever suffered by mankind.

Just to her left was the main counter, on which sat a giant of a cash drawer, ostentatious in its gilt-edged glory. Alongside it were glass jars filled with enough candy to tempt any child with a sweet tooth. Behind the counter were narrow shelves holding spices in small glass bottles that shone brightly in the single spear of sunlight able to poke through the cluster of ladies' dresses hung across the front window. Barrels of flour, crackers, and pickles squatted in front of the counter, and behind it a huge woman stood, hands on hips, watching her with interest.

"Good morning," Patience said, smiling at Treasure Morgan, owner of, as she claimed, "the best-stocked mercantile west of St. Louis."

"'Morning," she said, a wide smile creasing her round face as she reached to smooth her perfectly ironed and starched apron. "The stage in already?"

"The stage?" Patience asked.

"Don't you worry, miss," she said briskly, "I can have your order filled and you back on that stage before the driver gets his horses watered."

"I don't understand."

"You didn't come in on the morning stage?"

"No," she said, "of course not. Treasure, what are you talking about?"

The woman's small blue eyes narrowed slightly. "You know me?"

Patience felt a whiplash of irritation. What was wrong with everyone today? Had she suddenly become invisible? Completely forgettable?

And then the answer came to her. Brady. This was his doing. For some reason, he'd obviously convinced Treasure to go along with his little game of pretending to not know her. Well, she would put a stop to that quickly enough.

"Now Treasure," she said, paying no attention to the woman's stern expression. She knew very well that the storekeeper didn't have a mean bone in her body. "I really don't have the time to play this little game with you."

"Game? I'm not playing any game, Miss . . ."

At her hesitation, Patience said, "Please, Treasure. Call me Patience. We know each other far too well for formalities."

Consternation briefly clouded the woman's features as she said, "We do?"

"Don't you think so?"

"Well, I—"

"It seems silly for friends to stand on formalities, doesn't it?"

Treasure looked at the woman and studied her for a long minute, trying to figure out who in heaven she was. And why she would be acting as though they were old friends. But try as she might, nothing came to her. Still, she seemed a pleasant woman and Treasure wasn't about to chase off a potential customer, no matter how odd she might be.

"Yes," she said with a shrug of her wide shoulders, "I suppose it does at that."

"Good! Now Treasure, I'm in need of a few new things."

"Uh-huh," she said and slowly walked out from behind the counter to follow Patience toward the ladies' dresses.

Flashing her a quick look over her shoulder, Patience explained, "All of my clothes are missing from my room."

She wasn't sure where they'd gone, though, and that was a touch disturbing. The fog in her mind thickened a bit and she tried to will it away. But it wouldn't work. So, until she remembered exactly what she'd done with her clothing, she'd need more, wouldn't she?

"Your room." As far as Treasure knew there were no asylums near Fortune, so she had to wonder just where the woman was staying. She flicked a glance toward the closed door and the street beyond. Was someone even now running up and down Main Street looking for the woman? Had she escaped from some wagon on its way west?

"Now Treasure, I know you don't really approve of my staying above the saloon, but—"

"You have a room at the saloon?" She looked at the woman and privately thought that she didn't seem the type to be working abovestairs at Brady's place. Not enough meat on her bones, for one thing. And that simple gray dress wasn't really the sort her kind of woman usually chose.

"Only temporarily," Patience said blithely, waving one hand.

"You're working there temporarily?"

"Working there?" The woman's face went ghostly white and then scarlet as realization took hold. "I should say not! Why, Treasure, I'm surprised that you would even think such a thing."

"But you said—"

"Now," she said and shook her head. "I don't remember doing it, but I must have decided to throw all of my old clothes out and buy new ones." Reaching up, she rubbed at a spot on her forehead, as if trying to ease a headache.

"Are you feeling all right?" Treasure asked, half-afraid the woman was about to fall to the floor and have a fit.

"Aren't you kind?" Patience responded, forcing a smile she obviously didn't feel. "I just have a bit of a headache," she said, then added slyly, "Perhaps we should open another bottle of Doctor Moore's Female Tonic. Do you think Beatrice has recovered enough to enjoy another small party?"

Treasure reared back, clapped one hand to her chest and goggled at the woman. Now, how did she know about that?

"I suppose we shouldn't have," Patience was saying, "but we did have fun, didn't we?"

Yes, Treasure thought, they had indeed. She and Beatrice and Vonda Shales, the laundress, had cracked open a bottle of Doctor Moore's. The three of them had toasted each other with the "elixir" until none of them could see clearly.

And maybe that was why she couldn't recall this woman having been there. Because she had to have been there, else how would she know about it? Heaven knew it wasn't something she or her friends would have talked about. Some of the women in Fortune would be absolutely scandalized by the idea of single women playing cards and drinking elixir.

She flushed slightly, remembering the laughter and the shared confidences that night. Maybe it had been foolish, but it had seemed harmless at the time.

Patience laid one hand on her forearm and Treasure jumped, startled. But an instant later, a slow, easy warmth rolled through her, soothing her soul and wrapping itself around her heart like a cozy blanket.

"I won't tell a soul," Patience said and removed her hand, taking the warmth with her. "That night is just between the four of us."

The four of us, she thought and tried to affix this woman into the middle of the blurred memories of that night. And the longer she thought about it, the more confused she was. However odd it seemed, it was the only explanation. No one else knew about that little gathering and she couldn't imagine either Beatrice or Vonda mentioning a word of it to anyone.

Unless, she thought, as a small, worrisome thread unwound itself inside her, someone had been outside her windows that night. She bit back a groan at the thought of what her customers would make of her then.

Patience flicked through the selection of dresses, discarding every one that was the least bit dull or uninteresting. She had no desire for blacks and grays or even the dignified dark blue serge. She wanted color. Lovely spring colors that would make her feel alive and happy and . . . pretty.

Selecting a few, she draped them across her arm and headed toward the small room at the back of the store. "I'll just try these on, if you don't mind."

"Not at all," the woman murmured.

As she walked, her brisk steps kicking the hated gray skirt out in front of her, Patience called back, "Did you find those back issues of *Godey's Lady's Book*?"

She didn't see the confused expression cross Treasure's face. "The *Lady's Book*? Uh, no. Not yet."

"Oh, well," Patience said loudly, just before she stepped into the dressing room, "I do hope you'll be able to locate them. I want to find just the right pattern for my wedding dress. You did say you could get the fabric for me, didn't you?"

"Fabric?" she echoed before pausing to ask, "Wedding dress?"

Really, Patience thought, just a bit impatiently, why was the woman repeating everything she said? But even as the flash of frustration shot through her, she reminded herself that naturally her wedding wouldn't be as important to anyone else as it was to her.

"I really want to surprise Brady," she said. "So my dress has to be wonderful."

"Brady?" Treasure shouted. "Brady Shaw?"

"Of course Brady Shaw," Patience said, already undoing the buttons at the neck of her gown. As if she'd marry anyone else when she had loved Brady for so long.

"You're marrying Brady?"

"Not without that dress," she called, shaking her head as she reached for a lovely lemon-yellow gown.

Treasure sighed and slid a glance across the room to the shelf behind her cash box where Doctor Moore's elixir sat temptingly. Marrying Brady Shaw? Now she *knew* the woman was off her rocker.

Chapter Four

Brady wasn't sure how he'd lost control of the situation. But he damn sure had.

Patience Goodfellow—and what kind of name was that, anyway?—had stepped into his life and he had no idea how to get rid of her.

His back teeth ground together and he shoved one hand through his hair in frustration. He'd never met a female as hardheaded as this one. She looked at him through those golden eyes of hers and saw only what she wanted to see. And how in the hell was a man supposed to argue with that?

Logic didn't seem to be working. Just an hour or two ago, she'd complained about "her" room upstairs and demanded to know where her clothes had gone. Brady had pointed out that it wasn't "her" room and he didn't know or care where she kept her clothes. Naturally, she'd assumed that he was playing some sort of joke on her and had sailed right past any hint of reality.

Crossing the room, he pushed through the double doors and stepped onto the boardwalk. Leaning one shoulder against a porch post, he crossed one foot over the other, brushed the edges of his jacket back and shoved both hands into his pockets. Squinting into the morning light, he studied the town of Fortune.

Two years he'd been here. He'd stumbled across the town on his way west from Santa Fe and when he'd won the saloon, decided to stay put. He'd figured at the time that he could always move on again when the spirit grabbed him. But he hadn't. It wasn't easy for a rambling man to suddenly take root, but then he'd always been open to trying new things.

A wagon rolled past, the old horse that was pulling it straining every muscle to drag the heavy load through the mud. The man on the driver's bench looked as old as the horse he cursed and Brady wasn't sure which of them he was more sorry for. The beast for being in chains or the man, whose chains probably went a lot deeper.

Damn philosophical for so early in the morning, he told himself and shook that thought aside as he slanted his gaze toward the end of town. It wasn't far. Hell, the whole of Main Street was nothing more than a few clustered buildings sitting at the edge of a creek that ran high in spring from mountain runoff. Generally speaking, in desert country, a source of water was plenty enough reason for a town to grow. And about twenty years before, a few hardy prospectors, tired of looking for gold that remained elusive, had started this little place. Lord knew, it was a far cry from New Orleans or San Francisco, but until today, Fortune had suited him just fine.

Brady frowned to himself and absently watched his fellow citizens go about their morning business. He'd become accustomed to the town, he thought, and wondered when it had happened. He'd found a kind of comfort in knowing that every day would be much like the last. And after living the kind of life he had, that comfort meant more to him than it might to another man.

For instance, he knew the barber would open his doors, then pour himself a cup of coffee and plop his butt down onto a chair outside his shop. Vonda Shales would start the fires under her laundry tubs just a half hour before the blacksmith started pounding on his anvil. Treasure Morgan would be washing her windows in another hour or so and Sheriff Hanks would take his first of many walks up and down the street.

It was comfortable. Familiar.

But now, that was all changed. By one woman.

"Say, boss," Joe called out as he loped across the street, dodging another wagon and stepping wide around a horse and rider.

"Yeah?" Brady answered, straightening up from the post and pulling his hands free of his pockets.

"I found Davey down at the livery. Said he'd get right on it." Joe's broad face creased in confusion before he added, "I don't get it, though."

"What?" Brady muttered, shifting his gaze toward the livery stable. As he watched, Davey shot through the wide doorway and headed off down the street.

"This. Sending the kid around town asking about that woman." Brady looked at him and Joe shook his head while shrugging broad shoulders. "Why not just tell her to leave? Why're you tryin' to find out more about her?"

He scowled at his bartender and muttered, "Why don't you let me worry about that?"

"Okay by me," Joe said with a shrug, then added, "but Davey would've done the work for two bits. You didn't have to pay him a dollar."

One corner of Brady's mouth lifted as he watched the boy leap over a sleeping dog stretched out across the width of the boardwalk. "Yeah, I know," he said, but he knew only too well how hard Davey worked for the coins he earned every day. And a dollar, to a kid on his own, was a fortune.

Still, it wouldn't do his "bad man" reputation any good at all if people were to suspect he had a soft spot for the boy.

"You think he'll find out anything about her?"

"I don't know," he admitted and privately thought the chances were pretty slim. In a town as small as Fortune, he would have heard if someone was missing a crazy relative. But he had to try something, didn't he?

Shifting position, he braced his feet wide apart and folded his arms across his chest. Hell, he wasn't sure why he was doing this either. It would be a hell of a lot easier to just throw her out on her narrow backside. But she was clearly loco and Brady just didn't feel right about turning a woman whose bread wasn't quite done loose on the world. Besides, surely someone, somewhere, was missing her. No doubt looking for her. All he had to do was find out who that was and hand her over.

The sooner the better, he thought as, across the street, the door to the Mercantile swung open and

Patience stepped outside. Her arms were full of wrapped packages, her long, black hair fluttered lazily in the soft wind, and when she lifted her head and stared right at him as if she'd known he would be there, Brady's breath caught in his chest.

Even from a distance, he felt the punch of an invisible impact as her golden gaze locked with his. For one brief, strange moment, it was as though he were looking at someone he'd always known. Though that thought made him nearly as crazy as she was.

Still, her eyes shone in the shadows of the overhang and an uneasy sensation crept through him. It was as though she were looking deep within him, to the emptiness he knew was there and he damn well didn't like it. But he couldn't look away. Something inside him shifted uncomfortably as he met her stare, silently challenging himself to be indifferent.

He lost.

"Boss!" Joe's voice came loud and insistent and his tone let Brady know it wasn't the first time he'd tried to get his attention.

"What now?" he demanded, tearing his gaze from Patience's.

The bartender blinked at the near growl in his boss's voice. "You want me to head into Santa Fe today? That shipment of liquor's sitting there waiting to be picked up."

Santa Fe.

Of course.

Brady smiled to himself as a notion formed in his brain. But aloud, he said only, "No. I'll take care of it myself."

"Huh?" Joe asked, his surprise evident.

He couldn't blame the man. After all, Brady hadn't been to Santa Fe in months. But then, until today, he'd had no reason to go.

"I'll go to Santa Fe," he said, glancing briefly at Joe before stepping off the boardwalk headed for the Mercantile. "And I'll take *her* with me."

If Davey didn't come up with any information, then in a town the size of Santa Fe, surely Brady would be able to find where Patience belonged.

Everett Tuttle leaned his head back and laughed until he was forced to clutch his sides to keep his massive belly from shaking too hard. But when the gunsmith looked down at the unsmiling boy in front of him, he fought hard to get control of himself. Taking a deep breath, he let a few last chuckles escape him before saying, "Sorry, boy, didn't mean to laugh, it just hit me funny."

Davey's lips twisted. Some grown-ups had a right strange sense of humor. He'd been up and down the street for the last hour, talking to everybody, and hadn't found one soul yet who'd paid him much mind. Everett had been his last hope. And the way the man was laughing like a loon, Davey figured he just might be related to that crazy female Brady was so worked up over.

"Now boy," Everett was saying, "most women I've known are pretty much loco. Never met one yet with a lick o' sense."

"But do you know this one?" Davey prompted, eager to get his task done and his dollar collected.

"Can't say as I do, boy," the gunsmith said, leaning back on his chair until the wood creaked and groaned in complaint. "Pretty, is she?"

Davey thought back to his first glance of her. He hadn't thought at the time that she was pretty—not like Miss Lily or Miss Fern—but she had good eyes. Real warm and understanding.

But he wasn't about to tell Everett that. So instead he just shrugged. "I guess."

The gunsmith scraped one beefy hand across his whiskery jaw. "Well hell, boy, if she's pretty enough, a man's liable to be willing to overlook some craziness." He smiled to himself and added, "Why, I remember a time when—"

"I got to get back to work, Mr. Tuttle," Davey interrupted him quickly, knowing only too well how long Everett could talk once he got wound up.

"Ah," the man said, nodding toward a dismantled pistol lying scattered across his counter. "Well then, you best get going so's I can get back to fixing this Colt."

Disgusted, Davey turned for the door, shuffling his feet against the unswept wood planks. Disappointment crouched inside him as he realized he had no news to give Brady. It wasn't just knowing that he probably wouldn't be paid—after all, he hadn't found out anything—but he hated to let Brady down when the man had trusted him with work.

He was almost to the door when Everett's voice stopped him.

"What's that you've got slung over your shoulder there?"

Davey stopped and looked back, one hand going to the brass circle he'd looped up his arm and over his shoulder. "Just a little hoop's all."

"You're a caution, boy," Everett said, shaking his head. "Always pickin' up junk, aren't you?"

Frowning to himself, Davey walked outside, the big man's words ringing in his ears. Pulling the metal circle off, he held it in both hands and smoothed his fingertips across its warm surface. "It ain't junk," he muttered and stepped out of the way of Martha Higgins and her twins.

Jumping off the boardwalk, he sat down on the edge of it and, still holding the circle in both hands, looked up as Tommy Sutton ran past, chasing after his hoop, smacking it with a stick to make it roll faster. Envy puddled inside him briefly. Tommy had a ma and a pa and a house with his own bed to sleep in. He got to go to school so he wouldn't grow up ignorant.

Davey swiped one hand under his nose and looked back at the metal ring in his hands. "And on top of all that, he's got him a new hoop to roll." He sighed as he rubbed his fingertips around the brass circle and fought down a swell of regret. "If you was just a little bit bigger, I could roll you around town."

Instantly, the old brass hummed in his hands. Davey's eyes widened. He held his breath. The already warm metal blossomed with a heat that Davey felt clean to his bones, yet didn't burn his hands at all. He told himself to drop the durn thing, but he couldn't quite bring himself to do it. Instead, he held on tighter, harder, and felt it when the circle began to grow.

"Oh my," he whispered, completely unaware of anything but the near miracle happening right under his nose.

As he grasped that ring, it continued growing, stretching, and he was helpless to do anything but hold his breath and watch. It shifted, pulsing, pushing itself into a new size, while maintaining its perfectly round shape. And in only seconds, the humming stopped, the heat faded into its normal warmth, and Davey was sitting on the edge of the boardwalk, holding a hoop-sized brass ring.

He blinked at it in stunned surprise, but then slowly a smile built on his face and he rubbed the surface of the thing lovingly. "Well now," he murmured, "if that don't beat all."

It was a hard thing when a man was run out of his own place of business, Brady thought, stepping through the double doors of the saloon. A ripple of laughter followed him outside and he walked to the edge of the boardwalk in an effort to distance himself from it.

Hell, wasn't it enough that he'd been given a bill for all the new clothes Patience had bought at the Mercantile? Wasn't it enough that the woman had planted herself upstairs in the room right beside his? Or that she'd already started in on Joe, trying to help him rearrange the stockroom?

Nope, he thought grimly, leaning forward and

curling his fingers around the porch rail. Apparently it wasn't near enough for the crazy woman who was pushing him into insanity himself. No, she'd had to go and tell a few of his customers that she was Brady's fiancée. And now those men were having the time of their lives, laughing at him.

He shot a look heavenward and scowled, just in case there was Somebody up there. "Whatever you're doing, cut it the hell out," he muttered. "Find somebody else to play your games on. I'm not interested."

Naturally there was no answer and he hadn't really expected one anyway. He'd seen little enough in his life that would make him think there was some benevolent God up there worried about what everybody down here was up to. And if there was, he figured that God wouldn't have much to say to an ex-gunfighting gambler.

Which was fine by him, since he preferred running his own life anyway. Besides, from what he'd seen God hadn't done any of his believers a helluva lot of favors.

Frustration still bubbling inside him, Brady squinted against the bright sunlight and caught a flicker of motion out of the corner of his eye. Straightening up, he watched as Davey raced up, slapping at a hoop with a long stick. A reluctant smile curved his mouth as he realized this was the first time he could remember seeing the kid actually play. Usually, he was too busy running from one of his jobs to the next to take the time to just be a boy.

Davey grabbed his hoop, swallowed his own smile, and jumped up onto the boardwalk to stand in front of Brady. He bounced that hoop against his shin and shuffled his feet, scraping the worn soles of his boots across the uneven planks. Then he ducked his head briefly, looked up, and swung that fall of brown hair out of his eyes before saying, "I'm sure sorry, Brady." Clutching the hoop as though it were the deed to a gold mine, he said, "Nobody knows nothing about her."

"Anything," Brady corrected absently.

"Anything." Davey shrugged bony shoulders. "It's like she just fell outa the sky or something, 'cause nobody ever heard tell of her."

Brady frowned to himself. "The only thing that falls out of the sky is a bird, and she's no bird."

The boy chuckled, then stopped again quickly. "No sir, she ain't."

"Isn't."

"Isn't," Davey said, nodding, then added, "But she don't belong here either."

"Doesn't."

The boy sighed. "Doesn't."

Brady lifted his gaze to look beyond the boy, toward the edge of town. If she wasn't from here—and that piece of news hadn't surprised him any—then she had to be from Santa Fe. And if she was, he'd find where she belonged.

Today.

A shuffle of feet drew his attention back to the kid as he turned to leave, narrow shoulders slumped, chin resting on his chest.

"Aren't you forgetting something?" Brady asked and the boy turned around to look at him.

"Huh?"

"Your dollar?" he prompted, when the boy just stared at him.

"You don't have to pay me, Brady. I didn't find out anything."

Pride, he thought. A powerful thing in one so small. Digging one hand into his pocket, he pulled out a single coin and flipped it in the air toward the kid. Davey snatched it and held it clutched in one grubby fist.

"I didn't pay you to find something, Davey," he said softly. "I paid you to ask questions."

Looking from Brady to his closed fist and back again, the boy smiled before pocketing that coin. "Thanks, Brady."

He nodded, then jerked his head in the direction of the saloon doors. "Joe's setting out the bar lunch," he said. "Why don't you go in and help him? Then get yourself something to eat."

"Yes, sir," he said and headed right off.

The doors swung crazily for a moment, marking the boy's passage, and when they stilled, Brady told himself that at least the kid would eat one good meal today. And he wished all of his problems were so easily solved.

"I'm afraid I still don't understand," Patience said as she watched Lily tuck a lovely red feather into her upswept blond hair.

The woman glanced at her in the mirror and laughed. "What's not to understand, honey? I work here. I support myself. And I don't need a man to help me do it." She paused for a moment, then chuckled. "Well, all right, maybe I do need a man to help me do it."

Patience felt a hot flush of embarrassment race through her and flood her cheeks. Since finishing her shopping, she'd been at loose ends. She'd already helped Joe rearrange the stockroom and met a few of Brady's friends. And, she thought, remembering the stunned expressions on the faces of the men she'd spoken to in the bar, she had to wonder when people were going to stop pretending not to know her.

It was all very peculiar.

But then she dismissed the thought and returned her mind to the moment at hand. Until it was time to leave for Santa Fe with Brady—a drive she was looking forward to immensely—she'd decided to spend a little time with the women who worked at the saloon.

But Lily didn't seem to be open to conversation any more than Fern and Addey had. Though at least Lily was a bit more willing to listen than the other women. They'd run off the moment she'd said hello—why, they'd almost behaved as if they were afraid of her.

Which was certainly ridiculous.

Perched on the edge of the lone chair in Lily's room, Patience watched the woman opposite her.

Cupping her breasts with both hands, Lily pushed them higher into the black corset she wore atop a full red satin skirt.

Self-consciously, Patience glanced down at her own less-than-abundant bosom and sighed.

When the other woman was satisfied with the amount of flesh displayed, she turned her back on the mirror and looked Patience dead in the eye. "You're not here to try to reform me, are you?" she asked warily. "I mean, you're not going to start spouting Scripture at me?"

"Would you like me to?" Patience asked, already mentally searching for appropriate Bible passages. Though she hadn't really planned on this, she was sure, if given a moment or two, she'd be able to come up with something.

But Lily saved her.

"No, ma'am," she said quickly, giving her a tight smile. "I've heard 'em all, anyway."

"Yes, I suppose you have," Patience said agreeably. "And besides, if you were really interested, you could read them for yourself tonight."

Lily shot her a guarded look. "What do you mean?"

Patience smiled. "Lily, it's no disgrace to read the Bible every night."

"I don't—" The blonde straightened up, shot an almost guilty glance around the otherwise empty room, and then stared at Patience as though she had just sprouted another head. "How did you know about that?"

She opened her mouth to answer that question, then snapped it shut again. For heaven's sake. How *did* she know? She wasn't sure. But the knowledge was there. In her mind. She just . . . *knew*.

How very odd.

"Is somebody talking about me?" Lily asked, her voice quiet. "I mean, if word gets out that I—"

"That you're more than you pretend to be?" Patience finished for her.

Now it was Lily's turn for flushed cheeks. Uneasiness was written all over her face and she twisted her hands together at her waist as if looking for something to hold on to. Then defensively, she said, "It doesn't mean anything. The reading, I mean. It's just a comfort sometimes, is all."

"Of course it is. Why do you think so many people read the Bible?"

"For ammunition."

"I beg your pardon."

Lily pulled herself together, drew a long, deep breath, and said, "Folks don't read the Bible to be better people. They just read it to be better than everybody else."

"That's a hard thing to say."

"But true," Lily said, though she softened her words with a half-smile. "I've been preached at, around, and over for years."

Compassion stirred within Patience's breast and she stood up, crossing the room to stand beside the other woman. She laid one hand on her forearm and said softly, "If people knew why you'd chosen this life, perhaps—"

Openmouthed, Lily stared at her. "What do you know about—"

"Oh Lily, don't you remember that night just a few weeks ago?"

For a long moment, she said nothing, then realization dawned. "No," the other woman said, shaking her head and pressing her lips together tightly.

"Yes you do," Patience said, and let her memory drift back to that night when she'd found Lily here, in her room, sobbing as though her heart might break. "You were reading those old letters. And saying how you wished things had been different."

Lily shook her head again, as if silently denying Patience's words.

But Patience wasn't a woman to be stopped by denial. "I put my arms around you and held you while you cried. You told me all about how your husband died in the war and how you were left alone. To fend for yourself in a world that's seldom kind to women alone."

"I didn't—" Lily whispered shakily, but her gaze was soft in memory and her brow furrowed.

"You did," Patience told her softly. "And after a while, you felt better. Remember?"

Lily stared at her for a long moment. She licked dry lips and tried to still the wild racing of her heart. She *had* felt better after her wild cry that night when she'd mourned all that was lost to her. Her gaze shifted to Patience's hand on her arm and she took comfort in the warmth of the woman's touch. Lifting her gaze again to look into the golden eyes still watching her, Lily asked breathlessly, "Who are you?"

"Your friend," Patience said and gave her a smile bright enough to chase away any shadows still remaining in Lily's soul.

And for one brief, wonderful moment, Lily believed her.

Chapter Five

The wagon hit a rut in the road and Patience lurched forward on the seat, swaying dangerously near the edge. But Brady's reactions were quick. He caught her forearm in a firm grip and yanked her back squarely onto the seat.

"Hang on to something, will you?" he demanded and released her as quickly as he'd reached for her.

But it didn't seem to matter. Patience still felt the warm imprint of his fingers on her arm as clearly as if he'd branded her with his touch. She smiled to herself and ignored his snappish tone. After all, he'd probably only been afraid she was going to be hurt. She slanted a glance at him and found herself silently admiring his strong profile. His nose was straight and narrow, his jaw square with a no-nonsense chin. His mouth, even set as it was now, in a grim slash across his face, was a pleasant one and his pale blue eyes looked as clear and cold as the sky above them. His dark brown hair was a little too long, curling slightly over his shirt collar, and Patience made a mental note to speak to him about getting a haircut before the wedding. He wore a black hat, pulled down low over his eyes, a black coat and trousers, and a forest-green vest. A handsome man, she thought and felt the oddest sensation take up residence in her abdomen—and lower.

Slapping one hand against her stomach, Patience frowned and tried to calm the nest of butterflies whirling around within her.

"Something wrong?" Brady asked, shooting her a quick look before turning his gaze back to the long stretch of road in front of them.

"I don't know," she said honestly. "It's just—"

He turned a wary eye on her.

Instantly, she read the unspoken question in his eyes and stiffened her spine in response. "I am *not* going to fall into a fit, Brady Shaw, and I wish you would stop this ridiculous pretense of yours."

His jaw worked for a long moment as if he were chewing on the words he refused to let escape. Finally, though, he surrendered and blurted, "I'm not pretending anything, Patience."

She squirmed around on the seat until she was facing him. Clapping one hand to the top of her head to hold one of her brand-new hats in place—as she didn't want to see the lovely yellow creation bouncing off across the desert—she looked right at him. "You most certainly are. You're behaving as though you'd never seen me before and I must say I find it terribly rude."

"Well, pardon the hell outa me," he muttered, then snapped his mouth shut.

"I wish you wouldn't swear," she said.

"Lady, in this situation, that's about all I've got left."

Another rut shook the wagon and this time Patience fell against Brady. Her arms went around his neck and she held on for dear life until the wagon straightened itself and continued on. But even then, she was reluctant to let go of him.

Just being this close to him filled her with more wonderful sensations than she could possibly describe. Her breasts pressed against his upper arm, heat shimmered through her body and lit up her insides like a shower of falling stars in a night sky. His jaw was no more than a breath away and Patience licked suddenly dry lips as she inhaled the sweet scent of bay rum clinging to him.

It had always been like this for her. She'd loved him so long, she thought, it was as if he were a part of her.

"You can let go now, Patience," Brady said softly, never taking his gaze from the road.

"I know," she said, but kept holding on to him.

He inhaled sharply and blew the air out in a rush impatiently. "Patience," he asked, "why in the hell are you so all-fired set on marrying me?"

She drew her head back and looked at him. Her gaze moved over his so familiar, so dear features until he finally shifted his gaze to meet hers. Only then did she smile and say, "Because I love you, Brady."

A flicker of some emotion danced in his eyes and was gone again in less than a heartbeat. She couldn't identify it. Wasn't even sure she'd seen it. But at least she knew her words had had some effect on him—despite his efforts to deny it.

The word "love" rattled around inside his brain for a long minute before Brady deliberately chased it out. She didn't love him. Hell, she didn't even *know* him. And if she didn't take her arms from around his neck soon, he just might be tempted to forget that she was nuts.

Damned if he couldn't feel her warmth skittering through him. Her small breasts pressed to him, her thigh alongside his, he felt the brush of her breath soft against his cheek and he closed his eyes briefly in a futile attempt to ignore what she was doing to his body.

"Sit back, Patience," he said tightly, squeezing the words past the knot in his throat. Maybe traveling to Santa Fe with her hadn't been such a good idea after all, he thought. They still had a few more miles to go and then there was the ride home to survive.

But, he thought, perking right up, with any luck at all, he'd be *alone* for the return trip. And Patience would be tucked up in whatever attic was awaiting her.

And as that thought presented itself, he winced. He'd known her less than a day, but there was something about her that made him regret the fact that she would no doubt be locked away somewhere. It wasn't as if she were dangerous—to anyone but him. He shifted uncomfortably on the wooden bench seat and wished he had enough room to ease away from her a bit. But even if he had, it wouldn't do him a damn sight of good with her clinging to him like fresh wallpaper.

Gritting his teeth, he took one hand from the reins, reached up and disengaged her arms from around his neck. Sparing her a quick look, he said, "Just sit back and hold on, all right?"

She smiled and he sucked in a gulp of air. Damn, that smile of hers was enough to light up every dark corner in a man's soul. But as soon as that thought flashed through his mind, he dismissed it. His shadowy corners had been dark too long.

"What is it you're afraid of, Brady?" she asked, her face entirely too close to his.

"I'm not afraid, Patience," he said. "Just not interested."

And even he didn't believe that whopper.

Sure enough, she laughed and the sound of it washed over him, through him, and Brady knew he was headed for some serious trouble real soon.

"Oh Brady," she said and leaned in close, planting a quick, fever-inducing kiss on his cheek. "We're going to have a grand life together."

He wouldn't get mad, he told himself firmly. He wasn't going to let this little woman fire up a temper he'd been able to control for more than ten years. But he also wasn't going to let her keep talking foolishness.

"The only thing we're going to have together is a ride to Santa Fe," he said and snapped the reins in the air over the horse's back. Why wouldn't the damn animal run? Hell, an empty wagon couldn't weigh that much, could it?

"And home again," she said, easing back onto her corner of the bench, thank heaven. Then she smoothed her palms across her skirt and fiddled with the hem until even the toes of her shoes were decently covered.

Brady rolled his eyes.

"And then we'll have to start planning the wedding," she was saying. "We can meet with the preacher in town or—" She stopped and laid her hand on his forearm in a much too familiar fashion. "Would you rather be married in Santa Fe? Perhaps at the Loretto chapel?"

He shot her a quick look and tried not to notice the eagerness shining in those golden depths. Instead, he focused on what she'd just said. The Loretto chapel. She knew about it. So she'd been to Santa Fe. Probably lived there and somehow had wandered off and ended up in Fortune.

Keeping his voice even, he asked, "You've seen the chapel?"

"Oh my, yes," she said and folded her hands in her lap as any well-bred lady would. "It's a lovely little place, isn't it?"

"From the outside, sure," he agreed, though privately he thought it a little showy for a town where most of the churches were made of adobe.

"Oh, but the inside is even nicer," she went on and waited for his acknowledgment.

"I wouldn't know," he said, hoping she'd let it drop, but somehow knowing she wouldn't.

He was right.

"That's right. You've never been inside."

"Now how'd you know that?" he asked and felt a curl of suspicion unwind inside him. He had no satisfaction for it, though, since she answered his question with one of her own.

"Whyever not?"

"C'mon, horse!" he shouted, snapping the reins

again before he glanced at her and shrugged. "Why would I want to go inside a church?"

"To pray?"

He laughed at the absurdity of the notion and let the chuckles keep rolling despite feeling her stiffen alongside him.

"What did I say that was so funny?" she demanded.

His fingers tightened on the reins and he let his gaze slide to the left of the road. In the far distance, he could just make out the turtleback hump of the Sandia Mountains while off to the right were the Sangre de Cristos, and he knew they were closing in on Santa Fe.

For miles in any direction, there was nothing but scrub brush, piñon and juniper trees, and some scraggly mesquite. Farther up the mountains, the landscape changed, of course, with the piñon giving way to ponderosa pines, then higher up came the firs and aspens.

But down here, it was mainly desert with the occasional stretch of grasslands. The sky stretched on into eternity and a cold wind swept across the open land, plucking at the edges of his coat. The wheels on the road crunched over rock and dirt and the horse snorted its complaints at being rushed.

And still he didn't answer her.

"Brady?" she said, prodding as he'd guessed she would.

Sighing, he turned to look at her. "If you knew me as well as you claim to, Patience," he said quietly, "then you'd know I don't pray and so I don't have any reason to go inside churches."

She frowned at him, but it wasn't anger he saw in her eyes, it was a wealth of sadness. His spine stiffened instantly. He didn't need or want her pity. A humorless laugh shot through him. A crazy woman feeling sorry for *him*? That'd be the day.

"You used to pray," she said finally, and the words seemed to hang in the air between them.

Yeah, he had. If he tried, he could probably dredge up dusty memories of whispered prayers going unanswered. But why the hell would he want to?

"I used to be no bigger than Davey too," he pointed out, in a tone that said he didn't want to discuss it. "Things change."

"Not so much," she said, obviously intending to ignore his unspoken warning to drop the subject. Then, leaning toward him again, she added, "You're still lonely."

The observation hit him hard, but he wouldn't let her know it. Damn it, he'd been alone for a lot of years, but that didn't necessarily make him lonely. There was a big difference between alone and lonesome. He did what he wanted, when he wanted, where he wanted. Hell, most men he knew envied Brady's life.

Well, at least they had until Patience had stumbled into it. But by now, there were rumors and laughter racing through Fortune . . . at his expense. His back teeth ground together. Funny how a woman named Patience could cause so much *im*patience.

"There's Santa Fe," he said, diverting her attention as he lifted one hand and pointed.

She turned her head to stare into the distance where he pointed.

Like a far-off island seen from the deck of a ship, the squat buildings of Santa Fe called out to him. There, he'd find peace again. There, he'd find the people Patience belonged to. Then, he'd be able to get back to his life.

The one so many men envied.

One of the oldest cities—well, some said *the* oldest city—in America bustled with an eagerness that belied its humble buildings and dusty roads. Wagons raced up and down wide streets, children ran, laughing and playing, merchants pushed handcarts loaded with their wares, and pious old women draped in black shawls sat outside adobe homes, fingering their rosaries.

The scent of beans and beef drifted on the chill wind and Patience sniffed appreciatively. She was hungry. In fact, she was ravenous. She couldn't remember ever being quite so hungry. Her stomach rumbled and she glanced guiltily at Brady.

He grinned and her toes curled.

"We'll get something to eat, then go see about my shipment."

She nodded, and after he parked the wagon in front of a cantina, she stood up and let him help her down. His hands at her waist felt warm, solid, and sent a ripple of awareness rocketing down her spine. He set her on her feet but didn't let her go, and for one agonizing moment, she thought her knees might buckle.

Then she looked up at him and actually *watched* him distance himself from her. He released her then and took a step back just for good measure. Patience swallowed back the needles of hurt poking the inside of her throat and told herself that it didn't matter. All that mattered was that she was here. With him. Where she was meant to be.

Everything else would work itself out in time.

Being with Patience was like looking at the world for the first time.

Brady wondered if all crazy people had this special gift for enjoying everything around them or if it was simply Patience herself. He had a feeling that it was just her.

Watching her now as she walked through the plaza past the Palace of the Governors, he saw it all anew. The people, the colors, the long, squat adobe building that served as the seat of government. Under the overhang, on the porch, vendors sat, crouched in the shade, selling everything from silver jewelry to tamales.

Patience walked along, inspecting it all. And Brady accompanied her, hoping that someone would see her and recognize her. But that wasn't the only reason, he thought as he watched her oohing and aahing over the merchandise displayed. A small part of him—a part he didn't want to admit to—was enjoying this time with her.

She paused in front of an old woman selling glazed clay pottery, and as she chatted in fluent Spanish, Brady watched her, amazed. She fit right in here. As if she'd always belonged. And yet her smooth white skin told him she hadn't spent much time in the windy desert. Her Spanish was fault-less—unlike his own—and her warm smile drew people to her like children to a vat of ice cream.

She started walking again and Brady kept just a pace or two behind her. Her pale yellow dress stood out among the dusty browns and blacks like a single bolt of sunshine in the middle of a rainstorm. In fact, she damn near sparkled with an inner light that made her seem so much more alive than the people around her.

Hell, the city itself felt more alive to him because of her.

And all of this was beginning to worry him.

She seemed to recognize Santa Fe, yet she acted as though she were seeing it all for the first time. She knew places, and street names. She knew where his favorite cantina was and she'd greeted the owner, Eduardo, as if they were old friends.

Now, as they turned onto the Santa Fe Trail road, she quickened her steps, headed directly for the Loretto chapel. Just as if she'd known all along where it was.

When she threaded her arm through his, he felt an unwelcome spurt of warmth shoot through him and he told himself that none of this mattered. He'd been charmed by women before. And nothing had come of it. Just as nothing—no matter what Patience thought—would come of this.

"There," she said, drawing a deep breath and sigh-ing it out again. "Isn't it lovely?"

He glanced at the chapel, not the nearby cathedral with its two spires pointed straight at heaven. Most of the churches in town were adobe. Bricks made of mud and straw and then baked in the sun. But not the Loretto. This chapel was made of sandstone and volcanic rock. It looked like a smaller version of an engraving he'd seen once of a castle in England. Well, a castle with stained-glass windows and a slew of nuns who looked after the place and most of the children in and around town.

Just being this close to the little chapel made him want to turn around and head back to the cantina for another beer. But he had a mission, and he was damn well going to complete it.

Determinedly, then, he headed across the street, practically dragging Patience in his wake. She took two steps for every one of his, and when he glanced at her, he saw she was holding that silly little hat in place as she ran.

He slowed down a bit and she flashed him a smile that was well worth whatever else he had to put up with today. And even as that thought presented itself, he wanted to give his own ass a good kick. He wasn't going to get pulled in by a pretty smile and a warm touch. Instead, he was going to find a place to leave Patience and then he was going back home.

To the saloon.

Where he belonged a sight more than he did a church.

Striding right up to the double doors, he yanked one of them open and ushered Patience inside. Before he could talk himself out of it, he followed after her.

The whole place was hushed, as if the world had drawn a breath and held it. Whitewashed walls shone in the afternoon sunlight and that same sun came pouring through the stained-glass windows, dotting the gleaming wood floor with patches of brilliant color.

Releasing Patience, Brady reached up and took off his hat, while letting his gaze slide around the empty church. He'd been hoping to find a stray nun in here. Ask her some questions. But they were probably all over at the boarding and day school they ran. Uncomfortable in a place where men of his kind surely weren't wanted, he shifted and grabbed for Patience's hand. "No one here," he said quietly. "Let's go over to the school."

"Just a minute," she said, lifting one hand to stay him and slipping out of his grasp as easily as fog sifting across the ocean. She walked farther into the chapel, headed straight for the circular staircase to her right.

Brady tugged at the collar of his shirt. "Patience . . ."

"Look, Brady," she said, motioning for him to come closer. "Isn't it beautiful?"

He cleared his throat, swallowed hard, and went to her. Anything to get her to hurry up. "What?"

She looked at him and he swore he saw some strange brilliant light shining from her golden eyes. But in the next instant, he told himself he was imagining things.

"This. The staircase."

"Yeah," he said, giving it a quick look. "Real nice."

She huffed out a breath and planted both hands on her hips. "Don't you see the wonder in it?"

Impatient now, he took another look. What he saw was several different types of wood, all polished until they shone like multicolored mirrors, pieces fitted together to make a series of narrow steps that circled around in on itself up to a choir loft. He took another look and frowned to himself.

"There's nothing supporting it," Patience said.

"I just noticed that," he said and leaned in closer, turning his face up, to follow the curve of the staircase that by all rights shouldn't have been able to stand.

"When they built the chapel, the builder forgot to leave room for a staircase to the loft." Patience ran one hand lovingly along the dark banister. "They say the nuns made a novena to Saint Joseph, asking for help. And soon after, a wandering carpenter arrived and built this staircase before disappearing into the desert again."

"He did nice work," Brady said, nodding. "Damn—darn impressive." Being in church could really put a crimp in a man's vocabulary. Another good reason for avoiding them.

He glanced at Patience in time to see her expression put the lie to her name. "What?" he asked.

"Don't you see? It was Saint Joseph himself who built this staircase. *He* was the mysterious carpenter."

Brady just shook his head. How was a man to argue when there wasn't a shred of logic to grab hold of? "You expect me to believe somebody from heaven dropped into Santa Fe just long enough to build a staircase?"

"How else do you explain it?" she demanded.

"A carpenter," he said tightly. "Just a man. A talented one."

"And then he disappeared?"

"He left," Brady corrected, but judging by her expression, she wasn't willing to let go of her own little fable. "Patience," he started, then stopped himself. "Nope. Not going to do it. Not going to get into another argument with you."

"At last," she said.

He arched an eyebrow at her. "You ready to leave now?"

"Fine," she said abruptly and marched past him toward the door. "But if you think we're through discussing this, you're mistaken."

Shaking his head and gritting his teeth, Brady followed her outside. Somewhere in this town, someone knew this stubborn female and he wasn't leaving until he found them.

"Are we almost home?" Patience asked two hours later from the bench seat beside him.

The boxes of whiskey on the wagon bed behind them rattled and clanked together as they had over every inch of road from Santa Fe. The sun was setting and the wind had kicked up something fierce. He'd walked himself footsore all over Santa Fe and hadn't found a single soul who knew anything about a missing crazy woman. Patience recognized plenty of people in town, but no one claimed to know her.

Which meant that Brady had wasted most of the

day only to end up right where he'd started in the first place.

With Patience.

And very little patience.

He pointed to a curve in the road. "Just beyond there. Only a few more minutes."

"Good," she said and leaned against him, settling her head on his shoulder and threading her arm through the crook of his. "I confess, I'm tired."

Strange, he thought, shifting a bit on the seat again. With her this close, he wasn't feeling tired. In fact, his body was alive enough to worry him. He didn't need this complication, he thought. What he needed was his life back.

All too soon, they were pulling up in front of the saloon. Brady grabbed hold of the brake handle and yanked hard enough to snap the wood clean off. It didn't help ease the temper riding him. Muttering to himself, he jumped down from the bench seat, then looked up to see Patience standing there, waiting for his assistance.

Hell, he didn't want to touch her again. Touching her made him forget just how much he wanted her gone. But there was just no help for it.

Holding up his arms, he grabbed her waist when she bent over and placed her hands on his shoulders. He swung her down quickly and let her go as soon as her feet hit the mud-caked street.

She looked up at him, cocked her head to one side, and asked, "What are you thinking, Brady?"

What wasn't he thinking? His brain was racing at

such a pace he felt as though his head might explode. But it all boiled down to one thing.

He took hold of her wrists and pulled her hands off his shoulders. A horse and rider passed them, but neither of them made a move toward the boardwalk.

"I'm wondering," he said, giving in to the urge to be honest, "just why it is I haven't thrown you out yet."

Her brow furrowed slightly as she shook her head. Then reaching up, she laid one hand on his cheek and Brady tried desperately to ignore the stab of pure heat that nearly dazzled him.

"When you were twelve years old," she said quietly, and he had to strain to hear her over the everyday sounds of town life. "You were lying belowdecks on that awful riverboat where you worked."

Brady just stared at her as memories came rushing back, filling his mind.

"You were hurt. Hurt too badly to even cry," she said and tears filled her eyes as she spoke. Her thumb slid across his cheekbone in a soothing touch.

His throat tightened around a knot of emotion that felt as though it were choking him. Hurt. Yeah, he'd been hurt. Beaten black and blue by a gambler who hadn't appreciated a clumsy kid spilling a drink on his white suit coat.

"The sound of the paddle wheel was your only company, and there in the shadows, you prayed for someone to love you." Patience smiled then and her eyes glistened through the sheen of unshed tears. "Here I am, Brady. *I* love you. How can you want me to leave?"

Staggered, Brady felt everything inside him go cold and still. He remembered it all so well. The pain. The whispered prayer in the darkness—that had of course, gone unanswered. The sense of aloneness that had damn near crushed him.

But what he didn't remember was Patience being there.

Air. He needed air. And yet he couldn't drag a breath into his straining lungs. His heart thudded painfully in his chest. His stomach churned and his mouth felt like cotton. How? How did she know so much?

He stared into her eyes and saw a flicker of confusion and worry written in those golden depths and he knew that she'd surprised herself with that little speech.

Then she lowered her hand from his face and he felt the loss of her touch right down to his soul.

Chapter Six

"'Bout time you got back, boss," Joe shouted as he barreled through the double doors and set them swinging so hard they slapped the walls.

Patience shook her head, took a step back from Brady, and whispered tightly, "I have to go. Inside."

"Just wait a damn minute," Brady said, making a grab for her. But she sidestepped him neatly, jumped up onto the boardwalk, scurried through the still-swinging doors, and disappeared into the saloon.

"Boss?" the bartender prodded.

"Huh?" Brady said, tearing his gaze from Patience's retreating form to shoot an irritated glance at his bartender. "What?"

"I said, you've been gone so damn long, thought maybe you wasn't comin' back."

Grumbling to himself, Brady yanked his hat down lower over his eyes and snapped, "What the hell do you care how long I was gone?"

Joe's eyebrows shot straight up on his forehead and he lifted both hands, palm out in mock surrender. "It ain't me, boss," he said and walked a wide berth around Brady, headed for the tailgate of the wagon. Slipping the chains and pegs loose, he lowered the back gate and grabbed the first boxful of liquor bottles. Hefting them easily, he rested the edge of the box on one shoulder and shot Brady a cautious look. "Texas Jack was here lookin' for you."

Perfect, Brady told himself. Just what he needed to end a miserable day. Texas Jack Bigelow was a loudmouth and a cheat but he had a fair hand with a pistol and fancied himself a gunslinger. When he was sober, Jack was easy enough to dismiss with a hard glare. But when he'd been drinking, it took a lot more patience than Brady had at the moment to avoid a fight of some kind.

"He still here?" he asked, hoping to hell Jack had found someone else to bother. Because in the mood he was in right now, he just might have to whale into Jack and the devil take the hindmost.

"Nope. Rode out about an hour ago, headed for Cripple Creek. Said he'd be back in a week or two, though." Joe headed for the saloon, but paused alongside Brady for a moment. "Said you should be ready for him."

As long as he wasn't here today, Brady thought. Hell, if there was one thing he didn't want to deal with now, it was some drunk trying to build a reputation by killing Brady Shaw.

He had just a few more important things on his mind than some halfwit who thought himself a bad man. Like just who the hell Patience really was. And how she knew so damn much about him. And why she was here. And how he was supposed to keep sane.

Hell, if this kept up, Texas Jack wouldn't have to kill him. Dealing with Patience would take care of that job, real nice.

But as that thought registered, it put his back up. Damned if he was going to let some strange woman march into his life and cause more kinds of trouble than a brushfire in a drought. He wanted answers and, by God, he was going to get them. Now. Pushing past Joe, Brady stomped through the saloon. He ignored the catcalls of the men gathered around the poker tables. Apparently the news about him and Patience being "engaged" had already spread through town on the local gossip wire.

He didn't see Davey sitting at the bar helping himself to another meal. He didn't notice Lily sitting off in a corner by herself. He didn't pay the slightest attention to anything but the door abovestairs. Behind which Patience waited.

Davey cringed as he watched Brady take the stairs two steps at a time. The man looked mad enough to bite through a ten-penny nail. A twinge of sympathy for the strange woman squeezed Davey's heart. Heck, he figured she couldn't help it none if she was peculiar.

But Brady wasn't the kind to slap a female around, and from what he'd seen already, that Patience could take care of herself. So rather than worry about some problem between grown-ups, Davey turned his mind to something *really* important.

His hoop.

Reaching down to his knee, from which the brass ring was hanging, he ran one hand over the warm metal as if to reassure himself that it was still there. He took another bite of hard-boiled egg and washed it down with a sip of the sarsaparilla Joe had given him.

A small swell of satisfaction washed over him. He was tired, but it had been a good day. He'd earned durn near a dollar and seventy cents. He'd helped Brady. He'd found a magic ring—though as soon as he thought the word "magic," he looked guiltily around the room. He'd have to keep it quiet, this magic ring. Else somebody would be after taking it from him.

And then he wouldn't have anything.

His fingers curled around the brass protectively as Joe stomped up beside him and set a box full of liquor bottles onto the bartop. The big man shot a glance at the upstairs landing and Davey did the same, frowning at the sight of Brady standing outside the woman's door, a look of fury on his face.

"He sure looks mad."

Joe snorted and shook his head. "That's what a female will do to you, boy. You pay attention."

"Yessir," Davey muttered, keeping his gaze locked on the man upstairs.

"You see," Joe went on, warming to his theme as he folded his arms atop the liquor bottles. "A man's got to be careful about letting a woman into his life. Oh, they seem right handy to have around," he mused, almost to himself. A smile drifted across his face briefly before he shot a quick, guilty look in Davey's direction and cleared his throat noisily. "But the minute you get a female stickin' her nose into things, your life goes to hell in a handbasket."

"Yeah?" Davey asked, shifting his gaze from Brady to Joe.

The bartender nodded solemnly. "Just take a look

at Brady up yonder," he said, his voice low and deep, carrying easily over the noise in the saloon. "You recall ever seein' him that mad?"

Davey thought about it for a long minute and finally said, "Not since the last time Texas Jack was here." He remembered the fight that night real well. Heck, Brady had tossed Jack right through that front window and the man had durn near bounced across the boardwalk and into the street.

"There you go," Joe said. "See? The only thing that'll make a man madder'n a female is some fella wanting to kill him."

Seemed right, Davey thought as Joe turned to go outside for another load of booze. Still, he told himself, watching the goings-on upstairs again, he figured he'd rather be dealing with Patience than with somebody as mean as Texas Jack Bigelow.

Then he shrugged, kept one hand on his magic ring, and picked up his sandwich with the other. Wasn't his business what grown-ups did. He just thought it a shame that what had been such a fine day for him had turned out so bad for his friend.

Patience set her hat down atop the scarred chest of drawers and glanced into the small, square shaving mirror hanging on the wall. Heart pounding, mouth dry, she stared at her own reflection and tried to understand what she'd just said to Brady.

The words had come of their own volition. She didn't recall summoning them. She only knew that when he asked her why he should let her stay, the answer had come to her. But once she'd actually said the words aloud, they'd reverberated in her mind until her body nearly shook with reaction.

How had she known that? How had she known something so private? The scene she'd described to Brady rose up in her mind and Patience saw it all so clearly. She could almost hear the thump of the paddle wheel as it slapped against the water. She could smell the river, see the lightning bugs, hear the laughter drifting down from the upper decks. It was all true. It had happened just that way, she knew it. But how was it possible that she should know it? He'd been only a child. She would have been, too, that many years ago.

She folded her arms around her middle and held on. Backing up slowly until the backs of her knees hit the bed, she slowly sank down onto the edge of the mattress and stared blankly at the floor. Children. She and Brady had been children.

Yet the memories she had of her own childhood had nothing to do with riverboats. Scowling, she recalled log cabins, women in long black dresses, and men wearing short pants, black hose, and buckled shoes. But that couldn't be right. Could it?

If she actually *remembered* the Pilgrims, it would make her over two hundred years old! A choked laugh squeezed past the knot of worry lodged in her throat.

She swallowed hard and muttered, "Don't be foolish, Patience." And just hearing her own voice in the stillness of her room helped. From belowstairs came the muffled sounds of conversations, laughter, and the oddly out-of-tune tinklings of a piano. But here, in this one corner of quiet, she was alone with thoughts that plagued her.

What did it mean, she asked herself, hoping for an answer that wouldn't come. How could she recall someone else's memories so clearly? And why would she remember being a Pilgrim herself?

"Maybe I really am crazy," she whispered and just saying those words aloud sent a shiver along her spine. "No," she argued, "I'm just tired." Then continuing, her voice became a little stronger, more confident. "That's all it is. Exhaustion. The trip to Santa Fe. The coming wedding. Anyone would be a little confused. It's only natural."

Natural to recall someone else's memories? a small voice inside her asked.

She shook her head fiercely. That wasn't at all what was happening. That was impossible. Everyone knew that. So, obviously there'd been some sort of misunderstanding. There was, no doubt, a logical explanation. Now, if she could only think of one.

A knock at the door sounded out, sharp, impatient, and her head snapped up. "Yes?"

"It's me."

Brady. Of course it was him. Who else would it be? No doubt he wanted to talk about her "memory." And she could hardly blame him. She stared at the door as if she could see through it to the man beyond. Her heartbeat quickened until she wouldn't have been surprised to see it fly out of her chest. She swallowed hard, forcing the knot of emotion in her throat down, until it fell like a rock to the pit of her stomach.

And for the first time since she'd known him, Patience didn't want to see him. Well, she mused, amending that thought, to be completely honest with herself, she did *want* to see him. But what could she possibly say to him? No. Better to keep her distance until she was calm again. Until she'd figured out the answers to some of her questions.

"Go away, Brady," she called out.

"Not likely," he said through the door, and even muffled as it was, his voice carried a ring of frustration that she completely understood.

But she couldn't very well ease his frustration while still dealing with her own.

"I—um—have a headache," she told him, not lying, since a thrumming pain was just leaping to life behind her eyes.

"Well," he muttered darkly enough that she had no trouble hearing him. "Finally we have something in common." Then he rattled the knob and she jumped. "Damn it, Patience," he said, a bit louder this time. "Open this blasted door or so help me, God, I'll tear it off the hinges."

She gasped, drew her head back, and glared at the door. A quick jolt of anger flashed through her despite her own uneasiness, and since anger was so much easier to deal with than confusion, she gave in to it.

Instantly, Patience jumped up, crossed the floor, reached out, flipped the lock and grasped the knob. Turning it and pulling at the same time, she yanked the door open so forcefully, Brady nearly fell into the room. He caught himself, though, and, scowling at her, stepped inside. She slammed the door behind him.

Before he could open his mouth, Patience turned on him. Perhaps she might have been more restrained if her own nerves weren't singing at a fever pitch at the moment, but she'd never know for sure. But one thing she would always be certain of was that Patience Goodfellow was *not* a woman to be shouted at.

Tilting her head back, she met his pale blue gaze and said, "I won't be bullied by you or anyone else, Brady Shaw. And I resent having you threaten me."

"I didn't threaten you," he almost snarled.

"You threatened my door."

"I threatened to tear it off, and it's not your door. It's mine," he said. "My saloon, my door."

"My lock," she countered hotly, despite the ridiculousness of the argument. "And if I don't want to be disturbed I'll use it."

"Your lock is on my door and when I want to talk to you, you'll damn well open it or it'll come down."

Fury raged in his eyes and Patience met it with her own surge of temper. Crazy or sane, Pilgrim or not, she would never accept being spoken to in such terms. "I've told you before, Brady, I won't be cowed by a surly disposition."

"Surly?" he repeated, clearly astonished. "Lady, you haven't *seen* surly yet."

She ignored that comment and began walking a slow, tight circle around him, forcing him to turn if he wanted to keep his narrowed gaze on her. "I'm sure that men all over this town tremble in their boots when you give them that bad-tempered stare. But *I* will not."

"I didn't come up here to see you tremble," he muttered.

"Then why *did* you come?" she snapped, almost grateful for the chance to argue. At least it kept her from thinking and considering propositions that were clearly impossible.

"To talk to you," he ground out.

She stopped dead, sniffed haughtily, lifted her chin, and crossed her arms over her chest. "It is quite apparent to me that you're in no mood for a civilized conversation."

He loomed over her, but if he was hoping to intimidate her, he was doomed to disappointment.

"You're right about that," he told her. " 'Civilized' is not how I'm feelin' at the moment."

Neither was she, Patience thought. And when Brady's hands came down on her shoulders, any hope for calm dissolved. His touch only served to quicken her blood and send her heartbeat into a wild gallop.

She sucked in a long, deep breath, but it didn't help. She lifted her gaze to meet his and found no comfort in those pale blue depths. The man before her looked furious. And hard. And cold.

"I want to know, Patience," he said. "And I want to know now. How in the hell do you know so much about me?" His fingers tightened into her shoulders. "Who's been talking to you? And don't try to tell me you were there all those years ago, because I know for a fact you weren't on that riverboat when I was a kid."

"No," she said, wincing just a little as his fingers tightened even more on her shoulders. Instantly, he eased his grip, but he didn't let her go. "I suppose I couldn't have been there . . ." she shook her head, trying to make sense of it all. "But I remember it as though I were. And how else would I know?"

"That's what I'm trying to find out," he said through gritted teeth.

"You must have told me all about it," she said suddenly and as soon as she heard the words spoken aloud, she knew that was the explanation she'd been searching for. How silly of either of them to be so worked up over something so simple.

"No I didn't."

"Of course you did," Patience said, already clutching that truth to her chest. It explained so much. The clarity of the memory. The knowledge of Brady's despair, his pain. How could she possibly have known it if he hadn't told her?

There. She felt much better now.

Brady grabbed her tightly and pulled her close enough that she had to tip her head far back just to meet his gaze. Those eyes of hers glimmered with the sheen of innocence. She looked up at him with complete artlessness and he knew she believed what she was saying.

That momentary burst of surprise he'd seen in her eyes before was gone now. Obviously, she'd found an explanation and was sticking to it. Which didn't explain a thing as far as he was concerned. This was becoming stranger and stranger by the minute.

How did a crazy woman come to know so much about him? Hell, he'd never told *anyone* about that night on the riverboat. He hadn't thought of it himself in years. But the moment she'd mentioned it, that night had come racing back. Memory was so thick, he was choking on it and, damn it, he resented her for it.

He wasn't that lost kid anymore. And damned if he'd spend another minute thinking about the boy he'd been.

As the silence between them stretched on and on and he continued to stare into her eyes, he noticed something. That unshakable belief he saw written in her golden eyes began to dissolve. In its place came a shadowy hint of panic.

Something inside him shifted. He felt his frustration and anger slipping away to be replaced by a reluctant sympathy for Patience. Lord knew he hadn't asked for this, but had she? Was it her fault she was crazy? She'd sailed into his life full of her own confidence in the world and now he saw that sureness disappearing.

And despite how infuriating it was for him to put up with a woman who'd just attached herself to him . . . how terrifying must it be to be her? She had a whole world all made up in her confused head and when faced with its destruction she'd simply built another. Just to protect herself. And damn it, he couldn't really blame her for it, could he?

Wouldn't anyone else do the same? Hell, he'd

practically done the same thing himself. In choosing to ignore his beginnings, to forget his past, he'd really created his own reality.

Just because he wasn't crazy didn't make his pretense any more right than hers, did it?

Man, too many questions and not nearly enough answers. But as he stared into those golden eyes of hers, he knew one thing for certain. He couldn't turn her out into the street any more than he could marry her.

"Brady?" she said and it bothered him that her voice was less sure than it had been before. "You *do* remember telling me about that night, don't you?"

Hope. A wild, desperate hope glittered in her eyes and, damn it, he couldn't ignore it.

"Sure, Patience," he said before he could stop himself. "I remember."

She inhaled sharply, blew the air out again in a rush, and gave him that wide, brilliant smile that almost knocked him off his feet. "Oh, good," she said, shaking her head. "I was actually beginning to wonder if maybe I was imagining things."

Maybe it would have been better to help her discover the truth now. But he just couldn't do it. There was a vulnerability to her at the moment that had Brady thinking that if he tried to force the truth on her now, it would be like kicking a puppy.

The tightness in his chest eased back a notch or two. Temper slowly drained from him and he was left with a hollow feeling. Patience Goodfellow was his problem, he told himself.

At least until he could figure out how to get her

wherever the hell she really belonged. And until then, he'd just go along with her fancies, to keep her mind from shattering any more than it had.

With that thought in mind, he drew her closer, wrapping his arms around her in a move to comfort, not seduce.

She relaxed against him, nuzzling her head against his chest, right beneath his chin. He felt the tension slip from her body and he patted her back awkwardly. She sighed, slid her arms around his waist, and he was forced to remind himself that this wasn't sexual. The racing of his blood was just a normal reaction to the closeness of a female body.

It had nothing to do with Patience in particular.

He closed his eyes and gritted his teeth.

"It'll be all right, Patience."

"Of course it will, Brady," she whispered. "We're together. And that's all that really matters."

Brady bit back a groan and told himself this wouldn't last forever.

Chapter Seven

This was how it was meant to be, Patience told herself and closed her eyes, the better to enjoy standing in the circle of Brady's arms. Her earlier fears, the confusion, melted away in the face of such utter contentment. It felt as though she'd waited years to feel his arms around her—though that couldn't be right. Still, it didn't matter. Nothing mattered but being here. With him. The man she'd loved forever. She listened to the steady beat of his heart beneath her ear and smiled, when she held him closer, as his heartbeat quickened.

It was good to know that he, too, shared this wondrous sensation when they were close. Too many times, she knew that men and women felt no magic together. More often than not, those marriages became more of a prison sentence than a glorious bond of two souls becoming one. But that wouldn't happen with her and Brady. She felt it right down to her bones.

There was magic between them. There was rightness. There was . . . dare she think it? *Destiny*.

She snuggled in closer still, enjoying the feel of his hard, solid body pressed along hers. Her breasts ached. Butterflies took wing in her stomach, and her breath came in short gasps. But she ignored it all, far too intent on enjoying every moment of this time with him. His hands on her back felt warm, strong. His breath brushed across the top of her head and ruffled her hair and she sighed.

"Do you feel it, Brady?" she asked, her voice quiet, to keep from breaking the spell between them.

A groan sounded from deep in his chest and it seemed to her as though it were coming from the depths of his soul. "Oh," he said clearly through gritted teeth, "I'm feeling plenty, Patience."

"I'm glad."

He choked out a half-laugh. "You are, huh?"

"Oh yes," she said and reluctantly lifted her head from his chest to look up at him. She stared into his eyes and said, "I'm glad we feel this way about each other because I want our marriage to be a full and . . . *passionate* one."

A flash of something she couldn't quite identify darted across his eyes. "Patience—"

She spoke up quickly. "I know, it isn't seemly for a woman to speak about such things, but I want you to know that I'm . . . eager to be your wife."

"Jesus," he muttered, closing his eyes briefly before looking at her again. "Patience, we shouldn't be talking about this."

"Yes we should," she said, and moved her hands from his back to his chest.

His jaw clenched.

Her palms slid across his white shirt and she imagined the feel of his hard, muscled skin beneath her hands. A flush of excitement raced through her and stained her cheeks with heat. Her knees felt a bit wobbly, but determined to stay her course, she locked them and looked him dead in the eye. "I can see you're worried about me, Brady," she said, reading the concern and wariness in his gaze. "But you needn't be." She frowned slightly, then went on. "I'm not sure about some of my memories, but one thing of which I will always be certain is my love for you."

As soon as she said the words, he flinched. She felt it in the slight tightening of his grip around her body, saw it in the flex of his jaw muscle.

"Damn it, Patience—"

"Brady, don't you see?" she said, sliding her hands up higher until she was able to encircle his neck. "This was meant to be."

"What was?" he managed, though she swore he hadn't moved his lips at all.

"Us," she said, smiling, willing him to believe her. "*We* were meant to be."

He released his grip on her waist and reached up to pull her hands from behind his neck. Holding her hands in his, he shook his head and said, "Patience, you can't go on talking like this."

She held on to his hands, curling her fingers around his, refusing to let go. "You're right, Brady. We can't go on talking. We've already spent too much time talking."

Boldly, Patience went up on her toes then, tilted her head to one side, and slanted her mouth across his in a soft, gentle kiss. She gasped as, instantly, a bolt of lightning sparked through her from head to toe. She actually felt her blood sizzling in her veins and wouldn't have been surprised to find her hair was on fire. Deliberately, she swayed into him, giving herself up to the startling sensations coursing through her. She pressed her mouth, lips pursed, more firmly to his. She wanted more. Wanted to feel her blood race and her heart pound wildly in her chest.

Brady held perfectly still.

He told himself she didn't know what she was doing. Reminded himself that she wasn't right in the head.

But damned if she didn't *feel* right.

His body pulsing with a shock he never would have anticipated, he tried to figure out how a crazy woman could electrify his body with the briefest touch of her lips. But there were no answers. There was only hunger. A raw, pounding hunger that raged and clawed at his insides, demanding to be fed.

Her hands tightened on his and Brady squeezed her long, slim fingers until even in the grip of desire, he was afraid he just might snap them. And as that thought presented itself, he released her and let his hands drop to her waist. While he held her, she drew her head back to look at him.

"Oh my," she whispered and Brady looked into her eyes, drawn to the wild, excited gleam he saw there. "That was very nice."

He choked out a short laugh that scraped against his throat. "Nice? Patience, you are amazing."

She grinned at him and damned if that smile of hers didn't hit him almost as hard as that innocent, unpracticed kiss had.

"You liked it too," she said, "I could tell."

"You could, huh?"

"Oh yes," she said, nodding. "But if I'm not mistaken, I believe that I was doing most of the kissing."

"Is that right?" he asked, his hands spreading against the small of her back. Blast it, he knew he should let her go, but for some reason, he wasn't quite ready yet to release her.

"Of course, I'm not an expert," she continued, keeping her arms around his neck and pressing herself closer to him. "But I do think that if we both participated, it might be even better."

He sucked in a gulp of air and felt his resolve weakening. Brady'd never thought of himself as the kind of man to take advantage of a woman. Hell, he'd never *had* to. The women he spent time with were willing and eager and, more often than not, professionals. Women who were no more interested in hearts and flowers than he was.

Yet now a woman with stars in her eyes was looking at him like he was some kind of storybook hero. And damned if it wasn't working.

"Kiss me, Brady," she said and fire erupted inside him.

Hunger rode him hard and Brady wanted nothing more than to give in to it. But in one corner of his mind, a small, insistent voice of reason whispered, *She's out of her head. She doesn't know what she's doing. She thinks you love her.*

And even as that last thought flitted through his mind, he silently told that little voice to keep quiet and yanked her tight against him. How had he come to this? he wondered. Only a few minutes ago, he'd been furious. Now, that anger was forgotten in a rush of need so desperate, Brady nearly shook with it.

Her lips parted in surprise and he pushed all thoughts from his mind as he bent his head to claim the kiss he needed more than he cared to admit. He planted his mouth on hers and wrapped his arms around her in a viselike grasp.

If he'd thought that she might be a bit timid about a real kiss, he was mistaken. Patience gave as good as she got. And though her response was untutored, she made up for the lack of expertise in pure enthusiasm.

She pressed her body fully against his and he swore he could feel her nipples hard and erect, pushing into his chest. Brady groaned, parted her lips with his tongue, and took her mouth with a fierceness he hadn't planned. His insides lit up like a bonfire at midnight and every square inch of his body damn near hummed with reaction. He tasted her, exploring the secrets of her warmth, and with every stroke of his tongue, she held him tighter, closer. Her fingers curled into his shoulders. Her breath puffed against his cheek.

It was as if he'd touched a match to kindling.

Her passion erupted and all Brady could do was hold on to her and enjoy the ride. She clung to him, moving her mouth against his, slipping her tongue into his mouth with such wild sweetness, he felt the floor beneath his feet tilt and his world tip to one side.

He'd never expected such a response from Patience. But here, in the most unlikely female, he'd discovered more blazing desire than he'd ever encountered before. And Brady's body tightened until he thought he might explode.

He slid his hands up and down her back, tracing the line of her spine, and felt her shiver with his every touch. And still it wasn't enough. Suddenly, urgently, the desire to know her, to feel her beneath his hands came crashing down on him. She moaned gently and he swallowed it, feeding on it, feeling her urgency match his own. Fueling the flames within until he felt as though his skin were on fire. He'd never felt this before. Never knew he *could* feel like this, and damn it, he didn't *want* to. Staggered by the wild tangle of emotions nearly strangling him, Brady finally tore his mouth from hers and took a hasty step back.

Staring at her, he scrubbed one hand across the back of his neck and fought to draw air into straining lungs. Jesus, what had just happened here? he asked himself. He'd come up here looking for a fight and instead he'd come too damn close to bedding her. That thought sent another tremor shooting through him and it was all he could do to keep from reaching for her again.

Damn it.

Even now, his hands trembled with the need to touch her. He felt the warmth of her sliding deep within him and tried to stand against it. But Patience was a hard woman to ignore.

"Well, now," she said breathlessly. "See? Didn't I say it would be better?"

He shot her a glare that should have fried her to the spot. But instead, she only gave him another of those smiles of hers and it was as if some unseen hand had dropped a lit candle into the corners of his soul. Brady actually felt the edges of darkness inside him being pushed back and, damn it, he resented it. He didn't want anything from her. He didn't want to feel. He didn't want to be a part of her delusion and he bloody well didn't want to *want* her.

"Patience," he began, then stopped to clear his throat—using that time to also remind himself that she was nuts. It wasn't her fault that he'd overreacted to her kiss. Obviously, he'd been without a woman too long—something he meant to rectify immediately. But as for now . . . "Look," he said, searching for the right combination of words. "While you're here, it'd be best if you just stayed the hell away from me."

There, he thought. Simple. Direct. To the point.

"Oh, I don't think so," she said, and his gaze locked on her kiss-swollen lips.

Naturally she'd argue. He had a feeling that if the God she was so fond of actually stepped down out of the clouds to personally hand her the keys to heaven, Patience would find something to argue about.

"I do," he said bluntly, ignoring the quick shine of disappointment in her eyes. Hell, he told himself, she was crazy. By tomorrow she'd have forgotten all about this. "You just keep clear of me, Patience. And everything'll be fine."

He started for the door, determined to put as much distance between them as possible. Her voice stopped him cold.

"Are you afraid of me, Brady?"

Half turning, he looked over his shoulder at her

and told himself not to notice her mussed hair, the shine in her eyes, and the mouth that seemed to be calling to him. Her breath chugged in and out of her lungs and her breasts rose and fell in rhythm. His palms itched to touch her again and he licked dry lips that wanted nothing more than to taste every blessed inch of her.

He drew one long, shaky breath and looked directly into those golden eyes of hers. Then he admitted to something he'd never owned up to before when he muttered thickly, "Damn right I am, lady."

A few days later, Patience was forced to admit that Brady was determined to stay away from her. Any time she entered a room, he left it. When she looked at him, he turned his head. When she spoke, he acted as though he hadn't heard her.

This was not going well.

And for the life of her, she couldn't understand why. After the kiss they'd shared, she would have been willing to wager—even, she thought, smiling, with a professional gambler like Brady—that he would finally admit to his love for her.

But apparently Brady Shaw's head was just a bit harder than her own.

Still, she had the memory of their kiss to sustain her. He'd responded to her every bit as much as she had to him. Eventually, she would overcome his reluctance by the sheer will of her love for him. And he wouldn't be able to stand against the inevitable forever.

Until that happy time, though, she needed to be

busy. Which is why she was now standing in the center of what had once been a kitchen at the back of the saloon. Scowling to herself, she turned in a slow circle, letting her gaze sweep across the dust and grime. Apparently, no one had used the place in years. But, it was time to stop using Treasure's kitchen.

The cookstove on the far wall was encrusted with heaven knew what and the windows were nearly black with accumulated dirt. But appearances—as she well knew—weren't important. It was possibilities that mattered.

With that thought firmly in mind, she unbuttoned the cuffs of her old gray dress and rolled the sleeves up past her elbows. Then snatching up a long-unused broom from a cobweb-filled corner, Patience got busy.

The first brush of the straw against the floor sent a cloud of dust thick enough to choke her into the air. Instantly, Patience crossed the narrow floor to the back door and flung it open. A blast of sunshine spilled into the room, and when she turned back to face the kitchen again, she noted that the bright light defined every filthy inch of the place.

Patience sighed and just for a moment felt her spirits sink at the enormity of the task ahead of her. Still, this was important. Not only to her, but to Brady. If she were successful—and she had absolutely no doubt that she would be—he would see what an asset she really was. Besides, her new idea would keep her busy and everyone knew that old saying about idle hands.

Grabbing up her broom again, she attacked the

layers of dust on the floor with all the determination of an invading army.

Davey rolled his hoop past the saloon and around back, intent on following the thing wherever it went. After all, he had nothing else to do. Mr. Tuttle's barber shop was closed on account of him going fishing, so there was no hair to be swept up and no money to be made. He'd already finished his work for Miss Bea and at the livery. So he'd come to the saloon, hoping Brady would have a job needing doing.

But Brady, just as he had been for the last few days, was shut up in his office. Joe had told Davey to skedaddle, saying Brady was in no mood to be hearing a youngster clamoring around the place. That seemed sort of odd, since the gambler had never minded Davey hanging around before. But then, since Patience had come to town, lots of things were different.

He'd heard the talk. Folks whispering about her, wondering about her. But she didn't seem to care, or even notice.

The back door was open and Davey stopped, surprised. He'd never seen that door standing wide. As far as he knew, nobody used it.

A cloud of dust and dirt flew through the opening and sailed right past his nose. "Hey!" He grabbed his hoop and jumped backward, out of range.

Instantly, Patience was at the door, sticking her head out and staring right at him. "Pestilence! I am sorry, Davey. I had no idea you were in the line of fire, so to speak."

"That's all right, ma'am," he said and took a step forward, now that it was safe. Walking closer, he peeked into the old kitchen, glanced around, then looked up at the woman beside him. "Whatcha doin'?"

She sighed and leaned one forearm on the broom handle. "I'm trying to clean this mess."

"How come?" he wondered aloud, his gaze once again straying around the room.

"I want to be able to use it."

"For what?"

She smiled at him and durned if Davey didn't feel a curl of warmth settle in his belly. She surely did have a way about her, he thought. That was probably why Brady was having so much of what Joe called "female troubles."

She reached out and scooped his hair back from his face before he could duck. "I'm thinking of using this kitchen to supply hot food for the saloon."

Davey blinked at her. "But the saloon already has the bar lunch and all."

"True," she said, and turned to look around the room. "But that's merely meat and bread. If I can get this kitchen working again, we can have hot meals. And bakery goods."

His mouth watered. "You mean like cakes and doughnuts and such?"

"Exactly."

Now that sounded pretty durned good to him. And it occurred to him that she just might need a little help getting her kitchen ready for business. The wheels in his brain started turning as Davey realized that he could do his part to bring cookies and such to town and at the same time make him some money. If she was willing to hire him, that is. Well, he figured he'd never know if he didn't ask. He rocked back on his heels, real casual, like he'd seen Brady do sometimes. Then, holding tight to his hoop, he worked up the nerve and asked quietly, "Could you maybe use some help?"

Patience looked at him for a long moment then answered his question with one of her own. "Shouldn't you be in school, Davey?"

A sting of embarrassment tugged at him. Sure, he should be in school. But he'd rather eat. And if he didn't work, he'd get mighty durned hungry. Besides, someday, he figured to learn how to read and write and do his numbers. He just couldn't do it now, was all. Still, she didn't need to know all that, so he squared his shoulders, lifted his chin, and met her gaze.

"School's for children, ma'am," he said. "And I'm no child. I'm a man and I'd rather work."

She just stared at him for what seemed an awful long time and Davey had the strangest feeling that she was looking right into the heart of him. He wanted to squirm uneasily, but stood his ground instead. And even managed to straighten up, trying to look as tall and grown-up as he could manage.

Patience tapped the tip of one finger against her chin and looked the boy over. Her heart ached to see him so scrawny and in such ill-fitting clothes. But pride shone in his eyes and she had to be careful not to step on it. "And what kind of wage would you be expecting?"

"Uh," he said, shrugging shoulders that were far too narrow to carry the burdens he obviously did. "I don't rightly know. Whatever you think is fair, I reckon."

Trusting too, she thought, amazed at the boy's resilience. All alone. No family. No one to care for him. No proper home. And still he trusted adults to do right by him. Patience eased the ache around her heart by silently promising herself to do just that.

"All right," she said and pretended to consider the situation, despite the fact that her mind was already made up as to just what his pay would be. "As you said, you're a man, so it wouldn't be proper to pay you a boy's wage, would it?"

"Well . . ."

"Of course not." Patience answered the question herself. Turning slightly, she waved one hand to encompass the wreck of a room and, sighing, said, "Mind you, you'll earn every penny of your pay, Davey."

"I ain't afraid of hard work, ma'am."

"I'm not," she corrected.

He winced. "Yes'm."

"I will pay you one dollar a day—"

"A *dollar*?" His eyes went wide as saucers.

"That is what a man makes these days, isn't it?"

"Yes'm, usually," he said, then added honestly, "but folks around here don't pay me that much."

She smiled at him and watched as a matching smile lit his features when she said, "I believe in a fair day's pay for a fair day's work, Davey."

"Yes, *ma'am*." He nodded so fiercely that his hair

flopped down over his eyes and he was forced to swing it back and out of his way again.

As soon as they had this kitchen straightened out, she told herself, Davey was going to find himself in a barber's chair. And then, she mused, watching his shining eyes, they would do something about school. But for now, it was enough that she could assure Davey would be eating well.

Holding out her right hand, she asked, "Do we have a deal?"

He wiped his palm on his shirt before taking her hand in a firm shake. "Yes, ma'am, we sure do."

"Excellent." Then she handed him the broom.

He grinned at her and curled his fingers tightly around the worn stick. But when she held out one hand for his hoop, saying, "Why don't I put that away for you?" he shook his head.

"No, thanks, ma'am," he told her, carefully setting his magic ring to one side. "I'll just leave it right here."

"That's fine," she said, and gave the hoop a long, thoughtful look. There was something about that old brass ring that—She shook her head suddenly, turned her back on the hoop and said, "Now, then! Let's get busy, shall we?"

Chapter Eight

It was the noise that drew him.

And he was almost grateful for the distraction.

Brady'd been able to avoid seeing much of Patience for the last few days. But hell, a man couldn't hide in his office forever, could he? Besides, another day or so of staring at the water-stained walls in that cramped room would make him crazier than Patience.

Stepping into the saloon, he paused and let his gaze sweep across the familiar faces of the men gathered at the card tables. Only a few people were here this early in the afternoon. But he knew that by evening the place would be crowded, the air blue with smoke, and the only piano player in the States with ten thumbs would be banging out what passed for music around here.

Right now, though, the whole building was fairly quiet . . . except for—A crash sounded out from somewhere behind the bar and Brady started moving. That was the noise that had pulled him from his office in the first place. What the hell was going on around here? "And where the hell is Joe?" he wondered aloud as he headed for the closed door on the far end of the room.

"Maybe he run off with your fi-an-cée, Brady," someone yelled in answer.

"Yeah," someone else called out, "maybe she got tired of waitin' for you to come outa the office!"

"Very funny," Brady muttered darkly and didn't bother to respond. Damn it, he was never going to live this down. People were talking, and *had* been talking and *would* be talking. Apparently Patience wasn't exactly keeping their "engagement" a secret.

And he had no one to blame but himself. He should have put a stop to this days ago. He never should have kissed her. And he damn sure shouldn't have been tempted to do it again.

But he had.

Every night, he lay in his bed, in the room alongside hers, and thought about going in there. Touching her. Holding her. And every night, he talked himself out of it.

"*Somebody*'s got to have some sense around here," he muttered, to no one in particular.

"Hey, Brady!" Another voice from the sprinkling of people behind him. "What's goin' on in there, anyhow? Getting so noisy in here a man can't keep his mind on his cards."

He glanced over his shoulder right at the man whose voice he'd recognized and gave in to the spurt of temper inside. "Quiet won't help your game, Howard," he called back. "Why not save some time and just hand your money over?"

Laughter broke out as Irv Howard grumbled a complaint and hunched his shoulders, burying his face behind a hand of cards that was, no doubt, another loser.

But Brady didn't have time to appreciate the man's discomfiture. Instead, he rounded the corner of the bar and marched up to the door that hadn't been used as long as he'd owned the place. It opened into the old kitchen that had been closed up when the former owner had closed his hotel in favor of making the place a saloon.

Brady'd thought about maybe expanding sometime in the future, but for now, there was no reason for anyone to be in that kitchen. He grabbed the doorknob, turned it and pushed. The wood stuck in the jamb and he was forced to plant his shoulder against it and shove.

This time, it swung wide and Brady slapped one hand on the doorframe to catch himself before he could fall and sprawl across the kid kneeling directly in front of him.

"Afternoon, Brady," Davey said and waved with his scrub brush, flinging soap bubbles clear across the room.

Giving a quick look around the room, he noted the puddled soapy water on the floor, the halfway dismantled cookstove, and the hole in the wall opposite.

Naturally, standing right smack in the middle of the destruction, stood Patience.

"What do you think you're doing?" he demanded in a shout loud enough to rattle the windowpanes. If they hadn't already been broken. Which, of course, explained the crashing noises he'd been hearing.

Patience spun around to face the man she'd hardly seen in three days. He looked tired. As though he weren't sleeping well. He also looked angry. And so handsome he nearly stole her breath away. Even from across the room, just the sight of him was enough to quicken her blood and make her breath go fast and short. Good heavens, she'd obviously become a wanton . . . all on the strength of one kiss.

Wasn't it wonderful?

She smiled at him and was only a bit disappointed when he didn't return the smile.

Instantly, though, she realized that something must be terribly wrong. Judging by his expression, he was having some sort of difficulty. Perhaps he needed her assistance.

Lifting the hem of her skirt to avoid as much of the soapsuds as she could, she walked across the room and stopped just in front of him.

"What is it, Brady? What's happened?"

"That's what I want to know," he practically growled.

Davey ducked his head, picked up the bucket of soapy water, and scuttled to the far side of the room, clearly hoping to get out of range.

Brady glanced around the room again and then brought his gaze back to her. "What do you think you're doing?"

One black eyebrow arched and she lifted her chin. "I *think* I'm cleaning this disreputable room."

"Why?" he demanded, almost afraid to hear the answer. Whatever she had to say, he knew he wasn't going to like it.

"Because I'm going to reopen this kitchen," she said, confirming his darkest suspicions.

Reopen the kitchen? Hell, she was taking root. Settling in like some black-haired bird building a nest. In *his* tree! He shoved one hand through his hair and tried not to snatch himself bald while he was at it. He had been pushed further by her than by anyone he'd ever known. And he was feeling dangerously close to going over the fine edge he'd been straddling since Patience had walked into his life.

He took a deep breath and asked simply, "Who asked you to?"

"No one had to ask," she said. "It was my idea."

Well, sure it was her idea, he thought. Who the hell else would try to open up a kitchen that had been closed for years? *Someone else's* kitchen at that?

"Damn it, Patience," he muttered and grabbed her upper arm, half dragging her far enough away from Davey that what he had to say wouldn't be overheard. He tossed a quick look at the boy and noted that the kid had his head down and was whistling—loudly. Trying to drown them out, no doubt. Shifting his gaze back to Patience, Brady said, "You can't just storm into a man's place of business and take it over."

"You weren't using the kitchen," she argued.

"It's still mine."

"Is this going to be an argument like the one we had over your door and my lock?" she inquired and her voice was just a little too sweet.

"No," he said, remembering both that stupid argument and the kiss that had followed it. "It's not."

Definitely. Not even if he had to argue with her from a distance. He wouldn't get that close to her again. Mainly because he didn't trust himself.

"Good, because I have work to do." She half turned to walk away from him and Brady had to grab her again.

"I'm not through talking," he said, though he knew damn well he could talk until the moon fell out of the sky and it wouldn't make a damn sight of difference to her. She'd do what she wanted to regardless. "Just what is it you're planning on doing here, anyway?"

"I'm planning," she said, "on making food to be sold in our saloon. And perhaps even running a bakery. I noticed there isn't one in Fortune and I think—"

"*Our* saloon?" That one little word hit him hard.

She gave him a long-suffering look and sighed impatiently. "Fine. It's *your* saloon—"

"Thank you." A small victory, he thought, but one he'd take when she seemed to be winning all of the battles around here.

"—until we're married."

So much for a victory.

"Patience . . ." He was losing the thread of the conversation. He felt the whole damn thing unraveling and there didn't seem to be a thing he could do to stop it. Arguing with this woman was like watching a dog chase its tail. No beginning, no end, and no damn satisfaction if it actually caught its tail, just pain.

"Pestilence, Brady!"

She pulled free of his grasp and planted both

hands on her hips. Tipping her head back, she stared up at him with fire in her eyes. If he'd had any sense, he would have backed up a step. But lately, he'd noticed that when Patience was around, his sense went right out the window.

"How could you possibly be upset that I want to open a kitchen?" she asked and he heard the toe of her shoe tapping noisily against the floor. The echo of the sound seemed to pound out a rhythm in his head that throbbed painfully with every beat of his heart.

"This is my place, Patience," he said as calmly as he could manage. *His* place. He'd waited most of his life to have a place he could call his own. One spot in this whole damn world where he could belong. And blast if he was going to give it up so easily. Fortune, New Mexico, wasn't much of a town. And his saloon didn't hold a candle to some of the fine gambling houses he'd visited in San Francisco or New Orleans. But damn it, it was *his*. "Don't you figure I've got a right to know what you're trying to do to it?"

She folded her arms across her chest, completely oblivious to his obvious displeasure. "It was *going* to be a surprise."

"Well, it's that, all right," he grumbled, flicking another glance toward Davey. If he hadn't known better, he would have thought the kid was chuckling quietly.

The little traitor.

"With Davey's help," Patience was saying, "we should be able to get most of this done in a few days."

"Davey's working for you?"

"A dollar a day," the boy piped up excitedly, which proved to Brady the kid *had* been listening to their conversation.

Lowering his voice, Brady leaned in close to Patience and told himself not to notice the golden hue of her eyes or the soft blush of color on her cheeks. It didn't matter that her breath came short and fast, making her breasts rise and fall with a rhythm that set his own blood racing. The fact that the pulse point at the base of her throat made him want to plant his mouth there and feel her heart pounding her blood through her veins had nothing to do with what was going on now. It was all just another sign of his own mind beginning to dissolve.

He swallowed hard.

"Are you all right?" she asked suddenly.

"Nope," he admitted, shaking his head. And he probably wouldn't be all right until he could figure a way to get Patience out of his life. And the chances of that happening were beginning to look mighty damn slim. He hadn't heard one word about a missing crazy woman. He'd left word with the sheriff in Santa Fe and he'd checked with Fortune's sheriff a time or two in the last couple of days. But there was just nothing.

No one was looking for her.

No one but him seemed to care that she was here.

And there was absolutely no one to help him deal with her either. He was on his own in this. As he had been on his own for years.

So no. He wasn't all right. He was about as far from all right as a man could get and still be standing.

"Brady?"

"Patience," he said, speaking up quickly before she could go off on a tangent, "just where are you getting the money to do all this? The kitchen, paying Davey"—he glanced at the shattered windowpanes—"buying new glass."

He had her there, he told himself. She damn sure didn't have any money. Hadn't she charged all of her new clothes from the Mercantile to him?

"Now, the windowpanes were an accident," she said. "We were trying to open the windows to air out the room, but it had been so long, they were stuck in literally coats of grime and we shoved too hard and the glass broke. But I'll replace them."

"Uh-huh," he murmured, trying to remember to keep his voice low, despite his urge to shout. "And like I asked before, what are you gonna use for money?"

"Well," she said in a tone most folks used when talking to a particularly stupid child. "I'll have to borrow some money, of course."

"Of course," he said tightly. "From who?"

"Whom," she corrected.

"Patience . . ."

"From you, naturally," she snapped. "Who else?"

"Who else indeed," he mused, though he admitted silently that he'd known this was coming. She was convinced they were engaged to be married. Why shouldn't she also be convinced that he'd be willing to finance any of the notions that popped up in that pretty head of hers?

On the other hand, he thought, with an inward

smile, if she had nowhere to go for help but him, all he had to do was not loan her the money and at least this part of his nightmare would end.

He looked into her eyes and saw calm reason there and wondered why in the hell crazy people didn't *look* crazy. Anyone looking at Patience would see a fairly handsome woman with a too thin figure and a head full of beautiful hair. But they wouldn't see the side of her that could make a man want to run into the desert and howl at the moon just for the hell of it.

And they wouldn't see the woman who somehow managed to affect him more than any other female he'd ever known.

Dreams of her interrupted his sleep. Thoughts of her disturbed him all day. Thinking about how to get shut of her drove him to distraction. And desire for her made his body ache. All in all, Patience Goodfellow was slowly driving him out of his mind.

He reined in his temper and forced himself to speak slowly and calmly. "Why would I want to loan you money to do something I don't want you to do?"

She leaned into him, placing both hands on his chest, and Brady felt the heat of her touch slide deep inside him, and in that instant, he knew he'd lost this battle. How in the hell was a man supposed to stand strong against a woman who made his blood boil with a simple touch?

"Because this is a good thing, Brady," she said. "For me. For us. For Davey."

Had she guessed about his fondness for the boy? Was that why she was using the kid as ammunition?

Then as soon as he thought that, he dismissed the notion. She wouldn't do that, he told himself. Not Patience. Nope, she was simply trying to help the kid as best she could and, damn it, at least she'd offered the boy a decent wage. She hadn't tried to get by with paying him pennies, like some folks in town did.

Brady shot a look at the boy, busily scrubbing away at the dirt accumulated over too many years. And he knew that even now, the kid was busily adding up money he hadn't even made yet. A twinge of sympathy tugged at his heart.

Heck, Brady knew better than most how hard it was to be a kid, on your own. He knew the loneliness. The fear. The hunger. And he knew damn well that earning your keep was the only thing that kept that fear at bay.

Patience had given Davey that.

Well, she'd *offered* him that. Despite the fact that she didn't have the money to pay the boy.

Brady scraped one hand across his face and felt the scratch of whiskers he hadn't gotten around to shaving yet. Fine, he thought. She'd helped Davey. But she was still clinging to the whole engagement thing too. And he had to find a way to nip that in the bud. Fast.

He sucked in a long, deep gulp of air before telling her *again,* "There is no *us,* Patience."

A glimmer of hurt shone in her eyes and he felt a quick stab of guilt. Though why he should was beyond him. He had been a perfectly content man until the day Patience had marched into his life and set up camp.

She eased back from him, folding her hands at her waist and looking as prim as a spinster schoolmarm. Shaking her head, she set her long black hair to dancing about her shoulders and Brady had to curl his hands into fists to keep from reaching for it.

"I don't understand why you insist on denying our love, Brady Shaw," she said and the tremor in her voice caused another shaft of guilt to slice at him. "After all we've been through."

"We haven't been through anything, Patience!" he snapped and knew that the hold he had on his temper was beginning to fray.

"You might be able to convince yourself of that," she said simply. "But not me. I know you, Brady. I know what you want. What you need."

"I don't *need* anything," he told her and meant every word.

"You need *me,*" she said, shaking her head. "Maybe even more than you know."

"All I need from you is to be left alone."

"I've hardly seen you in four days, Brady," she pointed out. "You've been alone. And if you don't mind my saying so, it doesn't look as though it suited you."

"As long as you're here. In the saloon. Hell, in *Fortune,*" he said, throwing his hands wide, "I'm never alone."

She sucked in a gulp of breath, gave him a smile, and said, "Why, Brady, that's the nicest thing anyone's ever said to me."

His chin hit his chest. Jesus.

What could he say to her? He'd tried reason and it

hadn't worked. He'd tried getting mad and she ignored it. He'd tried finding the attic she belonged in and no one had claimed her.

He was running out of options. Gritting his teeth, Brady looked away from the shine in her eyes. Maybe this kitchen thing was a good idea, he thought. If nothing else, it'd keep her busy and away from him for a while.

"Fine. Have your kitchen," he said and hoped he didn't sound as defeated as he felt.

She threw herself at him, wrapping her arms around his neck and hanging on for all she was worth. He felt the impact of her body slam into his and instinctively his arms went around her and held her tightly to him.

He looked down into her eyes and easily read the sheer pleasure in those golden depths. Her joy was damn near contagious, he thought as a similar pleasure rippled through him despite the nagging thoughts plaguing his mind.

"You won't be sorry, Brady," she said. "You'll see. This will be wonderful."

He was already sorry, he thought, about a lot of things. But it was too late to change anything now. Besides, if he couldn't find where she belonged, maybe some cowboy would fall in love with her cooking and take her off Brady's hands.

It wasn't much hope.

But at least it was something.

CHAPTER NINE

"Don't see what else I can do, Brady," Sheriff Sam Hanks said and poured another cup of coffee from the battered tin pot. When he was finished he set the pot back down onto the top of the potbellied stove and walked to his desk. Dropping into his chair, he eased back, lifted his feet to the corner of his desk and crossed them at the ankle.

Cradling his cup in both palms, he shook his head and continued. "I've sent wires to everywhere I can think of. Notified other lawmen from here to St. Louis and even west to Frisco and Los Angeles. Nobody knows a damn thing about her."

"That's just perfect." Brady jumped to his feet so quickly, the chair he'd been sitting in fell over backward, clattering loudly on the wooden floor. He snatched it up, set it to rights again, and then stalked across the floor to the front window. Jamming his hands into his pants pockets, he stared unseeing at the town beyond the dirty glass.

He'd played his last card.

Brady's back teeth ground together, and in his pockets, his hands curled into helpless fists.

He wasn't a man to go running to the law for help. In fact, he usually did everything he could to avoid sheriffs or marshals. Back when he was a gunfighter, hiring his talents out to whoever offered the most money, he'd skirted the edges of the law—always aware that with just one slip he could find himself in prison. And now that he was a saloonkeeper, he still wasn't exactly a pillar of the community.

But desperate times called for desperate measures and Brady had taken the chance of coming to Sam Hanks for help in dealing with Patience.

Glancing over his shoulder at the man, Brady studied the sheriff's sharp green eyes that belied his indolent posture. Not much got past Sam, he told himself and thought idly that he and the sheriff were about the same age. Strange how two men could travel such wildly different paths in life.

Sam had been a Texas Ranger, a U.S. Marshal, and for some reason known only to him, had given that up and settled for being the sheriff in a one-horse town like Fortune. But then, Brady, too, had given up wandering to take root here. Maybe the two of them weren't so different after all.

"Don't know what else I can do," Sam said and took a drink of coffee so bitter it made him shudder visibly as it slid down his throat.

Reluctantly, Brady smiled. "If your own coffee's that bad, why drink it?"

"It's here," he said with a shrug.

Good enough reason to drink coffee, Brady told himself. Not a good enough reason to put up with a woman who kept insisting you were in love with her.

Snatching his hat off, Brady shoved one hand

through his hair and muttered, "Maybe I should place an ad in the papers back East."

"About Patience?"

He nodded.

Sam shook his head. "You can try. But chances are, that woman's from right around here somewhere. How's a light-in-the-head female going to make it all the way to Fortune from back East without being noticed?" He paused, then answered his own question. "She wouldn't."

"So if she's from around here, why is no one claiming her?"

Sam shrugged. "No telling."

"And that leaves me where, exactly?"

Sam grinned. "Engaged?"

"Real funny."

"Hey, you could do worse."

"Yeah, I could shoot myself accidentally."

Laughing, Sam lowered his feet to the floor, set his coffee cup onto the desk, and stood up. He walked across the room to stand beside Brady and looked out the window at Fortune. "I don't know why you're so busy trying to get shut of her," Sam said. "I remember at the town dance a couple weeks ago, you and her looked real cozy."

Brady shot him a look. "You're as crazy as she is," he said. "She wasn't at the dance."

Sam frowned thoughtfully, stroked one finger along his jawline, and shook his head. "She had to be there," he said. "We were talking about it just the other day and she mentioned how I'd had to leave the dance early to lock Otis Cummings in one of the cells to sleep it off."

Brady sighed heavily.

"How else would she know that if she wasn't there?"

How else indeed, Brady wondered. He still had no answers to that question. Patience knew too damn much—and not just about him—but about the whole town. She spoke to people as if they were old friends and more often than not folks responded to her. He'd even noticed a few people giving him dirty looks lately—as if they were blaming him and not Patience for all of the confusion around here.

But hell, that shouldn't surprise him. Since Patience had hit town, nothing had been the same. Grumbling under his breath, he peered through the layer of dirt on the windowpane. He watched as Vonda Shales left her laundry and started off down the boardwalk in the direction of the saloon. Shaking his head, he knew without a doubt that Vonda and Treasure and probably Beatrice as well were going to be helping Patience set up her kitchen. As they had yesterday. And the day before.

Despite all of his efforts, Brady's life was sliding out of his control and Patience Goodfellow was at the helm, steering his ship right onto the rocks.

And there didn't seem to be a damn thing he could do about it.

"I don't think this is such a good idea," Lily said and smoothed nervous hands down the front of the dress she'd borrowed from Patience. A simple green dress, it was nothing like the clothes she normally wore to work in the saloon. And silly as it sounded, she was a lot more nervous all covered up than she was when her breasts were on display.

Her blond hair was done up in a simple topknot and several loose tendrils had been left to dance along her cheeks and across the back of her neck. The collar of the dress seemed too tight, though, and Lily had a hard time swallowing the knot of fear lodged in her throat.

"Nonsense," Patience said briskly as she grabbed Lily's hand and nearly dragged her down the stairs after her. "You'll see. This is the perfect opportunity for you to make some new friends."

"Friends?" Lily muttered, trying to lift the hem of her skirt with one hand so she wouldn't tumble down the stairs only to land in a broken heap at the bottom.

"Yes," Patience said, throwing a smile over her shoulder. "Friends. Like you and I are."

A warm spot settled in the center of Lily's chest and she clung to it. Despite all odds, she and Patience had become friendly over the last few days. And it had been so long since any "decent" woman had spoken to her in anything other than a sneer, Lily had cherished the time they'd spent together. But being friendly with Patience and making friends with the other town ladies might be two very different things.

She knew darn well what God-fearing Christian women thought of her and her kind. And though it shamed her something fierce, Lily really couldn't blame them. Before her husband had died, leaving her penniless and alone, Lily, too, had looked down her nose at the women who made their livings on their backs. So maybe she'd earned the snubs and censure she received now.

But at the bottom of the stairs, when Patience made a sharp right turn headed for the door leading to the kitchen, Lily dug in her heels. "I can't do it," she said, staring at that door as if it were the gateway to hell. "I can't go in there."

"Of course you can," Patience said softly and her voice echoed solemnly in the early morning quiet of the empty room.

"No, ma'am," Lily said, shaking her head. "It's no use anyway, Patience. They won't talk to the likes of me."

"Why wouldn't they?" she asked.

Lily choked on the short, nervous laugh that shot from her throat. "Because I'm a whore," she said, forcing the words out and forcing herself to hear them.

In the shadowy light, Patience's features almost seemed to glow as she smiled and came closer. Lily felt herself warming to that smile as she had right from the first. But her friend's warmth couldn't protect Lily from the icy reception she knew she'd receive the moment she walked through that door.

Patience took both of her hands in hers and held them gently. "Lily, you don't have to be afraid."

"I'm not afraid," she argued and tried to pin down just what exactly she was.

"Yes you are. But don't you see, everyone has something they're ashamed of. Large or small, it doesn't matter. What matters," Patience said softly, "is who we are. Inside. In our core."

Lily wanted to believe that, but—

"Give them a chance," Patience urged her, squeezing her hands carefully. "Give yourself a chance."

How many times had she wished for a chance to be something different? Lily wondered. How many times had she lain awake at night and prayed for the opportunity to change things? To be the woman she once was. To have the life she'd always wanted.

And now that perhaps that chance had arrived, would she really turn her back on it because she was too afraid to risk it?

No. Nodding to herself, she squared her shoulders, lifted her chin, and tucked her protective shell around her as she had for years. She wouldn't be denied because she hadn't tried. And if the women treated her no differently than she expected, well, she would have lost nothing.

"All right," she said and was almost surprised to hear her voice work. "I'll give it a try."

"Good," Patience told her, still holding on to her hands as if afraid she might bolt. "You won't be sorry."

"We'll see," Lily murmured. But Patience didn't hear her. She was already pulling her toward the door.

"Grown-ups do the durndest things," Davey muttered and kicked at a rock in his path. His brass ring slid off his shoulder and he reached to shove it back into place.

He'd been all set to make him another dollar working for Miss Patience and now he had nothing to do at all. As soon as he'd run into Treasure Morgan on her way to the saloon, she'd shooed Davey off, saying they wouldn't be needing him today. Well, he figured he should wait and ask Patience, but Treasure had nearly pushed him out of her way, telling him to go on and play.

Play.

He stopped dead on the dirt track and swiped one hand beneath his nose. Hell, he wasn't a child. He didn't play.

But he wasn't working either, he reminded himself. At least not today. So what was a body supposed to do with himself when he had a whole day stretching out in front of him?

An idea wiggled to life in his mind. Slowly, Davey smiled and pulled that brass hoop down off his shoulder. Holding it in both hands, he hardly noticed the now familiar warmth of the metal anymore. But he braced himself for a blast of heat as he said, "If you was a fishing pole and line, I could maybe catch some nice fish for supper."

Instantly, the hoop hummed and shifted in his hands. The metal warmed considerably and as Davey hung on, it kind of melted out of its round shape and took on length and size. He held his breath as the magic unfolded. The brass straightened out, thicker at one end than the other. Heat sizzled his palms but didn't burn him as his pole took shape. And in seconds, it was over and the brass was silent, its heat cooling into a comforting warmth.

The fishing rod was twice as tall as he was and he stared as, from the tip of the pole, a long, slender thread of brass unwound to become a line, complete with a hook and a squirmy-looking brass worm.

"My, oh my," he whispered, never failing to be amazed at his good fortune. This magic ring just kept on getting better. Forgetting all about work and the dollar he wouldn't make today, Davey grinned. Then, clutching his new pole, he stepped off the road and cut across the open land between the back end of Fortune and the small, fish-stocked lake just a mile or two north.

Patience threw the door wide and stepped into the kitchen, pulling Lily in after her. She felt the other woman's reluctance and told herself there was no need for it. Treasure Morgan was a kindhearted woman, and as for the others, she was fairly certain that if Treasure accepted Lily, the others would as well.

"Morning, Patience," the short, round storekeeper called out when she heard the door open. As she turned around, she said, "I think I've got all the supplies you asked for and the others'll be here any minute."

"That's wonderful," Patience said and watched the woman's expression harden as her gaze locked on Lilly. Pestilence! This might not be as easy as she'd hoped it would be. Apparently, the lines between "good" women and the "not so good" were drawn deep. A shame, really, she told herself. Because when all was said and done, shouldn't women really band together? Help each other?

After all, she thought, in the war between men and women, aren't we all on the same side?

Beside her, Lilly straightened up defensively, as if preparing for battle. But there wouldn't be a fight. Patience would see to it.

"Treasure," she said abruptly, shattering the strained silence hanging in the air, "this is my friend Lily. Lily, Treasure Morgan."

"We've met," the storekeeper said and folded her arms across her more than abundant bosom.

"I told you this wasn't a good idea," Lily muttered and tried to draw free of Patience's grip, obviously bent on escape.

She didn't succeed.

Patience bit back an oath. The clash when two hard heads collided was nearly deafening. But she'd faced greater challenges, hadn't she? As that thought flitted through her mind, though, she frowned slightly and tried to remember just when that might have been. But an instant later, she gave it up and returned her focus to the matter at hand.

Looking meaningfully from one to the other of the women, Patience ignored the obvious drop in the room's temperature and said, "I just know the two of you are going to be great friends." Treasure sniffed and Lily muttered something unintelligible. Patience paid no attention to either of them. "You'd be surprised just how much you two have in common."

Treasure's mouth dropped open and her eyes widened until they looked as though they were about to pop out of her head. Lily's only reaction was a muffled, choked-off laugh.

But Patience wasn't finished. They were going to settle this right here and now.

"Treasure," she asked pointedly, "did you know that Lily's husband was killed at Antietam?"

The storekeeper flinched slightly and her eyes softened just a bit as Patience pressed her advantage. Turning to the blond woman beside her, she said simply, "Treasure's husband died in that same battle."

Lily blinked and took a short breath.

"How did you know about my Henry?" Treasure asked, her voice hardly more than a whisper.

"You told me yourself," Patience said gently, looking back at her.

She shook her head. "When?"

Sunshine drifted through the brand-new windowpanes and lay in an oblong pattern across the floor. The sounds of life from outside seemed very far away as the three women faced each other.

"Does it really matter, Treasure?" Patience asked, her voice soothing, tender.

The storekeeper's eyes filled with tears she battled to keep from shedding. Her jaw worked furiously and she blinked against the dampness blurring her vision. Finally, she reached up and rubbed one hand across her eyes before looking at Lily again. And this time, there was a softness in her gaze that had been sorely lacking before.

"No," she said quietly, more to herself than to anyone else. "I guess it don't matter at all."

Some of the starch had left Lily's posture and she watched the storekeeper through wary, yet almost hopeful eyes.

"My Henry," Treasure was saying, "fought with General McClellan and the Army of the Potomac."

Lily's chin lifted a notch and she folded her hands at her waist so tightly, her knuckles whitened. "My Tom was with General Longstreet."

Patience watched the byplay, hoping she had been right. Hoping that these two lost souls would recognize each other and take comfort in the giving and sharing of memories.

"A Confederate, eh?" Treasure asked.

"Yes," Lily said tiredly. "But is that really important anymore?"

The older woman thought about it for a long minute before saying, "No. No, it surely ain't. That damn war took too many from both sides."

"Amen," Lily said.

Treasure took a tentative step closer. "You couldn't have been much more than a child when your man died."

Lily smiled. "It seems like a lifetime ago."

"Don't it, though?" Treasure murmured. "I swear, sometimes I don't even remember being a wife."

"I remember," Lily said and her smile faded into a wistful expression. "I remember every day."

The storekeeper nodded to herself. "I expect that you do."

Patience held her breath. It was a tenuous peace, but she felt certain that, given time, these two women would bridge the chasm that separated them.

The back door swung open and Vonda Shales strode in. She stopped short on the threshold when she caught sight of Lily and her features screwed up as though she had a mouthful of vinegar. Patience sighed. She'd been so close.

"What is *she* doing here?" the laundress asked, her voice thin and tight with barely restrained outrage.

Once again, Lily seemed to fold in on herself even while stiffening her spine in self-defense. But this time there was no need. Before Patience could say a word, Treasure turned and spoke up.

"Vonda, you never did learn to wake up your brain before opening your mouth."

"What?" the tall, thin woman sputtered, lifting one hand and pointing at Lily. "She—she's a—"

"Widow," Treasure finished for her before she could say what she clearly had in mind.

"*She* had a husband?" Obviously stunned, Vonda stared at Lily as though the pretty blonde had two heads.

Patience wanted to smack her. Not a very Christian thing to do, granted, but it would have made her feel so much better. She shouldn't have been surprised at the woman's reaction, though. After all, Vonda had long been a woman too consumed with her own bitterness. A spinster, she'd given up on love years ago, and with that surrender, her heart had shriveled and her soul had dried up.

A sigh rippled through Patience. She'd tried many times to reach the laundress. She'd tried to open her heart, but Vonda was a stubborn woman. One who could very well destroy the fragile peace that had just been established.

But Treasure spoke up again and it was clear from the first that she was in charge now and wouldn't be putting up with any nonsense.

"Yes, she did," the storekeeper said, giving her friend a glare that should have curled her hair. "And she lost him. In a war that took too many from us."

"But she's—"

"A friend," Treasure interrupted smoothly, then turned her softened gaze on the saloon girl she would have walked right past only the day before. "A new friend."

Blindly, Lily reached out for Patience's hand and squeezed it tightly.

Chapter Ten

Two days later, the steamed-over windows in the kitchen framed a blurry picture of the outside world. But inside, the room was filled with warmth and shared laughter. A half-dozen women scurried about the kitchen, each of them helping Patience on her first official day of business.

She looked up from the mound of dough she was kneading and noticed how Treasure stayed protectively close to Lily, and Patience smiled. She only wished everything else were going as well as Lily's entry back into the world she'd left so long ago.

But there was a cold, hard knot of discomfort sitting in the pit of her stomach and Patience didn't know what to do about it. Probably lack of sleep, she told herself firmly. But sleep was hard to come by when your own dreams worked against you. Dreams that had chased her through the last two sleepless nights. Dreams that were flashes of memory. Bits and pieces of a past she couldn't—or wouldn't—completely remember. Odd, wasn't it, that she recalled so much of her time with these people of Fortune, but her own past was shrouded in a mist that refused to lift?

"Patience?"

She lifted her gaze to meet Lily's.

"Are you feeling all right?"

No, she wasn't. But that wasn't what Lily wanted to hear. "Of course," she said and forced a smile that felt strained and uncomfortable.

"If you're worried about how the men'll react to the food, don't be." Lily's gaze swept across the wide array of just-cooked snacks before coming back to Patience. "You're a wonderful cook. Everything you've made tastes . . . well, *heavenly*, I suppose, is the only word that fits."

"Thank you," she said and inhaled sharply. Enough worrying about dreams that were no more substantial than the frost on the windowpanes. Smiling at Lily again, she said, "Let's load up a tray for you to take into the saloon, shall we?"

Brady was hip deep in females.

Now, he was used to Lily, Fern, and Addey trotting in and out of the saloon. After all, they worked there. The customers wanted them there. They were good for business.

This, though, was something else entirely.

This was nothing short of an invasion.

"Everett Tuttle!" a woman shouted from across the room and the unlucky gunsmith jumped—along with every other male in the room—spilling his beer down the front of his red flannel shirt.

"Durn it, Rachel," he cried, "you about scared ten years off my life."

The short woman hurtled across the room as though she'd been shot from the barrel of a gun.

Brady sighed. In seconds, she was alongside her husband, snatching what was left of his beer out of his hand and slamming it down onto the tabletop. "You got no business whiling your day away here in this saloon. You get on home and finish repairing that back porch."

"Now, Rachel." The burly gunsmith damn near cowered from the tiny woman who was his wife.

"Don't you 'now, Rachel' me," she snapped and threw a baleful glance at a man who dared to chuckle at her husband's distress. Wagging a finger at him, she warned, "And don't you start in laughing, Hiram Vines. Miriam's right over yonder in the kitchen and if she hears that you're—"

The other man didn't wait for her to finish that sentence. He jumped up and scuttled out of the batwing doors, leaving them swinging in a wild goodbye wave.

While Zeke allowed Rachel to drag him out of the building, Brady shook his head and leaned against the bar. He scraped one hand across his face and clenched his teeth together hard enough to turn them to dust. He was finished. There had been scenes like that one every day, ever since Patience had opened that damned kitchen back up. He had females from all over dropping in right and left. They were chasing their husbands home and shaming the single men into leaving with a few well-chosen words and frosty glares cold enough to turn a man's blood to ice.

If this kept up, he'd be out of business in a month.

Lifting his head, he stared down the length of the bar toward the closed door leading to the kitchen. Even from a distance, he heard the chattering and the laughter that signaled to anyone who cared that there was a herd of women in there. Ranchers' wives. Townswomen. Hell. Even Lily had deserted the saloon and gone to work for Patience.

And not only was he being driven out of business, he reminded himself in disgust, he was paying for the privilege. Besides loaning Patience the money for supplies and Davey's wages, now he was anteing up Lily's paycheck as well.

"That kitchen better make some money," he muttered to no one, "because the saloon's damn near a dried-up well."

"Brady," Sam Hanks said as he walked up and took a position alongside him at the bar. "If your face gets any longer, you'll drown in your beer."

"Today, that's sounding like a good idea." Brady slid him a sidelong glance. "Some sheriff you are. There's a damn crazy woman in town, stealing me blind, and you're no help at all."

The tall, lanky sheriff chuckled, signaled to Joe for a beer, then said, "I offered to be your best man."

"Well now, that's real funny," Brady told him and curled his fingers around the handle of his beer mug. Lifting it, he took a sip, even though he really didn't want it, then set the glass down again. "You come by just to make me feel worse?"

"Nope," Sam said, accepting his beer with a nod of thanks and pausing long enough to take a long, satisfying drink. He wiped his mouth on the back of his hand and said, "Came to tell you I got an answer to that last wire we sent out to Sacramento."

"And?" A flicker of hope danced in his chest and was quickly extinguished again when Sam went on.

"And nothing." The sheriff shrugged. "Nobody knows anything about her."

He wasn't even surprised.

"It's like she dropped into town out of nowhere." Right into my lap, he added silently and focused his gaze on that closed door again, as though he could see through it to the woman at the root of the headache pounding behind his eyes.

"Hell, Brady," Sam was saying, "why don't you just ask her where she's from?"

He bit back a laugh that had no humor in it. "What makes you think *she* knows?"

The sheriff shrugged again and Brady gritted his teeth. His eyes felt sandy from lack of sleep. His temper was frayed and his body felt as tightly wound as a twenty-dollar watch. She'd been here nearly a week and already Brady could hardly remember what it had been like without her around.

She'd taken over his life and there didn't seem to be a damn thing he could do about it—short of selling the saloon and making a run for it. But even as that thought registered, he pushed it aside. Brady Shaw had never run from anything or anyone in his life and he damn sure wasn't going to start now.

"She seems to know you," Sam said. "And all of us."

"And that doesn't bother you any?" Brady demanded, keeping his voice down so that the few customers left in the saloon couldn't hear him. "You think about it, Sam. Here's this female showing up in town, claiming to know me—"

"To be engaged to you . . ."

"Shit." He inhaled sharply. "Right. And she's settling into town like she's been here all along."

"Hasn't she?"

"No, damn it!" Brady scowled as a few heads turned toward him and he silently reminded himself to keep his voice down.

Sam shifted position uneasily, resting one booted foot on the brass rail in front of him. Cradling his beer glass between his hands, he twirled it gently, sliding it through the water ring on the highly polished wood. "Y'know, Brady, I'm not stupid enough to get involved in a clash between a man and his woman—"

"She's *not* . . ." Brady muttered an oath and let his chin hit his chest. What was the use?

"But," Sam continued as if he hadn't been interrupted. "I'll say this. If you've changed your mind about marryin' Patience, then just say so and stop all this other foolishness."

"Foolishness?"

"Folks aren't taking kindly to you treating Patience the way you are."

"*Really.*" Sarcasm dripped from the single word, but Brady had a feeling it was sliding right past Sam unnoticed.

"Yep. Folks in Fortune are fond of Patience. Always have been."

Always. Hell, there *was* no always where she was concerned. But why did no one but him see that?

How had she managed to convince everyone in town that she'd always been there when he knew damn well she hadn't? For one thing, if they really were engaged, he'd have had her in his bed by now and his body wouldn't be constantly screaming for release.

What was it about Patience Goodfellow that had people ready to do whatever they could to help her? What was it she brought out in folks that turned them to her side—against *him*? Hell, even Sam was becoming one of her big supporters and Brady resented it. He hadn't had many friends in his life. But Sam had become one in the last couple of years.

He still wasn't sure how it had happened. Most lawmen he'd known wouldn't exactly be willing to be friendly with a gambler—let alone an ex-gunfighter. But Sam had. And over the last couple of years, the slowly building friendship had come to mean a lot to Brady. Now that, too, was dissolving because of Patience's one-track mind.

Damn it, why did she want *him*? Even to the most desperate spinster, Brady shouldn't look like a prize. A man alone, more comfortable in smoke-filled saloons and whorehouses than in cozy parlors. He knew more about thieves and shanghai queens than he did about quilting bees and barn raisings. He'd grown up on docks and riverboats, scrambling for a living like any other wharf rat. And on the road to adulthood, he'd learned one hard-and-fast lesson.

To trust only himself.

So why in the name of all that was holy would *any* woman want *him* for a husband?

"She's a fine woman, Brady," Sam was saying,

dragging him back to the conversation at hand. "And people in town ain't going to be happy with the man who treats her fast and loose."

"Fast and loose?" Brady repeated, astonished. "Hell, Sam, I'm trying to get rid of her, not lasso her."

Sam's features tightened, but before he could speak, the door leading to the kitchen swung open. And even though they stood at the far end of the bar, the aromas drifting through that doorway caught both men's attention.

Lily, carrying a large tray, stepped over the threshold and paused, glancing around the half-empty saloon. She looked almost nervous, Brady thought and couldn't figure out why. She'd been working in the saloon for two years, after all. What was so different now?

Then he glanced to his right and saw Sam's expression go slack. He looked like a man who'd just had the floor fall out from under his feet.

"Well now, Lily," a man in the back of the room called out. "You're surely a sight for sore eyes. You miss me, darlin'?

The blonde shook her head, lifted her chin, and said, "Miss you? Heck, Earl, you're the main reason I quit."

Laughter followed her statement but she paid no attention as she wandered down the length of the bar toward Brady and a clearly thunderstruck sheriff.

Sam's jaw had dropped and Brady was forced to shove him to wake the man out of his stupor. "What's wrong with you?" he muttered as Lily came closer, smiling.

She looked different these days, Brady thought. Her hair done up into a tidy knot on top of her head, she wore a simple blue dress with a high collar and long sleeves. A far cry from the short silk dress and feather-adorned curls he was used to seeing her in—but she looked nice. In a prim, schoolmarmy way.

His stomach rumbled in response to the delicious smells approaching and Brady's attention shifted to the tray she carried. Arrayed on it were several small frosted cakes and a few golden-brown half-circles, still steaming from the oven.

"Patience wanted you to be the first to try some of these," Lily said.

Even the mention of her name was nearly enough to kill his appetite.

"No, thanks," Brady muttered.

"They're real good, Brady," she told him and shoved the tray closer.

The blended aromas drifted to him and damned if he could resist the temptation despite wanting to show Patience that he didn't need her cooking in his saloon. Reaching out, he snagged one of the frosted cakes and took a bite.

Flavors exploded in his mouth and Brady pulled the cake back and stared at it even while he chewed. He'd never tasted anything like it. Soft and sweet and light and airy, the small cake could have dropped down from heaven itself.

He moaned gently as the glory of the thing slid down his throat.

"I'll try one," Sam said from beside him and reached for one of those flaky brown wedges of crust. One bite and he, too, was sold. He turned an amazed glance on Lily and then turned to Brady. Waiting until he swallowed, he gestured with the pastry and said, "Damn, this is good."

Lily beamed at both of them. "Wait until you try her doughnuts."

"Doughnuts?" someone from the far side of the room yelled. "Did you say somebody's making doughnuts?"

Her eyes sparkling, Lily turned away from Brady and Sam and carried her tray across the room. Men were jumping up from the tables to hustle toward her. "Doughnuts," she said, "cookies, pies, cakes, and these steak-and-potato pies too."

Brady watched as his customers abandoned their beers and whiskeys and hands of cards to inhale the food Patience had cooked. And the sweet, satisfying taste in his mouth dried up. She'd done it. She'd overrun not only his life, but his saloon too.

"You ever seen anything like this?" Sam was muttering almost to himself as he picked away portions of the flaky crust he held. "Look at this. She's got steak sliced thin and potatoes and gravy all wrapped up in a pie crust. Like a whole meal you hold in your hand. Hell, there's even peas in there."

"Wonderful."

Again, Sam didn't pick up on the sarcasm and instead turned a knowing eye on Brady. "You know, you and Patience ought to think about closing the saloon and just opening a restaurant once you get married."

That tore it.

Tossing the rest of his cake to the bartop, Brady straightened up and glared at his friend. "I am *not* closing down this saloon," he said and didn't care how loud he got. This was his place. And if he wanted to shout down the rafters, then by God, that's just what he was going to do.

"Now, Brady . . ."

He held up one hand and thought, briefly, about throwing a punch but restrained himself, considering Sam would probably only throw him into a cell for his trouble.

"No," he said hotly. "No more. I've stood by for nearly a damn week. I've let that female run roughshod over me and my place for long enough. I'm *not* getting married, you hear me?" he added, glancing at the men staring at him before looking back at Sam. "I *don't* love her. I'm *never* going to love her. And by damn, that ought to be the end of it!"

The six women moved around the room in a flurry of motion. Skirts flying, arms waving, they laughed and chatted as they helped set the newly operating kitchen to rights. There were pastries cooling on the counter and steak pies baking in the oven. Sunlight poured into the room through the gleaming windowpanes and the combined scents of her morning's work hung in the air like a blessing. By all rights, Patience should be happy. She should be feeling a sense of satisfaction.

Instead, she thought, letting her gaze shift around the room, from one face to another, she felt . . . isolated. But why? she wondered. These women were her friends. Weren't they?

Of course they were, she thought, it was just that—Frowning to herself, Patience worried her bottom lip as her mind whirled. They were all very nice. Well, almost all of them. Vonda still managed to throw a sour note into an otherwise happy chorus. But it wasn't the laundress. It was something else. Something she'd been noticing for nearly a week.

Despite the smiles they gave her, each of these women, like everyone else in town, had something else in their eyes when they looked at her. Confusion. It was as if they really didn't remember her. Didn't know her as she knew them.

Patience wiped her hands on her apron and swallowed back the small knot of fear lodged in her throat. In the last few days, she'd sensed a difference in those around her. At first, she'd told herself that it was merely a game people were playing with her. Pretending they didn't know her. But it had gone on too long. It involved people not only in town, but from the outlying ranches. And it didn't matter that she knew so much about them . . . they didn't seem to know her.

And what did that mean?

Through the fabric of her apron, she squeezed her hands together tightly and held on as if that grip alone meant everything. The voices behind her spun into a swirling rush of noise that became nothing more than a buzz in her ears. Strange that this was all hitting her now.

But when Miriam had arrived this morning, staring at her as though she were a complete stranger,

Patience had felt the weight of the last few days crash down on her at once.

Now she wasn't at all sure what to do.

The adjoining door to the saloon swung open and Lily stepped back into the room, a wide smile curving her lips and the flush of success on her cheeks. "They ate up every scrap of food we offered and they want more."

"That's a good sign," Treasure told her and rubbed her palms together. "Let's load that tray up again, Lily. Only this time," she said with a conspiratorial grin, "they *pay* for what they eat."

Patience hardly listened. Strange, she'd been so excited about opening this kitchen, and now that she knew it would be a success, it didn't seem important anymore. She had too much on her mind to care about baking. She needed—

The sound of Brady's voice reached her through the open door and instantly she knew that what she needed was him. The man she loved. The man who loved her. The man she'd pledged her life to. He would help. He would know what to do about the odd sensations she was experiencing.

Smiling to herself, she headed across the kitchen and stepped into the saloon. She followed the sound of his voice, and when her gaze landed on him, she saw that he was looming over Sheriff Hanks, a look of pure fury on his features.

And it was only then she heard exactly *what* he was saying. Or rather, shouting.

"Did you hear that, all of you?" he called out,

waving one hand at the men scattered around the room, sitting at the dozen or so card tables. "I said, I'm *not* engaged to Patience. I'm *not* in love with her. And I'll be damned if I'm turning *my* saloon over to a crazy woman!"

Every single word hit her body like an icy bullet. She felt their impact. She felt the slow shriveling of her soul. She felt her blood slow and cool. And finally, she actually felt her heart break.

The echo of his words still hung in the air when she noticed that the silence had become thicker. But her ears were ringing and a voice in her head was wailing, so she wasn't at all sure why.

The rush of temper left him as quickly as it had come on him and Brady greedily sucked in a gulp of air. He faced down the men in the room, ready to glare them all into submission. But as he looked at them, he saw that they weren't watching him.

Someone in the room cleared his throat.

A chair's legs scraped against the floor.

And slowly, Brady swiveled, following the direction of the other men's stares. He knew what he'd find when he turned. But it didn't help.

Patience stood statue-still in the open doorway to the kitchen. Behind her, he caught a glimpse of a few other women gathered close enough that they, too, had probably heard him.

But it was the hurt in Patience's gaze that jabbed at him. Those golden eyes of hers shimmered with a silvery sheen of tears that he hoped to hell she wouldn't shed. Because seeing her cry would surely finish him off.

"Patience," he said and his voice sounded as rusty as an old gate, long unused.

She only looked at him for another long minute. Then quietly, calmly, she turned around and walked away.

Chapter Eleven

For a couple of long heartbeats, nobody moved.

Damn it.

Regret choked him and he wished heartily he could have bitten off his tongue. But it was too late now to take the words back. They hung in the still air, as clearly defined as the scent of Patience's pastries. He swallowed hard, but it didn't help ease the knot of discomfort lodged in his throat.

"Well, now you've gone and done it," Sam muttered, breaking the spell that had fallen over the saloon.

"Shut up," Brady snapped without looking at him. He didn't need to be told what he'd done. One glance at Patience's hurt expression had accomplished that. He snatched up his hat from the end of the bar and jammed it down onto his head. Feeling lower than he ever had before, he crossed the room in a few long-legged strides. Only one thing to do. Find her. Talk to her. He slapped one hand down on the bartop as he rounded the corner but when he would have walked through the open doorway, he was forced to stop.

Every female who'd been in the kitchen was now blocking his way, standing between him and Patience. And right up front was Treasure Morgan.

"Get out of the way, Treasure," he said tightly.

"You oughta be ashamed of yourself, Brady Shaw," the storekeeper said, giving him a look that should have killed him and planted him six feet under.

A pang of guilt jabbed at him. But an instant later, he asked himself why he should be feeling guilty. Sure, he wished Patience hadn't heard him yelling like that. But damn it, he'd been mighty fair about this for nearly a week.

"You had no call to be talking to Patience that way," Lily chimed in from beside the big woman, and Brady shot her a look, noting for the first time that she had a real mean glare when she wanted to.

An itch settled between his shoulderblades. The same kind of feeling he used to get when his body was warning him that somebody, somewhere, had a gun aimed his way. But that was ridiculous. These women weren't armed. And, he thought, letting his gaze slide from one furious expression to another, that was probably a good thing.

"I wasn't talking to Patience," he reminded them all. "I was talking to Sam."

As one, they all turned their heads to stare at the sheriff. Disgusted, Brady saw the otherwise fearless lawman actually cringe. But an instant later, the women forgot about Sam and focused on Brady again.

And he had to fight the urge to do a little cringing himself.

"You should apologize," Lily told him.

Well now, that was just what he'd planned to do. But doing it on his own and being told to do it were two different things. Set a man's back up to be told how and when to do anything.

"Apologize?" Brady echoed.

"Crawl," Treasure suggested.

He just stared at her.

"Never did hurt a man to do a little crawlin'," the storekeeper went on. "And there's nothin' a woman likes more than to see her man willin' to do a little crawlin' to win her forgiveness."

Crawl?

Even the thought made his spine go ramrod straight. He'd never begged anybody for anything. And he damn sure wasn't going to start now. He'd try to ease her hurt feelings, but he'd be standing on his own two feet when he did it. But before he could say so, an unidentified man spoke up in his defense.

"Now, you women back off of Brady there," someone called out from the back of the room.

"You hush, Rudy Mendez," Treasure snapped, shooting the cowboy a narrow-eyed glare that would have given a paid gunman second thoughts.

Brady couldn't blame the man for doing what he was told.

The storekeeper was a formidable woman at any time, he thought, but at the moment, she looked downright menacing. Her jaw was set and those eyes of hers were shooting fire. Brady took a small step forward and Treasure moved to block him. She crossed beefy arms over her mammoth bosom and planted her feet far apart in a battle stance.

Brady scraped one hand across his face and briefly considered his chances of getting past her.

Then she tilted her chin toward him defiantly and silently dared him to try.

Wasn't hardly fair, since they both knew he wouldn't raise a hand to a woman.

And short of throwing her to the ground and walking across her prone body, he figured there was no way he was getting through that kitchen. Why was it that females were suddenly becoming the enemy? He'd always gotten along just fine with women. He generally liked all of them. And his charm had always stood him in good stead.

Until today.

Sucking in a gulp of pastry-scented air, which only served to remind him of Patience, Brady gritted his teeth and asked, "Are you going to move or not?"

"Not until I know that you're going to make things right with Patience," Treasure snapped.

"She was crying," Lily told him.

Ah, hell.

Guilt stabbed at him again and he resented it like the very devil. Hadn't he done everything he could for her in the last week? Hadn't he gone out of his way to be understanding? He'd given her a place to stay. He'd bought her new clothes. He'd lent her the money for the damn kitchen that was going to put him out of business.

Not many other men would have been so generous, he assured himself silently. So kind. So . . . *stupid*.

That one word settled in his brain and he had to own up to it. This was his own fault. He should have told her the truth a week ago. Should have made her listen. Shouldn't have allowed those delusions of hers to take root.

Shouldn't have hurt her.

His gaze drifted across the faces of the women watching him with murder in their eyes and he didn't blame them one bit. Hurting Patience had been like taking a stick to a child. There was just no excuse for it.

He had to find Patience and he for damn sure wasn't going to be able to get past these women. So he'd just have to go around them. Doing a quick about-face, he marched across the barroom in impatient strides, headed for the batwing doors and the main street beyond.

As he went, one corner of his mind noted that the folks in the saloon were still tearing into each other.

"It's lettin' females into a saloon that's caused this mess," some man called out.

"Letting?" one of the women challenged. "Buster Franks, the day hasn't come when the likes of you *lets* a woman do anything!"

"Y'know you women don't belong in here," another foolish man called out.

"And are you thinking to try to make me leave?" Treasure countered.

Brady kept walking, quickening his steps, eager to leave what looked like a brewing war behind him.

"Gettin' so's a man can't have a drink in peace anymore."

"You want peace, you old goat?" Miriam Vines shouted.

"Who you callin' an old goat?"

Brady's outstretched hands hit the swinging doors so hard, they smacked against the wall and rattled on their hinges. He kept walking and paused at the edge of the boardwalk under the overhang. Drawing a deep cooling breath, he let his gaze sweep across Main Street.

A dozen or so horses were tethered to the hitching rails dotting the road. A dray wagon rolled along the street, kicking up dust as its ancient wheels groaned like an old man getting out of his bath. The barber's old yellow dog lay stretched out in the sunlight, heedless of the traffic that moved around him. A handful of shoppers strolled along the boardwalks and a cold wind shot in off the desert, wrapped itself around Brady briefly, then went on its way.

He shivered slightly, narrowed his gaze, and studied it all again. She had to be here. Where else would she go? Out into the desert? No. Patience wouldn't do anything that stupid. She was here. Somewhere.

Brady hunched his shoulders deeper into the folds of his jacket and shoved both hands into his pants pocket. Leaning against the handy overhang post, he taunted himself with the memory of Patience's face.

Why the hell had she chosen *that* moment to step into the saloon? Why had he shot his mouth off when he'd managed to keep his temper for nearly a week? And why did it matter so damn much that he'd hurt her?

A curl of something he didn't want to acknowledge as remorse unwound inside him. It had been a lot of years since he'd felt sorry about anything he'd done. Well, not counting the night he'd won the saloon. But that was something he tried not to think about anymore.

Still, it figured that Patience would awaken in him the ability to feel bad about speaking his mind. He'd been alone so long, he'd pretty much done and said whatever he wanted to without having to worry about stepping on tender feelings. And Patience *was* tender. And sweet. And innocent. It wasn't her fault she was nuts.

That thought propelled him off the edge of the boardwalk. He had to find her. And if that meant turning everything in this town upside down, then that's what he'd do.

But he hadn't taken more than a step or two before that old yellow dog lifted its head, sniffed the air, and slowly pushed itself to its feet. Brady watched as the hound glanced first one way then the other before taking off in a slow trot around the edge of the barbershop.

Instantly, images of the last week raced through his mind. How many times had he seen that old dog rising from its continuous nap to greet Patience when she walked down the street? Until she'd arrived in Fortune, old Lightning had been known to sleep through fire, flood, and famine.

Most folks thought it cute that the old dog was apparently sweet on Patience.

Right now, Brady was just grateful for it.

Playing his hunch, he followed after the dog, stepping into the shadowy alleyway and trailing behind it at a safe distance.

Sure enough, as the dog left the alley, Brady heard

a familiar female voice whispering, "Oh, you sweet thing."

The dog's whine of pleasure drowned out the rest of Patience's words, but not the aching break of her voice. Disgusted with himself for making her cry, Brady plunged ahead, and when he stepped out of the alley, he found Patience on her knees in the dirt, her hands buried in Lightning's thick coat.

"Patience," he said softly.

She went absolutely still.

"I want to talk to you about—"

Her head snapped up and teary eyes flashed damp temper at him. "I think you've said enough, don't you, Brady?"

That now familiar stab of guilt jabbed at him and he took the pain as only what he deserved. "You weren't meant to hear that."

"Oh," she said, releasing the dog to stand up. One foot caught in the hem of her dress and she stumbled. He reached out to steady her, but she pulled back as if his hand were diseased.

Amazing how much that hurt.

"So then," she went on, "you meant what you said, you just didn't want me to hear you."

"Yes. No." He shook his head, stared into those golden eyes of hers, and fought to regain his resolve. Yes, he wanted to apologize for hurting her. But could he really take back what he'd said? Wasn't it better if they had this out now? If she understood that her delusions were just that? How much crueler would it be to play along with her only to eventually let her down?

He reached out one hand to her again, and when she took a step back from him, he let his hand fall, fisted, to his side. "I never wanted to hurt you, Patience."

"But you don't love me."

"I don't know you."

She actually winced and the pain written on her features rippled through him too.

"Then why?" she demanded. "Why do I know you?"

"I don't have an explanation for that."

"I do," she said and he was relieved to see the sheen of unshed tears had disappeared from her eyes. Temper was still there, of course, but anger was so much easier for a man to handle than tears. "The explanation is that you *do* know me, Brady. As well as you know yourself."

"Patience," he began, but she cut him off neatly.

"There's something between us, Brady Shaw. It's good and strong and wonderful."

He shifted uneasily.

"But you don't want it," she continued and her voice broke again, ripping out the last corner of his heart. "You don't want me."

His hard, taut body thought otherwise, but he was in no position to argue the point. "Patience, I don't want a wife. Any wife. Not just you."

"You're making a mistake," she told him.

"Won't be the first," he admitted.

"No," she agreed, "it won't be."

He shifted again, uneasiness crawling along his spine.

Patience watched him and wondered how everything could have gone so wrong. She'd loved him for so many years, it was hard to see him look at her as though she were a stranger. And yet . . . her mind raced, one thought after another presenting itself and then scurrying on.

Only an hour ago, she'd wanted to run into his arms, to have him tell her that everything would be all right. Now, she felt as though even their love was drifting away from her and there was nothing she could do to stop it.

Unless . . .

She knew Brady better than anyone else did. Perhaps even better than he knew himself. He could be pushed and argued with only so far and then he would draw a line in the figurative sand and stand his ground. And no amount of pushing or cajoling would get him to back down.

In memory, she heard him telling a roomful of people that he didn't love her and had no intention of ever loving her. And though that pain simmered in her breast, the rational side of her brain asserted itself, demanding she pay attention.

This wasn't about his lack of love for her. This was about his own need to be in charge. To draw that line in the sand. Brady Shaw wasn't a man to be *told* anything. She had to make him realize that loving her was something he *wanted* to do. She had to force him to remember exactly why they'd become engaged in the first place. The best thing she could do for both of them now, she told herself, was to pull back. To ease away from him. To give him the chance to see what his life would be like without her in it.

Then, he would know. Then, he would realize that what was between them was meant to be. Though she ached inside at the thought of being separated from him, this was the only way to be sure that they would never be apart again.

Decision made, she announced, "I'm leaving you, Brady."

His mouth dropped open. A second later, though, he regained his senses and asked, "You're leaving me?"

"Yes." In fact, the more she thought of it, the better the idea sounded. This could be just what they needed. Time. Time for him to see that what they shared, what they were *meant* to share, was worth everything.

"And where will you be going?"

"Don't you worry about me," she said and Patience smiled despite the niggling doubts inside her. She fought for courage. Fought for the strength to walk away from the only man she'd ever loved.

"Patience," he said tightly, "you don't have any place to go."

"Nonsense."

"You don't have any money."

"Piffle."

"You don't have a job."

"Unnecessary."

He reached up, tore his hat off and threw it to the ground. It bounced once, was picked up by a sharp blast of wind, and danced off out of sight. Shoving both hands through his hair, he stared at her as though she'd grown another head in the last moment or two.

"Damn it, you can't just walk out like this and not know where you're going!"

Lightning took a step toward him, curled back his upper lip and growled.

Instantly, she stiffened as a flash of memory darted across the surface of her brain and disappeared again into the mists. "I've told you before, Brady Shaw. Don't shout at me. And cursing is not acceptable."

"Acceptable?" He laughed, but there was no humor in it. Shaking his head, he shot a glance heavenward before meeting her gaze again. "Lady, around you a man *has* to cuss. It's the only way to stay sane. But you know what? You were right before. It's none of my business where you go."

"Well, you needn't be so nasty about it."

"This ain't nasty," he assured her. "But if you want to see nasty . . ."

The hound growled again and Brady looked at it. "Go ahead, dog. Bite me. That'd make the day perfect."

One of her eyebrows lifted and Patience laid a hand on Lightning's neck, calming him. "Apparently, you're in no mood for a rational conversation."

"And haven't been since you hit town."

She sniffed. Oh yes, a short separation was just what they needed. He'd see. He'd find that life without Patience Goodfellow was simply not worth living. One day soon, he'd come after her, begging her to return and marry him. She smiled at the notion. And maybe, she thought, with a long, last look into those lake-blue eyes of his, if he was very lucky, she'd accept his next proposal as readily as she had the first one.

"Goodbye, Brady," she said and, keeping one hand on Lightning, walked away, leaving him standing in the cold wind alone.

Just as he wanted to be.

That night, Brady lay in his bed and listened to the silence. He'd closed the saloon early, something he'd never done once in the two years he'd been in Fortune.

But tonight was special. Tonight was the first night he'd had to enjoy his reclaimed life.

Moonlight shimmered through the crack in the curtains hanging across the only window in his room and lit up the darkness with a silvery glow. Tucking one hand behind his head, he stared up at the beams overhead and told himself he was a lucky man.

Patience was gone. With the help of her newfound friends, she'd packed up everything and moved out of the room beside his that afternoon. Everything was as it should be, he told himself, smiling into the shadows.

But even as he thought it, his smile faded. "So," he mused aloud, just to hear the sound of his own voice in the quiet. "If everything's so great, why aren't you asleep?"

Disgusted suddenly, he pushed himself up and swung his legs off the bed. Buck naked, he stood up and walked across the bare wooden floor to the fireplace. There, he crouched, laid another log onto the fire, and stood up again to watch the flames devour the wood.

Fire-thrown shadows danced and jumped about the room like demons let loose of hell. Well, that was the kind of company he deserved, he supposed. He'd practically forced a crazy woman out into the street.

Slapping one hand down onto the narrow mantel, Brady scowled into the fire and told himself this was ridiculous. She wasn't his responsibility. She wasn't his problem.

But instead of making him feel better, all that thoughts of Patience did was to bring her image to the forefront of his mind again. Those eyes of hers. That smile. The warmth in her touch and the sound of her laugh. She was so clear in his mind, it was almost as if she were there. In the room with him. He could almost smell her.

A ripple of desire coursed through him and his body tightened in raw hunger. Need pulsed in his veins and he nearly shook with the strength of it.

"Damn, Brady," he muttered thickly, "there are other women in the world. Prettier women. *Saner* women."

Too bad it was the crazy one he wanted.

Whirling around, he snatched up the blanket off the end of his bed, threw it around him against the cold in the hall, and walked to the door. Flinging it open, he took three steps, stopped outside Patience's now empty room and hesitated just a moment before opening that door, too, and stepping inside.

Emptiness rushed at him.

The room still smelled of her, and somehow that made the abandoned room seem even more vacant.

Gritting his teeth, he told himself it was the cold that had him breathing hard as he walked toward the bed. But he knew a lie when he heard it, even if he was the one telling it.

Moonlight filled the room, defining every empty inch of the place. The bed had been neatly made, as if awaiting her return, and in the center of the mattress lay a long piece of ribbon, apparently overlooked by Patience and forgotten in her haste to leave.

He reached for it, and as his fingers curled around the silky scrap, he recognized it as coming from that silly yellow hat she'd worn the day they went to Santa Fe. Brady's thumb traced over the fabric lightly as he tried to shut his mind to the memories of her.

But they came anyway, one after the other, Patience laughing, Patience with temper in her eyes, Patience warm and liquid from his kiss—and he figured he'd just have to get used to them. And as his fist clutched the ribbon tightly, he walked to the window overlooking Main Street. He stared blindly into the darkness and tried to sort through the racing thoughts in his mind.

Only a few minutes ago, he'd been congratulating himself on just how lucky he was. He scowled to himself as his fingers stroked the cool strip of silk. For years, he'd counted on luck to see him through. For most of his life, he'd thought himself blessed with the luck of a survivor. A man who could get through anything as long as Lady Luck didn't desert him.

A cold wind rattled the window glass and crept beneath the edge of the sash, sighing around the empty room like a heartsick lover.

Still holding on to that bit of ribbon, Brady muttered, "Yeah. You're a *real* lucky man."

Chapter Twelve

The wind howled and hammered at the door of the little cabin, sounding like a damned soul futilely pounding on the gates of heaven. Rain spattered the windowpanes fitfully and hissed as it jumped down the chimney to land on the fire in the hearth.

Patience huddled on the narrow bed, drawing the quilt up close under her chin. She looked around the inside of the long-deserted cabin and wondered what it had looked like when Treasure had come here as a young bride. Naturally, she assumed the walls had been well chinked against the wind that now slipped between the time-warped logs. And she guessed the chimney hadn't been missing a mantel and several bricks and there'd probably been a few more pieces of furniture than this one narrow bed, a tiny table, and the one chair drawn up beside it.

"But maybe not," she mused and gratefully listened to the sound of her own voice. "They had each other so maybe what was in the cabin hadn't really mattered to them."

She knew very well that if Brady were here, she wouldn't mind the howling wind or the narrow bed or the empty room. Or the darkness crouched just outside.

Windowpanes rattled and the door shook on its hinges as another blast of wind slammed into the old cabin, and Patience shivered. Leaving town had seemed like such a good idea a few hours ago. Yet now, a hollow feeling settled in the pit of her stomach and Patience dearly wished she was safe in her room over the saloon. With Brady in the room beside her.

A rising tide of self-pity rose up inside her, and as she recognized it for exactly what it was, Patience scowled into the firelit shadows. She should be ashamed, she thought. Lying here feeling sorry for herself.

Slowly, she straightened out on the bed, unwinding her body from the curled-up, hopeless position she'd been in for too long already. She was a strong, sensible woman. Whimpering and whining was *not* the way to win the heart of a man like Brady. "And if it were," she whispered firmly, "I wouldn't want him."

No. She knew him well. Knew what he wanted and needed. And knew that her strength was exactly the right match for him. All she had to do was make him see it. Believe it.

And she would, she told herself, closing her eyes and giving in to the languor stealing over her. His image instantly appeared in her mind and she wondered if he was already missing her. If he was thinking of her. Regretting letting her go. She smiled as she comforted herself with the hope that he was miserable without her, and with that smile still on her face, Patience drifted into sleep.

The dream came without warning and she moaned softly. Faces, blurred and indistinct, rose and fell in front of her. Murmurings drifted past her and she strained, trying to hear, trying to see, until finally one face became clear. Fury contorted the man's features and his voice lashed like a whip as he shouted, "You're my daughter and you'll do as I say!" He wore a long black coat, knee britches, and black shoes with pewter buckles. Nothing shiny. Nothing fancy. Nothing pretty.

And his expression hardened as he stared at her. Patience saw herself, shoulders straight, spine rigid, as she faced him down, refusing to cower one more time from her father's rage. Her simple gray dress was dirty, as though she'd been knocked to the ground earlier.

She felt his anger. Felt her own pride and stubbornness—and fear. He lifted his right hand and slapped her face hard enough to draw tears from her eyes, but still she wouldn't bend. "I won't marry that horrid old man you've promised me to," she shouted back at him. "I'd rather die."

Her father's familiar face went a deep purple shade and she thought his heart might burst in his chest. "You're a plain woman, Patience. You've had no other offers. I'll not support you, and Jacob Pennyworth is willing to have you."

"Willing?" she countered, feeling a strange sense of pride for having finally found the courage to stand up for herself against her father's bullying. "Of course he's willing. No one else will have him."

"Enough!" he shouted again, looming over her until Patience took a step back instinctively. He raised his fist and . . .

She woke up. Jolted from sleep, she sat straight up on the tiny bed. Her heart pounded fearfully in her chest. Her breath came short and fast. Sweat beaded her upper lip and her mouth was dry and bitter with the taste of fear.

Dragging breath after breath into heaving lungs, she told herself it was only a dream. Consoled herself with the fact that nightmares couldn't hurt her. But the images were so clear. The voices more of memory than dream. The fear so overpowering she nearly choked on it.

And staring into the darkness, she wondered if maybe Brady wasn't right after all. What if, she thought, as a chill tingled along her spine, what if she really was crazy?

A baby screamed and its harried father jiggled it unsuccessfully. Another man, just as bewildered, offered advice. "Try giving him a bottle."

"He already ate everything."

"Then maybe you should change his um . . . you know."

"No, sir." The father shook his head emphatically. "I ain't doing that again. It's disgustin'."

Brady sighed and looked away from what had become a familiar sight in the saloon. Men were suddenly in charge of the children. They were straggling in here at all hours, looking for companionship and help. But there was just no help to be had.

"The whole world's gone crazy," he muttered.

"It's war, that's what it is," Sam complained and slammed his closed fist down onto the bar and gave the other man a glare he usually reserved for the men he locked up.

Brady just stared at him, amazed as he interpreted that look. "And this is *my* fault?"

"You're damn right it is," the sheriff said. He paused just long enough to pick up his beer, take a long swallow, and slap it back down again. "This all started 'cause you shot your damn mouth off about Patience."

A knifepoint of regret, topped off with a little guilt, stabbed him in the guts.

Jesus. Three days since he'd spouted off in the bar—three days since Patience had up and left—and the ache the mere mention of her brought was still fresh as a daisy. He muttered a curse and told himself, as he had for the last three days, that this was just temporary. Soon enough, Patience Goodfellow would be nothing more than a bad memory and his life would be just the way it used to be.

Simple.

Uncomplicated.

Lonely.

Shit.

Brady reached behind the bar for a bottle of good brandy he kept there for special occasions. Like when he wanted to drink and not poison himself with the rotgut that passed for whiskey around here. Pouring himself a healthy dose, he brought the glass to his lips and drank it down like bad-tasting medicine.

Fire roared through his insides and it was the first time in three days he hadn't felt cold.

"Sheriff's got a point, boss," Joe piped up. "Ever since you and Patience had that go-round, the females in town have been on the warpath."

"And it's getting worse," Sam told him, gesturing with his drink until the beer inside the glass sloshed over the edge and splashed onto the bar.

Joe wiped it up without a word.

"You're not blaming this on me," Brady argued. "Just because the men in this town can't get along with their wives—"

"Oh, it ain't just the wives, boss," Joe said before Sam could. "It's every blessed female alive, from the Widow Thornton right down to Sallye Beth Hartsfield and she's just four or thereabouts."

"He's right," Sam said, giving the bartender a look that said this was *his* story, and *he'd* tell it. "This is a war just like what the preacher was talking about in his sermon last Sunday."

Well, that explained nothing, Brady thought and poured another drink.

"He don't go to church," a man called out from the room behind them.

Brady lifted his drink in a mock salute toward Hiram Vines, then turned back to Sam. "What did the preacher say?"

"He was talking about a story one of those Greek fellas wrote a long time back," Sam started and furrowed his brow briefly. "Don't remember the man's name exactly, but that's not important anyhow. This story he wrote—"

"Lasissy something—" Joe threw in.

"Yeah," Sam agreed, nodding. "It was about how the women in this town of Athens, they got mad at their menfolk and figured a way to get even."

"Yeah . . ." Brady still didn't understand what this had to do with him. But he was beginning to understand why his saloon had all the earmarks of a nursery.

Joe leaned one forearm on the bar and ducked his head to whisper, "Seems them Athens women started holding back 'favors' from their men, so's they'd stop going to war at the drop of a hat."

Sam huffed out a breath. "Don't you have a beer to pour somewhere?" Then he waited for Joe to move off before saying, "Like he said, the women stopped kissing their men, stopped sleeping with 'em, hell. Stopped doing anything for 'em. No clothes washing. No caring for the children. No cooking. Nothing. And it nearly tore that ol' city apart."

Brady knew the story of *Lysistrata*. A man alone tends to read a lot. The women of Athens had punished their men in the only way they could. By drawing back and pretty much leaving them to fend for themselves. As he recalled, it had caused all manner of problems.

But if the women of Fortune were turning this town into another Athens by holding out on their men, he wasn't going to take the blame for it.

"And what do you expect me to do about it?"

"Apologize to Patience. Bring her back here. Marry her."

Brady choked on a sip of brandy. "You want me to marry her so the folks in town will stop fighting?"

"Hell, yes," Sam said.

"Hell, no," Brady told him.

"Well, why the devil not?" Sam argued, then lowered his voice. "You know as well as I do that you miss her."

That cut deep. All right, he thought, maybe he did miss her. But it was the kind of missing you did when a toothache finally stopped hurting, he told himself. You knew the pain was gone, but you weren't exactly longing to have it back.

He lowered his gaze to the bartop and trailed his fingertips along the path of the wood grain. All right, he acknowledged silently that maybe he missed her more than that. Maybe he missed hearing her laughter first thing in the morning. Maybe he missed feeling the warmth of her hand on his arm. Hell, until she'd come to town, he hadn't realized just how little "touching" there'd been in his life. Patience had always seemed to be taking his hand or laying her own hand on his forearm. And damned if he didn't miss those small displays of affection.

Admitting that, though, only served to point out that he'd done the right thing. There was no room in his life for a woman like Patience. It was better this way, he told himself. Even if she wasn't clearly crazy, she was a good woman. Too good for the likes of him. And he had no business even thinking different.

A wharf rat had no place with a lady.

Why didn't *she* see that?

"Things are gonna start getting ugly around here soon," Sam warned him.

Brady frowned and shook his head. "Not my problem, Sam. You're the sheriff. You take care of it."

"You're the only one who can fix it," Sam said.

"Why's that?"

"'Cause you're the damn fool that started it!"

A spurt of anger shot through him. "*Patience* started it," he reminded his friend. "The day she showed up." And then, he added silently, she'd made it worse by leaving him.

And apparently, she was doing much better without him than he was without her. After all, she hadn't been back in town, looking for him. She hadn't come around asking for his help. Yet every day he wondered where she was. If she was all right. Every day, he listened for the sound of her voice. Waited to hear the rapid click of her heels against the floor.

Hell, he even missed arguing with her and that was really saying something.

The nights were the worst, though. He'd lie there in the dark, so hungry for her, every inch of his skin feeling as though it were on fire. And there was just no relief for the wanting.

"Have you even seen her since she left?" Sam asked, breaking the silence.

"No." He'd looked for her that first day she was gone. Wanting to make sure she was all right. Telling himself that he'd have done the same thing for anyone. Though he knew damn well that was a lie.

But he hadn't been able to find her.

Which went to prove how badly she wanted to

stay lost. The town just wasn't big enough to hide in unless you really worked at it.

"I think Lily knows where she is."

"Huh?" Brady's head snapped up and he looked at his friend, waiting for more information.

"Lily's staying with Treasure now—"

"I know." Brady shook his head, amazed anew at how much had changed because of Patience. Lily had not only quit working at the saloon, she and Treasure had become such good friends, she'd moved out of her room upstairs and into the spare room above the Mercantile.

"—and when I went to see her last night, she—"

"You went to see her?" Brady asked, interrupting the other man. "Why?" After all, when a town sheriff went to talk to a saloon girl, it generally meant trouble. And if Sam thought he was going to throw Lily into jail on some trumped-up charge, just when she was finding some happiness . . .

Sam worked his index finger around the inside of his shirt collar and swallowed hard. Then narrowing his gaze, he told Brady, "I went calling on her, that's all."

Yet another surprise. It was a good thing he didn't have a bad heart, he thought.

"You're courting Lily?"

"Nobody said anything about courting," Sam muttered. "Can't a man go to call on a woman without folks getting the idea that—" He broke off, shook his head and started over. "Anyhow, Lily said something about what Patience was up to, then I guess she remembered it was supposed to be a secret and she closed up tighter than a wet boot. Wouldn't say another word about her."

Brady's fingers tightened around his glass. Lily knew where she was. Lily knew if she was all right. All he had to do was talk to Lily. And thereby admit he gave a damn, which was probably just what Patience was hoping for.

Nope. He couldn't do it.

No matter how much he wanted to.

"All finished, Brady," Davey said as he came in from the storeroom. "Got them boxes all straightened out and lined up like General Custer's boys."

"Those boxes," he corrected, without even thinking about it.

"Those," the kid echoed.

Brady shifted his gaze to the boy beside him and an idea slowly took shape in his mind. Laying one hand on Davey's shoulder, he smiled.

The little cabin rocked with laughter as the townswomen told story after story, entertaining each other with tales of their men's tribulations.

Miriam Vines laid one hand against her chest, pulled in a deep breath, and said, "You should have seen the look on Hiram's face when he sat down to dinner last night and I told him he'd be cooking for himself. That man wouldn't have been more surprised if I'd pulled a pistol on him."

"And Dennis?" another woman piped up from the far corner of the small, crowded cabin. "When I left the twins with him this morning, you'd have thought it was the end of the world." She grinned and added, "I saw panic in his eyes."

The women laughed and Patience smiled, since she knew it was expected, but inside, her mind was whirling. Her fight with Brady had taken on monstrous proportions. She hadn't meant to instigate a revolution. But whether she'd planned it or not, the town of Fortune had been set on its ear.

The lines had been drawn.

Women against men.

Wives against husbands.

And though she knew she should be touched by the support of these women, all she really wanted was to be in Brady's arms again. To have this settled. To know who she was and where she belonged.

To love him and be loved.

But the chances of that seemed slim. Patience stood up and walked to the far side of the cabin. Bending down, she stoked the fire and resettled the tea kettle onto the hob. Voices rose and fell around her, laughter punctuated the air, but she wasn't listening.

Instead, her mind turned, as it usually did, toward Brady. Three days she'd been gone and he hadn't even tried to find her. She wasn't that hard to find, after all. This little cabin that Treasure's husband had built when they were first married was only a short distance from town.

Lily pushed herself up from her seat on the floor and left the circle of women to join Patience at the stove. It just wasn't fair, she thought as she watched her friend's wistful expression. Lily was happier than she'd been in years and the woman responsible for her happiness was clearly miserable.

Patience looked up as she neared and forced a smile that was so overly bright, it was sad. "Are you enjoying living with Treasure?" she asked.

"It's surely different," Lily said and smiled to herself. It was all so new. Having friends. Living in a place where you didn't hear drunks whooping it up. Where you didn't lie in your bed waiting for the knock on the door telling you it was time to go to work again.

For the first time in too many years, her life was her own once more. And she felt . . . *good.* But she'd feel so much better if Patience would come back to town and help end the nonsense that was spreading like a wildfire.

"That's wonderful, Lily," Patience said and turned back to watching the kettle as it simmered on the stove.

"Aren't you going to ask about Brady?"

Patience stiffened slightly and a pang of sympathy tugged at Lily's heart.

"Of course," she said and her voice sounded so chipper it scratched at the air. "How is Brady?"

"Miserable," Lily said simply and waited while Patience turned to her with a hopeful smile.

"Really?"

Nodding, Lily leaned in close and said, "Fern and Addey told me he's like a bear. Just wanders around the saloon grumbling and muttering. Got a look dark as thunder on his face all the time and spends half of every night just sitting in the empty saloon. Guess he's not sleeping any better than you are."

"Oh, I'm fine," Patience told her, straightening her shoulders and lifting her chin as if that were enough to convince anyone.

"Sure you are," Lily said. "That's why you've got shadows under your eyes dark enough to plant corn in."

Patience ducked her head, then turned around to snatch up the whistling kettle. As she poured boiling water into the waiting teapot, she said, "I'm a little tired. That's all."

And stubborn, Lily thought. Don't forget stubborn. This small woman and Brady were either a match made in heaven or hell. They were so much alike. No bend in either of them.

Laying one hand on the woman's arm, Lily asked quietly, "Why don't you come back, Patience? He needs you."

"But he doesn't know that yet," she said. "And until he does, I'm not coming back."

CHAPTER THIRTEEN

Billie Sue Simon smiled at him.

Right there in the middle of Main Street, with folks walking all around. Then she lifted one hand and gave him a wave.

Davey's insides turned to mush and his knees went a little trembly. Those big blue eyes of hers latched on to him and her long, blond curls almost seemed to glow in the haphazard morning sunlight peeking out from behind the clouds. He felt hogtied and dizzy. About as out of place as a cow on a front porch. He wasn't sure what to do about it. Durn it, no girl had ever smiled at him before.

"I'm not s'posed to talk to you," she said and Davey almost looked behind him, thinking she must be talking to somebody else.

"How come?" he asked, when he could get his voice to work.

"My mama says we can't talk to you men, not till you come to your senses."

Men? His narrow chest puffed out a bit with pride. It was nice being counted as one of the men—even if the menfolk weren't real popular here lately. And remembering that made him remember what it was he was supposed to be doing.

"Our senses?" he said. "Brady says it's you females who're acting plumb loco."

"Are not."

"Are too."

Billie Sue sniffed like she had a cold or something, then turned her back to him and marched right off like a soldier on parade.

Davey straightened up, clutched his magic ring tighter, gave Billie Sue a fierce scowl, and forced his legs to work as he turned around and walked off.

Imagine that. Prettiest girl in town and she'd actually smiled at him. His feet got all tangled up together and he durn near sprawled out face first in the dirt. But he caught himself and kept going. His face felt all red and Davey figured he looked like a durn fool, so he hurried his steps to get away as fast as he could.

Besides, he had to follow Miss Lily, didn't he?

At the edge of town, he ran to make sure and keep the blond woman in sight. She surely did walk fast, skirts snapping with every step. Little puffs of dust shot up from her heels and an icy wind whipped her long hair out like a yellow cape behind her. He hoped she really was going to see Patience—'cause he surely didn't want to disappoint Brady.

Made him proud that Brady trusted him like this. Why, he guessed Brady Shaw was about the best man he knew. He didn't get drunk and loud like most men and he never had raised his hand to Davey. Not once, he thought, swiping one hand under his nose. Not like his pa had on more than one occasion.

But he didn't have time to think about his father, so he ignored the ripple of old fear that moved through him. After all, the old man was dead now. He didn't have nothing—*anything*—to be afraid of anymore. He was all grown-up now and doing for himself. Nodding, he shoved that ring up higher onto his shoulder, bent low at the waist, and hurried along. The money Brady had promised to pay him for finding Patience wasn't even important. Well, not the *most* important thing, he told himself. He wanted to help Brady.

The man just didn't look right since Patience had left town. It was like the heart had gone out of him. But it wasn't just him either. Most of the menfolk were complaining now that the females were being so ornery.

Davey frowned to himself and scuttled off the road, ducking and crouching in back of a piñon tree as Miss Lily stopped and looked behind her. When she set off again, Davey let her get a little ahead before he followed.

It wasn't long before the woman walked right up to a tiny cabin like she'd been there before. The door opened up and she disappeared inside. Davey glanced around, then shifted his gaze back to the cabin. Place looked like it had been around for a hundred years. Chinking was falling out of the log walls and the short, tumbledown chimney was missing more than a few bricks. But there was smoke curling from the top and Davey knew without a doubt that Patience was in there.

Still, he told himself as he started walking toward the cabin, he had to make sure.

"So you know where she is?" Brady asked a little more than an hour later.

"Yes, sir," Davey said and swung that shock of hair back out of his eyes.

"And you're not gonna tell me."

"No, sir," the boy answered on a sigh. "I reckon not."

Brady bit down hard on what was left of his back teeth. He was pretty sure that by now, they'd been ground down into nothing more than a speck of bone. Staring at the kid who stood before him, head hanging, he told himself that he shouldn't be surprised by the boy turning traitor on him. After all, since Patience had arrived in Fortune, nothing had been the same.

But damn it, he'd thought he and Davey were friends. That they understood each other. Two souls, alone in the world. He frowned to himself. The boy suddenly siding with Patience was a little hard to take.

Easing down into a chair, Brady used the toe of his boot to push another one out. Motioning to the boy to sit, he used the armrests and folded his hands atop his middle. Once the boy was perched on the edge of the chair opposite him, he asked, "Why won't you tell me?"

The kid clutched at an old brass hoop he held in his hands and studied the damn thing like it had the secrets to the universe written there on the scratched-up metal. Never lifting his gaze, he muttered, "It don't seem right, is all."

"Right?" His voice echoed in the empty saloon.

"Yes, sir."

"How's that?" he asked, forcing himself to remain calm when what he wanted to do was shout until the roof fell in. Damn it, he wanted to know where the hell Patience was and he wanted to know now. Why wouldn't anyone cooperate? And why did he want to know so badly?

That was the real kicker, he told himself, and another cold, hard knot of worry joined the others that were already stacked up in the pit of his stomach. He wasn't sure anymore if the worry was over Patience or over the fact that he *was* worried about her.

Damn it, he'd never in his life given a damn about anyone. And it had been a real easy way to live. Looking out for himself. Caring about nothing and no one.

Although, he was quick to point out to himself, he wasn't admitting to actually *caring* for Patience. It was more a sense of responsibility that had him pacing the saloon all night long. That kept him from sleeping. That kept her face and her voice looming in the forefront of his mind every blessed minute.

It wasn't her, he told himself, and even as he thought it, he knew it for a lie. Somehow or other, that crazy woman had eased her way into his life, and now that she was gone, his world was in a shambles.

He had to get her back. So he could well and truly find out where she belonged and get rid of her. He wasn't going to be able to put her out of his mind until he knew that she was where she was supposed to be.

Yeah, he thought, now *that* made sense. Much more sense than believing she mattered to him.

"Davey, I have to know where she is."

The kid finally lifted his gaze from that damn ring of his and looked Brady dead in the eye.

"Patience don't want you to know where she is, though, Brady. And I promised her I wouldn't say."

Frustration coiled inside him, but he'd had too many years of practice at keeping a poker face to let the boy see it. Instead, he said, "I thought we were friends, you and me."

"We are, but . . ."

"And friends help each other, don't they?"

"Yes sir, but . . ."

"You know I don't want to hurt Patience."

"'Course not." The kid looked appalled at the thought.

"Then why won't you tell me?"

"Because she's my friend too," Davey said, remembering the feel of her hand as she smoothed back his hair. He recalled her smile of welcome when she'd opened the cabin door to find him. She wasn't mad he'd followed Lily, though Lily sure enough had been. Nope. Patience had just gone down on her knees and taken him into a tight, hard hug. Then while she was holding on to him, she'd said how she'd missed him and fussed over him not wearing a coat with the weather turning so bad.

Even now, he could feel the gentleness of her touch and something inside him hungered for it again. It was so long since his mother had died, he didn't even remember her. But when he was around Patience, he didn't feel that emptiness of loss. She filled a spot in him that was no longer cold or lonely.

And if she needed him to keep secret her whereabouts, then that's just what he'd do. Even if it meant disappointing a man he thought as much of as he did Brady.

He shook his head and firmed up his lips. "Can't tell on her, Brady. Not even for you."

A long, silent minute ticked by. Then, to his relief, Brady reached out and gave his knee a pat. "I understand," he said as he stood up, put on his hat, and walked outside.

"Wish to hell I did," Davey muttered and leaned back in his chair.

Patience sat down in the rocking chair Treasure had brought out to her and scooted closer to the fire. Heat reached out warm fingers toward her and eased her into sleep she sorely needed.

Just for a moment, she told herself as her eyes slid closed and her body seemed to sink into the worn, comfortable curves of the polished wood. She'd just rest her eyes for a moment or two, then she'd get up and bake a little more.

Keeping herself busy so she wouldn't have time to think of Brady and how she missed him had filled the little cabin with stacks of cookies and bread and cakes. Treasure kept her larder full and, in return, Patience gave her the baked goods to sell in the store.

It was a good bargain, she told herself as she felt

her heartbeat slowing, her body sliding into sleep. But it would have been better if she were in town. In her own kitchen. With Brady.

Loneliness crept up on her and tugged at her insides.

She missed him so. But she missed the others as well. In fact, she could still feel Davey's arms hugging her neck and a warm thread curled around her heart. He responded so eagerly to the love his soul hungered for. The poor child needed loving nearly as much as Brady did. And she had so much to give if only they'd accept it. Why couldn't either of them see that? Her heart thudded painfully in her chest, but she reminded herself that all was not yet lost. She would convince them both, she thought, a soft smile curving her mouth as sleep claimed her.

Instantly, the dream started again. Patience moaned and her fingers curled tight around the ends of the chair's arms.

"You'll not defy me," her father shouted.

"I won't marry him," Patience yelled at him, for what felt like the one hundredth time. Why couldn't he see what he was doing to her? Why didn't he care?

It seemed that she'd been a disappointment to him all her life. And no matter how she tried to belong in the tiny community, she didn't fit in. She was too stubborn. Too prideful. Too independent.

Her spirit was simply too big for the tidy confines of the Puritan village. She couldn't bear to be less than she was, even to please the man looming over her now.

Her father, enraged, raised his fist and this time

he plowed it into her face with such force that Patience dropped to the dirt like a stone. Fear came first. Then the pain. Stunned, she shook her head, trying to clear the stars from her vision. Agony screamed through her jaw and she lifted one hand to cup the broken bone tenderly.

But there was no time.

Wrapped in a blind fury, her father continued to beat her. With fists and boots, he attacked her, avenging himself for all the times she'd defied him.

She cried out. Whimpered. Begged. Tried to crawl away. But he wouldn't be denied. Not this time. His fists and feet slammed into her body over and over again and finally all she could do was curl up, hoping to make herself as small a target as possible.

Dirt bit into her cheek. Stones scraped her skin. Tears pooled in her eyes and trailed down her cheeks. She curled her fingers into the ground, tearing at the wisps of grass still clinging to the frost-hardened earth.

She couldn't draw a breath. Her lungs clamored for air she couldn't provide. Sunlight from heaven shone down on her as she lay helpless on the ground, a captive to the misery tearing through her.

And then, like a blessing, the torment stopped. She felt the blows continue to land. But there was no more pain.

How odd.

She drifted away from the poor huddled girl lying at her father's feet. Absently, she watched as a crowd of men, all dressed in the same Puritan garb as her father, gathered around them, shouting encouragement, urging him to beat his daughter into submission.

And she didn't care.

She looked at the girl curled up in the dirt and knew none of it mattered anymore. The pain, the longing, the deep well of sadness that was as much a part of her as her thick black hair, were all gone. In their place was a warmth like none she'd ever known before.

Patience smiled to herself and enjoyed the sense of freedom racing through her. A voice called to her then and she turned, searching for the source. Her back to the crowd still thirsting for vengeance, she watched a brilliant, shimmering light form directly in front of her. It pulsed with warmth, with welcome, and the heart of it reached out to her.

She took a step toward it and stopped, looking behind her one last time. But the people and the village were already clouded in mist. Images blurred and were swallowed by the light encompassing her.

Comfort radiated through her and Patience felt the incredible sense of belonging. Here she was wanted. Here she was appreciated. Here—

A voice, familiar, soft, whispered, "It's time to come home, now. Remember, Patience, remember—"

The crash of sound woke her and she jumped from the rocker in response. Outside, the wind caught a loose shutter and slammed it against the wall. Startled, she slapped one hand to her chest.

"Remember, Patience, remember . . ."

Blinking, breathing hard, she whirled around in a circle, searching for the source of that voice.

But there was no one there.

She was alone.

The voice seemed to echo over and over again in her mind, teasing, taunting. Memory rushed in but was gone so quickly, it left her with nothing to grab on to. She knew that she *should* recognize that voice.

But one part of her turned away from that recognition. It was almost as if she were *afraid* to remember.

And that made no sense whatsoever. "I'm certainly not afraid of anything," she said and pretended not to notice that she sounded a bit less than convincing.

But it wasn't just the voice that worried her. It was that dream. It was too real. The people too familiar. The pain almost palpable.

The shutter slammed into the wall one more time, and her heart still racing, she went outside, following the noise that had awakened her. After she'd fixed the loose shutter and bolted it closed, she turned her face into the frigid wind, hoping to blow the last lingering wisps of that dream out of her mind for good.

A wall of gray clouds covered the sky, and as she stared heavenward, the first few snowflakes fell, whipped by the wind that seemed fierce enough to pick up the little cabin and carry it away.

But it wasn't strong enough to chase off the remainders of her dream. The images were still with her.

And standing there in the blast of chill air, Patience knew the cold she felt went far deeper than the weather.

* * *

"Snow."

Brady squinted into the sudden snowstorm and cursed the luck. By afternoon, slate-gray clouds had rolled in to completely cover the sun and sky. Wind roared across the desert, picking up sand and stones to pelt the poor folks who found themselves scurrying to get to shelter.

And Patience was out there . . . somewhere.

Another knot of worry dropped down his throat and bounced in the pit of his stomach. He reached up to tug his hat down more firmly on his head, then dipped the brim to block some of the wind.

"She doesn't even have a damn coat," he muttered thickly and stepped off the boardwalk.

Loping across the street, dodging the occasional rider, and easing past a freight wagon, he jumped up onto the boardwalk that ran in front of the Mercantile. Pausing briefly, he glanced through the wide front window into the heart of the store.

Treasure hadn't spoken to him since their little showdown in the saloon. And truth to tell, he hadn't exactly been sad about that. After all, the women in town were making their menfolk so miserable, Brady'd counted himself fortunate to be single.

But that was then. He didn't have a choice now, he told himself. With this storm blowing up, he *had* to find Patience. For her own sake. Hell, she was crazy. Someone had to look out for her.

Nodding to himself, he kept that virtuous thought firmly in mind as he stepped up to the front door and pushed it open.

The bell overhead jumped and clanged and Brady took a moment to scowl at it. Damned irritating sound. He snatched off his hat and slapped it against his thigh.

"Well, well, well," Treasure said from her seat behind the counter. "Look who's decided to do that crawlin' after all."

His spine stiffened and he bit down hard on his tongue to keep from arguing with the woman. Instead, he steeled himself to be calm and reasonable. "Treasure, I need to know where Patience is."

"I expected you before this," the older woman said and pushed her bulk up and out of her chair. Leaning her elbows on the gleaming counter, she propped her rounded chin in her hands and watched him. "Miss her, do you?"

More than he'd admit to her, he thought. But that wasn't the point.

"There's a storm building up out there," he told her, jerking a thumb in the direction of the window. "Patience shouldn't be out in it alone."

Treasure didn't even blink. "What makes you think she's alone?"

A spurt of completely irrational jealousy shot through him, though he'd never confess to it. Still, apparently, she could tell what he was thinking by the look on his face, because she took pity on him.

Pity. For *him*. That was galling as hell. He shifted uneasily beneath her stare.

"Don't get your long johns all bunched up," she said, shaking her head. "For heaven's sake, Brady, a fool could see you care for the girl."

"I care *about* her," he said tightly. "There's a difference." Hell, he didn't want to see her freeze to death in a freak snowstorm. That didn't mean he loved her, for God's sake.

"You are the hardest-headed man . . ." She sighed and shook her head wearily.

"Are you going to tell me where she is?"

"She asked us not to," Lily said and walked down the stairs to join them.

Brady half turned to look at her. "That was before this storm blew up. It's bad and getting worse, Lily. Do you really want her out there in it all by herself?"

The woman's soft heart shone in her eyes and Brady took his first easy breath since walking into the Mercantile. Lily's worry for her friend would outweigh her promise.

"It does look grim out there," Treasure said as the other woman walked over to stand beside the counter.

Lily nodded to herself and thought about it for a long moment. Finally, though, she lifted her gaze to Brady's and stared at him for what seemed forever.

He held his breath, waiting. Damn it, if she turned him down, he didn't have any idea where to start looking for Patience.

And he *needed* to find her.

"I swear to God, Brady," Lily said, giving him a glare that was sharp enough to slice a man clean to the bone. "If you make her cry again, I'll hunt you down like a dog and shoot you myself."

"And I'll load the gun," Treasure assured him.

His fingers curled into the brim of his hat and held

on tight. He'd be damned if he'd stand here and defend himself to a couple of mother hens.

"I'm not looking to make her cry," he managed to grind out through gritted teeth. "I just want to make sure she's safe."

The two women looked at each other briefly before turning back to him. Lily said, "All right, then. I'll tell you."

And Brady felt the first stirrings of relief.

CHAPTER FOURTEEN

Remember.

Patience picked up the bread dough and slapped it down onto the tabletop. Shoving her fists into the sticky mass, she kneaded, using the tension coiled inside her for strength. Again and again, her fists pounded the dough in a rhythm that danced along with the word repeating over and over in her mind.

Remember.

But she didn't want to remember.

"And why would I?" she asked the empty room. After a dream like she'd had, what person in their right mind would want to recall *more*?

"But then," she whispered, her hands stilling their nervous work, "that's the problem, isn't it?" She *wasn't* in her right mind. At least, not according to Brady.

She didn't *feel* crazy. She didn't feel any different than she had yesterday or the day before or the day before that. Nothing had changed. Nothing except for the fact that she'd watched herself die at the hands of a furious Pilgrim. A Pilgrim who was, she knew without a doubt, her *father*.

And that had to make her crazy, didn't it? A person alive and well in 1880 couldn't possibly have died in the 1600's. Reborn tension tightened her shoulders and fear curled up and settled in the pit of her stomach.

Outside, a storm raged. Inside, oil lamps and a cheerful fire kept the shadows at bay. She was warm and cozy . . . and alone.

She swallowed hard and pulled a shuddering breath into her lungs. Abandoning the mound of dough, she wiped her hands on her apron and walked across the small cabin to the front door. Bracing herself for the bite of the wind, she pulled the door open and stared out at a world she hardly recognized.

White.

There was so much white, it was nearly blinding. Wind-driven snow pelted her face and darted past her, demanding entrance to the cabin. A heavy blanket of gray clouds hung low over the landscape and showed no signs of moving on. A deep, bone-biting cold reached out to her and Patience shivered, one hand clutching the door, keeping it from flying open wider. Behind her, the fire blazed, but staring at the storm, she knew she was cut off from everyone. No one would brave this snow. No one would be coming to see her today.

She would be alone with the memories of the dream that still rattled around inside her mind. And for the first time since leaving Fortune, Patience was frightened.

The saloon was empty.

No one would be out looking for a drink or a card game today, Brady told himself. At war or not, the families in town would be hunkered down together, waiting out the storm.

Like he should be. But no, what was he doing? He was riding out into what had all the earmarks of a blizzard, to chase down a woman he didn't want. *Couldn't* want. He lifted his head and stared into the mirror across the room from him. But instead of seeing his own ragged reflection, he looked deeper into the glass and saw the echo of Patience's image.

Something inside him tightened, shifted, and he swallowed hard against the tight knot of an unfamiliar emotion clogging his throat. How had she done it? he wondered. How had she managed to dig herself so deeply into his life in such a short time? How had she taken a perfectly content man and made him into the haggard mess he was now?

And why in the hell was he riding out into the mouth of a storm to go fetch her?

"Because," he muttered, lowering his gaze to the gear stretched out across his bed again, "it's better than sitting here by yourself worrying that she's freezin' to death."

Calling himself all kinds of a fool, he snatched up his sheepskin coat and shrugged into it, quickly doing up the buttons. Then he checked his saddlebags again, making sure he had everything he wanted to take. When he was satisfied, he slung the saddlebags across one shoulder, grabbed the extra blankets rolled up on his bed, and slammed his hat down low onto his forehead. Instinctively, he dropped his right hand to the holster at his hip, checking to make sure his pistol was where it should be, then, satisfied, he left the room. His bootheels clomped against the wooden floor, sounding like a too rapid heartbeat.

He didn't even glance at the closed doors as he passed them. Fern and Addey were locked away in their rooms, probably enjoying a good rest. And Patience's room was just too empty. He stalked down the long landing to the head of the stairs, then went down in a rush.

At the bottom of the stairs, though, he stopped. Davey stood there, looking for all the world as though he'd lost his best friend. First time in memory that Brady could recall seeing the boy actually looking exactly like what he was. A scared kid.

"You goin' after her?" he asked.

"Yeah," Brady assured him. "I am."

"You figure she's all right?" Davey tossed a quick look over his shoulder at the storm raging just beyond the windows. "It's mean weather."

"It is," Brady said, anxious to be on his way. But staring into the kid's eyes, he knew he had to take an extra minute or two to ease the shadows haunting Davey's gaze. Muffling a sigh, he said, "Don't you worry. I'm sure she's fine. Patience isn't the kind of woman to go all weepy because of a few snowflakes."

"That's true enough," Davey said and a hint of a smile curved his mouth. "She's real brave."

Brady thought about it for a minute and damned if he didn't have to agree. She'd come into town a complete stranger and inside two weeks she'd practically taken over. Brave or crazy, he thought and decided he leaned a bit more toward the "brave" theory.

"Yeah, I guess she is at that," he said aloud. Then something came to him and he asked, "Where are you staying tonight?"

Instantly, the boy stiffened up. Hell, Brady could almost see the defiant, too proud gleam in his eyes that was a perfect match for the independent tilt of his chin. "I got a place."

If it was the place he usually stayed, a straw-filled stall at the livery stable, it wasn't good enough. Brady tried not to push his way into the kid's life. After all, he'd lived that life. And he knew all too well that people butting their noses in weren't welcome.

But there was a damn blizzard blowing up outside and he'd be double damned if he was going to be worrying about Patience *and* Davey freezing to death.

"I want you to stay here," he said, prepared to do battle the instant Davey's back went up.

It didn't take long.

"Thanks, but—"

"Look," Brady interrupted him, eager now to be off and not willing to leave until he knew the boy was going to be safe. "There's an empty room upstairs. There's plenty of wood for you to have a fire."

"I don't need—"

"You *do,*" Brady snapped and the kid blinked at the forcefulness of his tone. Sighing, Brady said, "Sometimes you just have to let your friends help you, Davey."

The boy gave it some thought. In fact, Brady was pretty sure he could see the wheels in the boy's brain turning as he considered his options. A breezy stall in a half-frozen barn and keeping his independence . . . or a cozy bed with a fire and being beholden to somebody.

Jesus. Two years he'd known this boy and he still had to fight him to take anything that even resembled a handout.

Exasperated, Brady finally blurted out, "Do it as a favor to me, all right?"

"Huh?" He swung that hair back out of his eyes and looked up.

Thinking fast, Brady searched his brain and came up with an explanation that just might work. "I'd feel better about leaving Addey and Fern alone here if there was a man in the place."

Davey blinked at him, but obviously the notion appealed to him. It would have been laughable under any other circumstances, Brady thought. Hell, Fern and Addey were tough enough to take on a grizzly bear and have him dressed out and made into a rug inside a few hours.

But if the little lie was enough to keep Davey safe tonight, then that was good enough for him.

"Well," the boy was saying, "if it'd help you out . . ."

"It would," Brady said shortly. "You hunker in here till I get back. There's food down here behind the bar and plenty of firewood."

"Yes, sir."

Relieved, Brady nodded and walked toward the door. Davey's voice stopped him before he could walk through it, though.

"Brady?"

Curbing his impatience to be gone because he heard the strain in the boy's tone, Brady glanced back over his shoulder at him. "Yeah?"

"You're gonna bring her back home, aren't you?"

Home.

That's what Patience had called this place.

Home.

He'd never thought of it like that before. Always it had simply been a place. A place to belong. To stay put. But nothing more.

Now, though . . . he thought of the emptiness in this place since she'd been gone. His own restlessness. The vague sense of uneasiness that had been his constant companion for the last few days. Patience had changed everything, damn it. He recalled the echo of her laughter haunting him. The feel of her touch. The taste of her kiss.

His body tightened into the now familiar state of complete discomfort he'd grown far too accustomed to.

A groan erupted in his chest, but he refused to let it loose.

"Brady?"

He shook his head and stared at the boy as if seeing him for the first time.

"I said, are you gonna bring her home?"

"You stay put," he said, narrowing his gaze to make his order plain.

"I will," Davey said. Then obviously not about to let his question go unanswered, he prodded, "Well? Are you gonna?"

Bring her home? He finished the kid's question

silently. His insides battled. Heart and mind tore at each other. Logic versus emotion. But he knew only too well which one was going to come out the victor. At least this time.

Then clenching his jaw, Brady tightened his grip on the extra blankets, looked the kid dead in the eye and said, "You're damn right I am."

Patience slapped both hands over her ears and tried to block out the sound of the voice that had plagued her all day.

Remember.

But it didn't help. The voice was *inside* her. It came from the heart of her. From her soul. And it wouldn't go away.

Tears stung her eyes, blurring her vision, but then there was nothing here she wanted to see anyway. She was alone. Too alone. That's what made the voice so hard to ignore.

"I won't surrender to this," she muttered, squeezing her eyes shut, until the tears banked behind her lids, streamed down her cheeks like tiny rivers. She shook her head and her hair, long and loose, flew about her shoulders like a wild black cape.

Sucking in a gulp of air, she muttered, "Whoever you are, *stop* this." Yet the voice she recognized but couldn't name went on, whispering, prodding, taunting her with the urge to remember things she had no desire to recall.

What more did she need to know? Patience let her arms fall to her middle, then she wrapped them around herself and held on. Tipping her head back, she stared up at the open beams of the ceiling. But she wasn't looking at the knotty, smoke-stained wood; instead, she saw the sky beyond it and the heavens beyond that.

"Blast you, make this stop," she said, firming her voice when it would have broken. "I am Patience Goodfellow. I live in Fortune, New Mexico. I'm engaged to be married to Brady Shaw. I love him with all my heart." Just saying the words aloud gave her strength. "I *refuse* to be insane, do you hear me?" Releasing her tight grip on her own waist only long enough to plant her hands at her hips, she continued. "I won't lose my life here. I won't lose Brady. I won't lose our future because you want me to remember something that has nothing to do with who I am!"

Remember.

Frustration bubbled over inside her. Her nerves felt as frayed as an old tapestry. The walls seemed to be closing in on her. The air felt thick, almost too thick to breathe. Her heart pounded in her chest and she knew if she didn't move, didn't get out of this place and away from that voice, she would be as crazy as Brady kept telling her she was.

Swinging around, she marched to the door, grabbed the heavy wooden latch, and stopped. Her fingers curled into the old wood, picking at the slivers poking up from the edges. "It won't help," she told herself aloud, more to hear the comfort of a voice—even her own—than for any other reason. "Wherever I go, that blasted voice will go with me."

Besides, there was the snow to consider. She wouldn't get fifty feet in this storm. As if to prove it to herself, she yanked the door open and was instantly pelted with a rush of frigid air and stinging bullets of wind-driven snow. She squinted into the swirling mass of white and told herself that no one would be able to travel in this weather.

No one, that is, except the man striding toward her from the direction of the dilapidated horse stall. Her heart leaped and then plummeted again all in the space of a few seconds. She'd wanted to see him so badly these last few days. But not now. Not when her mind was whirling and strange voices were haunting her and she felt as tightly strung as a badly tuned piano.

Her hands came together at her waist and she dug her fingernails into her skin as she watched him approach. Why was he here today? What could she say to him? If she told him about the voice she'd been hearing, he'd think her more crazy than he did already.

Oh God, Brady, go home.

But he wasn't going home. He was almost upon her and he had the look of a man who was planning on staying a while.

"Brady?"

Snow sifted down the neck of his jacket and beneath the collar of his shirt, dragging cold fingers along the length of his spine. But Brady was beyond cold and working on numb. His bones ached with it. His feet felt like blocks of ice. Still, the fire in his belly kept him plenty warm.

Seeing her standing there in the open doorway like a damn fool filled him with both relief and frustration. It was good to know she was all right, but if she didn't get back inside, she'd have pneumonia inside a week.

"Damn it, Patience, get into the cabin," he shouted to be heard over the wind.

"Don't you curse at *me*, Brady Shaw," she countered.

Something inside him leaped with excitement at hearing her snap at him again. And damned if that wasn't a sign that he was getting contrary. What man in his right mind would enjoy a woman's temper?

In a few more strides, he was beside her. Grabbing her arm, he turned her around and all but threw her into the warmth of the cabin. He stepped in after her and closed the door firmly, shutting out the snow and wind.

The first thing he noticed was the heat. Waves of it, crashing around him, gnawing away at the cold that had held him in its grasp for what felt like forever. He felt the ice melting from his hair, his hands, his clothes, and as he looked at her, he felt the ice begin to melt from his heart as well.

Her hair was a wild, tangled mess, her eyes looked red and puffy, and he knew she'd been crying. Why? Over what? Over *him*? A flicker of something close to hope sputtered to life inside him. Did she still care about him, despite what she'd heard him say about her to Sam? And if she wasn't crying over him, what else had her upset enough to wring tears from her?

He swallowed hard and let his gaze continue raking over her. Her dress was splotched with flour and God knew what else and her skin looked paler than he'd ever seen it before and that was saying something.

But still she was enough to prod his heart into a fierce gallop that threatened to choke him. God, he hadn't even realized how much he'd missed seeing her until he was actually facing her. Every instinct he possessed told him to reach out and grab her. Bury his face in the curve of her neck and inhale the sweet, soft scent of her.

But something in her eyes stopped him.

There was an anxiousness that had never been there before. A sense of worry that jabbed at his own happiness as surely as a hatpin stuck into a child's balloon.

And to cover up his own sudden uneasiness, he looked away from her golden eyes to survey the inside of the old place. Sparsely furnished, it looked pretty much like what it was . . . an abandoned cabin. Except, he told himself, for the trays of baked goods that were stacked on the chairs and the end of the table. And the stores of flour and coffee and sugar and what all standing like soldiers along the length of one wall. He thought of the meager supplies he'd brought along with him and almost laughed. Obviously, she wasn't hurting for food. But before the chuckle building inside him could escape, he noticed something else. Something that damn near took his breath away.

The adobe chinks between the logs of the cabin were splashed with color. Everywhere he looked, flowers were growing from the walls. White, yellow, blue, red, pink, every color he could think of was represented. Trailing vines of green leaves stretched themselves across the old, battered logs and supported the flowers that by all rights should never have been there.

For one thing, it was the dead of winter.

And for another . . . flowers just didn't grow out of adobe. Especially adobe that was probably older than he was.

Openly staring, Brady turned in a slow circle, trying to make sense of what he was seeing. But there was no explanation for it. The flowers were simply . . . *there,* filling the tiny cabin with their scent.

"What the—"

"Beautiful, isn't it?" she asked, following his gaze. "I don't know how it happened. Maybe it was the warmth of the fire that started them growing."

"Not likely."

"Well, what other explanation is there?"

"Good question," Brady said, bringing his gaze back to her. Staring into those golden brown eyes that had haunted him for days and nights on end, he forgot about the flowers. Forgot about the storm and everything else in the world but Patience Goodfellow.

He'd come here to rescue her and that's damn well what he was going to do.

"If you get your things together fast, we can get back to town before the heart of the blizzard kicks in," he said.

She took a step back from him. "I'm not going back to town."

Stunned, he just looked at her for a long minute. He hadn't figured on this. Oh, he knew she'd likely be a bit stubborn, but he'd also thought she'd be damn glad to get away from the solitude. But she didn't look glad. In fact, her expression looked nothing short of downright unfriendly.

He sighed. "Damn it, Patience, you can't stay out here all alone with a blizzard blowing in."

"Don't swear at me, Brady," she said, her gaze darting all around the room, looking anywhere but at him. "And I'm fine here."

"Oh yeah," he said, snatching his hat off and slapping it against his thigh. Clumps of snow dropped to the floor at his feet. "I can see that. You look half-crazed . . ."

Her gaze snapped to his.

"I'm *not* crazy."

"I didn't mean that, exactly," he said, cursing himself for choosing the wrong words. "But you look—Hell, Patience, a blind man can see you've been crying."

Well, perfect. He probably shouldn't have said anything about that either. Instantly, her chin went up a notch or two and her golden eyes narrowed defensively.

"You shouldn't be here, Brady."

Well, that was new. And damned discomfiting. That one short sentence stung bad. He scowled and wondered why it bothered him so that she was finally wanting him to leave her alone.

For damn close to two weeks now, he'd wanted nothing else. But up until today, she'd been all over him. Telling people they were going to be married.

Insisting that he loved her. Insinuating herself into his life. Forcing him to accept her and put up with her craziness.

Making him actually give a damn.

And now that he did, she wasn't interested?

He shifted position and crumpled the brim of his hat in one tight fist. The heat of the room did nothing to dispel the chill in her eyes. A fine thing, he told himself in disgust. She'd made him ride into a snowstorm just to save her and now she didn't want to be saved?

"Are you asking me to leave?"

"Yes," she said flatly.

Brady blinked and stared at her. Hell, he'd never been thrown out of *any* place. And he'd been in some of the worst saloons and bars in the country. There he was welcome. But apparently not in this little cabin in the middle of nothing.

"You expect me to just turn around and ride back to town in this blizzard? Without you?"

"I didn't ask you to come out here," she reminded him.

"No, you sure didn't," he said, stomping across the room to the fireplace. The flames licked and danced at the neatly stacked wood in the hearth and heat streamed out at him. But he still felt chilled to the bone. Glancing quickly at the fire, he looked back at her and said, "No, you came out here to the middle of nowhere and set up house in a cabin that's about to fall down around your ears."

"It's fine."

"Oh yeah." Brady nodded shortly and waved one hand to encompass the tiny place. "It's a damn palace, Patience."

"Don't—"

"Curse at you," he finished for her.

She swallowed hard and he wondered if she was biting back a few curses of her own.

"Go away, Brady."

"I'm not leaving you here alone."

She laughed shortly. "I've been alone for three days and it didn't bother you until now?"

He used the palm of one hand to dust what was left of the snow from the front of his coat. "In case you hadn't noticed, we didn't have a storm until today."

"Fine," she said, folding her arms across her chest. "If you're worried about the snow, I can promise not to go out in it."

"That's not good enough."

"It will have to be."

Frustration, something he'd become all too familiar with since Patience's arrival, rose up inside him, threatening to choke him. But he wouldn't give in to it. Not now, anyway. There'd be time enough later to figure out what the latest mystery concerning Patience was. For right now, though . . . There was something going on here. Something that she wasn't saying. Something she didn't want him to know.

And he wasn't about to leave her until he knew just what that was.

Shrugging out of his jacket, he tossed it across the back of the nearest chair. Throwing his hat onto the table, he planted his feet wide apart, inhaled deeply and crossed his arms over his chest, mimicking her defensive stance.

"Just ease your mind around this one fact, Patience," he said tightly. "I'm not leaving until I find out why you're so anxious to get rid of me."

Chapter Fifteen

"I'm not trying to get rid of you," she lied and hoped he didn't see the untruth in her eyes. "But I'm . . . enjoying the peace and quiet out here"—another lie—"and I'm not ready to give it up yet."

"That's too damn bad," he said, much too quietly.

"Don't—"

"Swear."

Her gaze flicked up to his and she watched his pale blue eyes muddy and darken. Anger sputtered there, along with a frustration that almost shimmered around him. But she couldn't do anything about that. How could she possibly help him when she couldn't help herself?

"Brady," she said, running her hands up and down her forearms, to stave off a chill that seemed to be seeping into her bones. "Can't you see that I don't want you here?"

"Yeah," he said tightly, barely moving his mouth to form the words. "I can. And I want to know why."

Was that hurt she saw flash briefly across the surface of his eyes? Guilt tugged at her heart and changed nothing.

"What difference does it make?" Patience asked, wishing he would just leave. Now. Before she forgot that she didn't want him to see her as she was at the moment. Nervous. Worried. Even silently she didn't want to acknowledge the word "afraid."

A part of her was so happy to see him, so grateful to not be alone out here with the wild thoughts plaguing her. But she couldn't let him stay. No matter how much her heart urged her to.

Steeling herself to do the right thing, she said, "You've made no secret of the fact that you're not happy to have me around." She shrugged, easing the pain of that statement off her shoulders. "Well, now I'm not. So go home. Enjoy being without me."

"Is this about what I said to Sam the other day?" His voice came soft and she heard the tinge of regret coloring its tone.

Instantly, the memory of his words slapped at her and she recalled perfectly the sting of hurt she'd felt. The humiliation of hearing him deny her to his friends. And yet, that awful moment paled beside what she was feeling now. Shaking her head, she said simply, "No."

"Then what is it, Patience?" he snapped, his tone more forceful now. More demanding. "What the hell has got you so upset that you're willing to stay out here by yourself in what looks to be the worst blizzard in these parts in years?"

She couldn't tell him. Couldn't share the fear that had its claws dug deep into her stomach. So she stiffened her spine and lifted her chin even higher than it already was. "That's none of your business, Brady."

"That's where you're wrong, Patience."

"Pestilence!"

"The minute you waltzed into my place telling everybody and their uncle that we were engaged, you became my business."

She whirled around, turning her back to him briefly before turning back to face him. After all, there was nowhere to go in the tiny cabin. She couldn't very well rush off in a huff. She'd freeze to death—and dying wouldn't solve her problems. It would only create more of them. "If you aren't the most stubborn—"

"Hah!" A short, sharp bark of laughter that was absolutely insulting in its lack of humor. "*I'm* stubborn? Patience, you could give lessons to a rock."

"If I'm so horrible," she countered, nourishing the anger inside, hoping it would devour the fear crouched in a corner of her soul, "why are you here? Why do you insist on being in my company?"

"Because I can't very well leave you out here unprotected."

Not because he loved her, she told herself. Not because he couldn't bear to be away from her any longer. But because she'd become a sort of responsibility. His duty. His charge.

Fresh pain lanced at her, but she buried it and answered him. "Unprotected from what?" she nearly shouted, but caught herself just in time. "The snow? I have a roof. I have a door. And a fire."

He shoved one hand through his hair. "Not just the storm, though that's enough by itself." He crossed the room to her in a few long strides. "There's animals out here too, you know. Some with four legs and too damn many with two."

She swallowed hard. "No animal is going to be able to open the door and I'm not going out—I've already told you I won't."

"And what about the two-legged kind?"

She flushed as he laid both hands on her shoulders and squeezed hard. Heat rushed into her body and she wanted nothing more than to lean into him. To take advantage of his hard, solid strength. But she couldn't. Couldn't risk that. Not until she understood what was happening to her.

"You mean men?"

"Yes, I mean men," he told her, giving her a shake as if she were a foolish child. "Somebody out riding in this mess spots the smoke from your chimney and comes right on in. How're you going to keep 'em out?"

She didn't have the slightest idea. And in fact that particular worry hadn't occurred to her even once during the last three days. "I—"

"You won't be able to."

Probably not. But planning for an attack by imaginary intruders was the least of her problems at the moment. "I'll be fine."

"If you say that enough, maybe you'll believe it. But I sure as hell won't."

She stared up into his eyes and read the fury banked there. He narrowed his gaze on her and she felt the strength of his pale blue eyes boring deep into her soul. She had the feeling that he was seeing far more than she wanted him to see.

Outside, the wind screamed past the tiny cabin and the old wooden logs shuddered. The window glass rattled from behind the safety of the shutters and Brady slid a glance toward the door.

"And you want me to go out in that storm—to head back to town, *alone,* and leave you the same way?" He shook his head firmly.

Patience frowned to herself. She did want him gone, but as the storm raged beyond the safety of the four walls surrounding them, she knew she couldn't let him go back out into the blizzard. He would have to stay. Whether she wanted him to or not. And somehow, she would have to find a way to hide from him the growing panic inside her.

Wrenching free of his grip, she took a step back and shifted her gaze away from him, to the fire. "All right, then, Brady," she said and walked to the hearth. Bending down, she picked up another of the logs and carefully laid it across the glowing, crumbling wood. "You can stay until morning. But then you have to leave."

Damned insulting this was, Brady told himself as he watched her deliberately ignore him. He'd ridden through a storm folks would be telling their grandchildren about just to save her pretty ass—and she couldn't care less.

Or did she? he wondered, noting the stiffness of her spine and her shaking hands. She stared into the flames as if seeking answers and Brady wondered what in the hell the questions were.

He'd seen folks act like this before. And he recognized the signs.

Patience was scared.

Bone-deep afraid.

And somehow seeing this brave, no-nonsense woman shaking from a terror that she wouldn't tell him about cut at him. Did she think so little of him that she couldn't bring herself to say what was bothering her? Over the last couple of weeks, she'd claimed to know him better than anyone else. So why didn't she know that he was willing—*ready*—to help?

Damn it, his hands practically itched with the need to reach out to her. But she'd made it plain enough that she wouldn't welcome his touch. Hell, she was just barely tolerating his presence. And that was a bitter truth to try to choke down.

Scrubbing the back of his neck with one hand, he reached out with the other hand and grabbed the nearby chair. Dragging it closer, he dropped onto it and continued to watch her. How long could she continue to stare into the fire? How long would she pretend he wasn't there, in the room with her?

And what would he say when she finally did turn around to face him?

Something inside him shifted, coiled, then struck at his heart, with the speed and deadly accuracy of a rattler.

He cared. Damn it, he actually cared about her. He hadn't planned to. And God knew he wasn't at all pleased about it, but there it was.

And he wished to hell that little voice he'd listened to for most of his life would come back and tell him what to do now.

But there was nothing. Just emptiness. A silence so vast and deep he cringed from it.

With the raging storm outside, he and Patience were locked in a warm world all their own. Two people, alone too long and yet somehow connected. Brady frowned at the thought, but couldn't deny it, not even to himself. There was something between him and this woman who'd dropped into his life out of nowhere.

He felt her terror as if it were his own. He sensed her anxiousness. He understood the isolation shimmering off her in waves of desperation.

And he knew that if he could only find a way to help her through this, he would be saving himself as well.

Davey looked out the window at the swirling wall of white just beyond the glass. "I sure hope Brady got to the cabin all right," he whispered and his breath made tiny clouds of frost on the cold pane.

He dragged the tips of his fingers through the frost, making railroad-track streaks that looked like arrows pointing to nowhere.

Heaving a sigh deep enough to empty his lungs, he told himself he ought to be feeling pretty good right now. He wasn't freezing his behind off in that drafty stall. Instead, he had a nice room with a big fire and a wide bed to curl up in.

But none of that seemed to matter. Not when he knew Patience and Brady were stuck out in the snow. "Still," he said, wanting to hear the words aloud, "Brady's a smart man. He'll find Patience. And he'll bring her back. Just like he said he would."

Easing away from the window, he picked up his magic ring from the edge of the bed and grasped it tightly. The warmth from the metal soothed him somehow and when he sat down in front of the hearth, drawing his knees up against his chest, he kept a firm grip on that ring. As if just holding it close would keep safe the two people he cared most about.

"It looks bad, doesn't it?" Lily asked, watching as Sam stared out the front window at a Main Street almost totally obscured by the wind-blown snow.

"It ain't good," he said, not bothering to turn around to face her.

Shadows loomed from every corner of the darkened store. The only light in the room came from the single oil lamp on the counter and the reflected, eerie glow of the snow piling up in drifts outside. From upstairs came the echo of Treasure's snoring, and but for that soft sound, the world was blanketed in silence.

Lily's whispered question seemed overly loud in the stillness. "But Brady will get through to the cabin, won't he?"

Sam snorted a half-laugh. "Brady's about the most stubborn man I know. If he sets out to do something, it usually gets done."

Usually, she thought, picking up on the one word in that sentence that worried her. Besides, Lily heard the hesitation in Sam's voice and knew there was something else he wasn't saying.

"But . . ." she prodded.

The sheriff glanced back at her over his shoulder and Lily saw the worry in his eyes. "But even Brady can't stand against nature when she kicks up her heels like this."

Lily's nerves prickled as they had so often in the last few hours. She should have insisted Patience return to town with her. She should have seen the signs of the coming storm and ordered Patience to give up this silly notion of teaching Brady a lesson. But even as she thought it, she had to smile. Lily couldn't imagine *anyone* ordering Patience to do anything.

"It's not your fault," Sam said softly.

"Of course it is," Lily snapped, unwilling to forgive herself that easily. "I was there today. With her. I saw the stormclouds coming in. I should have made her come back to town with me."

"Uh-huh," he said, turning his back on the window to stare at her. "And how would you go about that? *Making* Patience do something she didn't want to do?"

The very question she'd asked herself only a moment ago. "I probably couldn't have, short of holding a gun on her," she admitted, wrapping her arms around her middle and hanging on. "But I should have tried."

"You couldn't know the storm was going to be this bad."

"That doesn't help any," she said.

"I know." Sam walked toward her, and with every step he took, something inside Lily shook and shivered in expectation. It had been too long since she'd felt anything like real interest in a man. And she wasn't entirely sure what to do about it.

After all, up until a week ago, she'd been one of

the town whores. And maybe that's all Sam saw when he looked at her. *Maybe?* Of course that's how he saw her, she told herself an instant later. Why wouldn't he? A change of clothes didn't change what she was. Who she was.

Shame rippled through her in small, insistent waves. Foolish, she thought. Foolish to still be mortified by the choices she'd made to survive. Foolish to still wish things could be different.

And then he was there. Right in front of her and his nearness sparked a slow fire deep in the pit of her stomach. He looked down at her and one corner of his mouth tilted in a half-smile.

"I'd say don't worry," he said, "but I can see that'd be a waste of time."

"I can't help being worried," she told him. "Patience is my friend." She dipped her head briefly, then lifted her gaze to meet his squarely. "The first friend I've had in too many years."

That quirky smile of his slowly faded and he lifted one hand to cup her cheek gently. His touch set off a trail of small fires, burning along her spine, tingling just beneath her skin.

Unexpected passion shot through her veins. God, how long had it been since she'd felt *anything* when a man touched her? A long empty part of her yearned to be filled, craved the magic she'd once found in the circle of a man's arms.

She fought the feeling, though. She couldn't give in to the need welling within. There were other things more important than the unfamiliar sensations rattling around inside her.

Patience.

The woman who had single-handedly changed Lily's life. Patience had looked past the feathers and the lip rouge to the woman within and had given Lily a chance to find herself again.

And now it was up to Lily to return the favor.

"I have to go find her," she muttered, more to herself than Sam.

He caught her upper arm in a firm grip as she turned to head for the stairs.

"You're thinking to go out in that storm?" he asked. "Are you out of your mind?"

She pulled free. "Patience needs help."

"She has Brady."

"We don't know that." The more she thought about it, the surer she was that this was the right thing to do.

"My money's on him," Sam said.

"But it's not your money we're betting on him," Lily reminded him. "It's Patience's life."

"Damn it, Lily," Sam said, grabbing for her again when she would have started up the stairs.

"I have to do something," she said. "I have to—"

"What?" he demanded. "Ride out in the storm? Get lost yourself? Freeze to death?"

She opened her mouth to argue, then was forced to snap it shut. She hated it, but he was right. She'd be lost in that blinding snow before she even got out of town. She'd never be able to find that cabin in this mess.

"I know it's not easy to wait," Sam said, as if reading her mind. "But sometimes it's all we can do."

Lily chewed at her bottom lip.

When she didn't speak, Sam went on, pulling her toward him. "Brady's got sense. Plus, he started out after her before the storm got so bad."

She moved stiffly, reluctantly, but once he had his arms around her, she leaned into him and he drew his first easy breath all night. Damn, but he'd needed to hold her. And now, inhaling the clean, sweet scent of her, it was near impossible to keep his mind on the conversation at hand. But he fought for control and found it.

"Patience is safe. You just have to trust that."

"I'm trying," she said, her voice muffled against his chest.

"If we're lucky, the storm'll ease up some soon."

"And . . . ?"

"And," he finished, holding on to her more tightly, "if they're not back before then, I'll head out in the morning. Go find them."

Lily tipped her head back and stared up at him. "You will?"

"I will," he promised and knew that he would do anything to keep that shine in her eyes focused on him. Even ride out into a storm that was bad enough to give a mountain man second thoughts.

Brady fed another log into the fire, then sat back. Leaning against the stone hearth, he drew one knee up and rested one forearm atop it as he watched Patience sleep.

She'd fought hard against her closing eyelids, but exhaustion and the warmth of the cabin had finally done her in. She lay curled up on the narrow bed, huddled beneath a couple of the blankets he'd brought with him. In the glow of the firelight, her black hair shone like a starlit midnight and her fair skin looked as pale and creamy as moonlight.

As that thought registered, he scowled to himself. Jesus, he sounded like some damned poet. He leaned his head back on the stones and just barely resisted the urge to bang his skull against them for the hell of it.

How had he come to this? he wondered. Until two weeks ago, he'd been content with his life. Now, he was sitting in a cabin with flowers growing out of the walls, watching a sleeping woman who knew too many of his secrets. A woman who touched him when he didn't want to be touched. A woman who saw things in him no one else ever had.

She shifted on the bed, moaned quietly, and his heart twisted in his chest. What was running through her mind now? Was it thoughts of him, images of him that brought such pain?

Damn it, if he'd never opened his big mouth, she never would have run off to this cabin in the middle of nowhere. And he wouldn't be sitting here, his body hard and tight, his control stretched to the breaking point.

He scrubbed one hand across his face, easing the tired ache behind his eyes. There'd be no sleep for him. Not tonight. Not while she was so close. Hell, he'd had a hard enough time getting sleep with her in the next room, separated from him by a couple of doors and a few feet of hallway. Here, in this tiny cabin, it would be impossible.

Besides, somebody had to keep the fire stoked. Although, if he could get the damn thing blazing as hot as his blood felt at the moment, it'd never go out.

"I don't *want* to remember," Patience shouted in her sleep and Brady pushed away from the hearth, already moving toward her.

"No," she called out, twisting and thrashing on the bed, tangling the blankets around her legs as she tried in vain to run from whatever dream image chased her.

Just as he reached her side, Patience screamed and shot bolt upright on the bed. Eyes wide open, but unseeing, she struggled for air, gasping like a fish tossed from a stream to lie dying on the bank.

Brady grabbed her shoulders and eased down onto the mattress beside her. "Patience," he said, "Patience, wake up. It's just a dream."

She turned those blind eyes on him and he waited what seemed forever until she recognized him and sighed in relief. Then she shuddered so violently, her whole body shook with the motion, and Brady pulled her close, wrapping his arms around her and holding tight. Her arms went around his middle and he felt her hands splayed against his back as she turned her face into his chest.

He sucked a huge gulp of air into his lungs and drew her scent deep inside him.

"Brady?"

"Yeah," he whispered, soothing her tremors with

his voice and hands, "it's me." Tenderness welled up within him and he was startled by it. Never had he felt this protective instinct, this urge to comfort. But holding her like this, he knew that he would do whatever it took to keep her safe.

"Oh God." Another shudder wracked her body, but her breathing slowly evened out as she held on to him.

"It was just a nightmare," he told her and indulged himself by stroking the palm of one hand across her hair. Soft, silky, the long strands caressed his fingers, but it wasn't enough. He wanted more. Needed more. And that shamed him, since she was still trembling in his arms.

"It was terrible."

He cradled her close, enjoying the feel of her head against his chest, her arms around his waist. He contented himself with the closeness and determined to put his own desires aside for her sake.

"That's why they call 'em nightmares."

"You don't know," she said, but didn't elaborate.

He drew another long, deep breath and heard himself admit, "I know all about nightmares, Patience. Trust me on that."

"Not like this, Brady." She shook her head and burrowed closer. "Not like this."

"Like what?"

"I can't tell you."

All right, now that bothered him. Though why it should, he couldn't say. After all, he'd never told anyone about his own nightmares, had he? Still, he wanted her to trust him enough to tell him what was bothering her. Wanted her to need him. And that fact hit him hard.

He'd spent most of his life trying to be needed by no one. How had this one woman slipped inside his heart, his soul, in two short weeks? And why all of a sudden was she so intent on keeping him at a distance?

"What don't you want to remember?" he asked, recalling the words she'd shouted.

"I—don't know."

He frowned at the flowers on the wall behind her and tried to figure out if she was lying to him or to herself or both.

"Brady?"

"Yeah?"

"I think maybe you were right. Maybe I *am* crazy," she whispered in a voice so soft he barely heard her.

An invisible fist squeezed his heart until he winced with the pain of it. Instinctively, he tightened his hold on her, pressing her into his body, letting her feel the solid slam of his heartbeat against her ear. Oh, he'd done a helluva job with her, he told himself in disgust. He'd taken a proud, strong woman and made her doubt her own sanity.

His mind raced with images of the past couple of weeks.

Patience, in his saloon. Patience smiling. Helping Lily. Loving Davey. Turning the whole damn town upside down. Making him so hungry for her that he couldn't sleep at night. Was it crazy to go after something you wanted, despite all the opposition some damn fool threw into your path? Was it crazy to help people and expect nothing in return? Was it crazy to offer a blind idiot love, even when he was too stupid to accept it?

No.

Damn it, no.

He eased back a bit, then tipped her face up to his and cupped her cheek in the palm of his hand. His thumb stroked across her cheekbone as he said quietly, "Patience, you're probably the least crazy person I know."

She blinked up at him and his heart did a slow roll in his chest.

"Do you mean it?"

"Yeah," he said, giving her a small smile that earned him one in return. Her whole face lit up, and not for the first time, he wondered how she managed to pack so much warmth, so much love, into a simple smile.

"I think I'm the crazy one," he said, mostly to himself. "For not seeing how much you mean to me."

Her breath caught, then shuddered from her lungs. She lifted one hand to touch his cheek and the heat of her hand slipped down into his soul, warming him through. Damn it, he hadn't wanted to miss her. Hadn't planned on it. But blast if she didn't leave a big hole in his life when she was gone from it.

"Kiss me, Brady," she said. "Kiss me like you did before."

Need tightened inside him and he knew that right now, one kiss would lead to a hell of a lot more. "I want you, Patience. Bad."

"I know," she said and lifted her face for his kiss.

Chapter Sixteen

Of course, Patience knew that she should close her eyes when she was kissed. But she kept her eyes wide open, not wanting to miss anything. And so she watched as Brady slowly lowered his head toward hers. Watched as his eyes darkened with passion. Saw his lips part.

He held her face in his hands, tipped his head to one side, and then slanted his mouth across hers.

Lightning flashed within her.

Brilliant, white-hot light sizzled her blood, clouded her mind, and blurred her vision.

His lips, full and soft, caressed hers in a gentle motion that became more insistent, more demanding, as the seconds ticked past. Patience sucked in a small gasp of air and knew it wasn't enough—but she didn't care. All she could think of was the touch of Brady's lips on hers.

Warm, tender, he held her and tasted her as if she were a particularly luscious dessert. Her breath shuddered in and out of her lungs. Her heartbeat quickened, pounding in her breast with enough force to send it smashing through her rib cage.

And she wanted more.

As if sensing her need, her urgency, Brady parted

her lips with his tongue and the magic she remembered with such clarity came rushing back to her. Again, she felt his soul touch hers. She felt the bone-deep assurance that they belonged together. That this was destined. That they were truly soul mates, fated to be complete only when joined together.

His tongue swept into her mouth and she relished the sensations pooling in her center and then spreading to every inch of her body. Heat filled her. Liquid fire raced along her veins, igniting within her a passion she'd never known before. This was what she'd waited for, hoped to find. This was why she couldn't have married the man her father had chosen for her.

Because only with Brady Shaw could she find such . . . *completeness*.

His hands slipped down to her shoulders, his fingertips kneading her skin, and even through the fabric of her dress, she felt the wonder of his touch. And yet, it wasn't enough. She needed more. Needed to feel all of him.

Boldly, she lifted her hands to the front of his shirt and slowly, clumsily, began to unbutton it. He broke the kiss, pulling his head back to look at her, and Patience ignored the quick slash of embarrassment that heated and no doubt colored her cheeks with bright red splotches. This was no time to be shy.

She was finally where she was meant to be. In the circle of Brady's arms. And as he looked at her, she felt the strength of his gaze and it gave her power. Flush with the sense of it, she continued down the length of buttons, opening his shirt, baring his chest.

Patience breathed deeply, then slid her hands under the plain white cotton material, to feel his hard, solid muscled flesh beneath her palms.

He hissed in a breath and narrowed his gaze. "Jesus, Patience," he managed to say, "you're killin' me."

"That's not my intention," she said, sliding her fingertips along the wall of his chest, exploring his skin, loving the feel of the dark, soft hair curled on his flesh.

He choked out a laugh. "It's not, huh?"

"Oh no," she said, looking up into his eyes, "I want you very much alive." Then she ran her palms across his flat nipples and smiled when he groaned and clenched his jaw tight.

"Honey," he whispered, "I'm more alive than what's good for you."

"*You're* good for me, Brady."

"I almost wish that was so, Patience," he said through gritted teeth.

"It is, Brady," she said, leaning into him, scraping her hands up his chest, across his shoulders, feeling his muscles bunch at her touch. "It *is* so. Can't you feel it?"

His hands fisted at her back as he lifted her up and gathered her close, pressing her against him with enough strength to squeeze the air from her lungs. "What I feel," he said, looking up to meet her gaze, "is you. Only you."

She stared back at him, recognizing the flash of desire in his dark blue eyes. She felt his strangled breathing, sensed the tightly leashed power in his body. And made a decision.

"That's enough, Brady," she whispered, leaning down to kiss his forehead. "For now, that's enough."

"All I can promise you is now, Patience."

"Then give it to me," she said. "Give me now and tomorrow can take care of itself."

Slowly, deliberately, he lowered her, letting her body slide against his until she was sitting in his lap with the strength of his arms encircling her. He lifted one hand to smooth her hair back from her face, his fingertips sliding across her cheek.

"Beautiful," he whispered as he lowered his head to hers. "So beautiful."

And as his lips came down on hers again, Patience *felt* pretty for the first time in her life.

He tipped her back, cradling her head in the crook of his left arm, and while his mouth worked magic on hers, his right hand slid up and around to cup her breast. Patience sighed into his mouth and he swallowed it, taking that small rush of air for his own.

Her breasts ached.

Actually ached.

She'd never known a sensation like this. His hand cupped her and even through the fabric of her dress she felt the impression of each of his fingers. Then he touched her nipple and that small bud of flesh tightened, springing to life with his attentions. A tingling raced from her breast to her abdomen and then lower. A soft, slow, burning ache settled between her legs and she squirmed uncomfortably, trying to ease it.

But there was no relief. Only more of the same. He touched her, running his free hand up and down her body. First her breast, then her waist and her hip. Then he cupped her behind and kneaded the soft flesh there until she moaned, the sound muffled by his mouth.

Brady took every sigh, every gasp, every sound she made and buried it deep within him, like a treasure to be protected and guarded. He kissed her and felt himself falling into the golden depths of her eyes. He touched her and experienced her reactions as well as his own. He'd never known anything like this.

Her untutored responses drove him wild. Fed the flames threatening to engulf him. Made him want to take more, to give more. To *feel* more.

It was as if they were one. Everything she felt, he did too. Magic shimmered in the air around them. Unexplainable. As impossible as the flowers growing out of the walls. It couldn't be happening, and yet it was.

His tongue laid siege to her mouth, caressing, stroking, exploring, and her every whimper echoed inside him, reverberating right down to his soul. He felt it all with her as if for the first time. And the strength of the passion rising within nearly choked him.

Yet he wanted . . . *needed* more.

Sweeping his right hand up to the row of buttons that began at the neck of her dress, Brady undid them expertly, one by one, with a flick of his thumb and forefinger. He felt her stiffen slightly, but when he slid his hand beneath the fabric, to cup her breast through the fine lawn material of her chemise, Patience sighed, her body melting into his.

Breaking the kiss, he lifted his head to stare down at her. She opened her eyes, meeting his gaze, and

Brady's heart swelled at the damp emotion blanketing the golden eyes he knew so well.

"Brady," she said, arching into his touch, "it feels—"

"Perfect," he finished for her and slipped the chemise down far enough to bare her breast to his gaze.

"Yes," she whispered, nodding, "perfect."

He dipped his head and took her nipple into his mouth and was nearly swamped by the rush of emotion pouring through him. Hers, his, he couldn't distinguish between them anymore. And he didn't care. It was enough to be here. With her. Holding her. Loving her. If he died tonight, he'd leave this world a happy man for these moments with Patience.

His tongue circled the hardened bud of flesh, and with every sweeping caress, she arched higher into him, offering herself, silently asking for more. And he gave it to her.

He suckled her, gently at first, and then as she grabbed at his shoulders and clung to him, he drew at her breast with tight lips and the edges of his teeth.

Wonder sparkled through her and Patience nearly forgot how to breathe. And it didn't matter. Nothing was as important as the feel of Brady's hands and mouth on her body.

When his lips closed around her nipple, she almost shot straight up into the air. She'd had no idea. No way of knowing what intimacies were shared between a man and a woman. His mouth teased her, caressed her, tugged at her breast until she felt the drawing of his lips to the bottom of her heart.

He shifted, turning her in his arms so that he could

lavish attention on each of her breasts in turn, and while he did, his right hand swept down the length of her. Sliding beneath the hem of her skirt, his palm moved up her calf, past her knee, up her thigh and to the damp, warm spot that joined her legs.

Patience held on to his shoulders, digging her fingers into his flesh to stabilize her grip on the world. If she let go of him now, she knew she would slide off the edge of the planet.

He cupped the most intimate, private part of her body and the moment he did, Patience felt a shuddering sensation surge through her. She gasped, threw her head back, and stared blindly at the ceiling overhead.

"Brady—"

"It's all right, darlin'," he whispered, lifting his head long enough to reassure her. "Just let it come, Patience. Let yourself feel it."

"It's too much," she said, fighting against the powerful tingling rising up from her middle.

"It's never too much," he said, and dipped one finger through the slit in her drawers to slide deeply within her.

And Patience's body bowed. Her back arched high off his lap. She dug her fingers into his shoulders until she wouldn't have been surprised to learn she'd drawn blood. Her eyes widened. Her breath caught.

He touched her again, deeper this time, and she cried out his name as wave after wave of sensation washed over her, nearly drowning her in the onslaught. Her body trembled. Brilliant colors flashed in front of her eyes. She gasped wildly for air only to sigh it out again as the last few ripples of feeling eased through her, leaving her limp and tingling.

"Oh, sweet heaven," she murmured, blinking until her vision cleared enough to see Brady smiling down at her.

"That about describes it, I suppose," he said, shifting position again until she was lying on the narrow bed and he was on his side next to her.

"I had no idea," she said, licking dry lips. "Really, you should have warned me."

He chuckled. "Then you wouldn't have been surprised."

"Surprise is part of it?"

"The first time," he said.

Regret pooled inside her briefly. "I wish it had been your first time too."

His smile slowly faded and he reached for her, spearing his fingers through her hair, turning her head until she was looking directly at him. "This is better than my first time, Patience. Because it's my first time with you."

Her heart melted, then instantly swelled to life again, full of the love she'd always carried for him. Reaching up, she cupped his cheek and asked, "Can we do that again?"

"That and a whole lot more," he assured her and moved to help her out of her dress.

In seconds, it seemed, Patience was lying there naked, and she watched with interested eyes as Brady stood up and quickly got out of his own clothes. His broad, tanned chest was finely muscled and dusted with a smattering of tight, dark curls. His waist was narrow, his legs incredibly long, and his . . . Her eyes widened at the size of him.

He must have read her expression because he lay down beside her, gathered her into his arms, and whispered, "Don't worry. We'll fit fine."

And then every thought in her head disappeared. All she could concentrate on was the luxurious feeling of being surrounded by his warm, strong flesh. Pressed along his length, she felt his arousal and experienced a brief flash of sensual power. She did this to him. She created a fire in him that could only be quenched by their joining.

And with that power came a new confidence and the courage to follow her own heart's desires. Turning around in his arms, Patience shifted until she was able to kiss his chest. Her mouth slid across the hard strength of him, tasting, exploring, and with every kiss, she heard his quick intake of breath and knew that he was as moved by this experience as she.

She found his flat nipple and flicked her tongue against it as he had done to her. He groaned tightly and cupped the back of her head in his palm, holding her to him. Her hands moved over his body, getting to know the feel of him, teaching herself everything about him. But when she reached down and nervously curled her fingers around his hard length, Brady gasped and instantly flipped them over until she was lying beneath him.

"What is it?" she asked. "Did I do something wrong?"

"God, no," he told her, levering himself up on one

elbow. "But one more touch of your hand and it would have been over."

She wasn't entirely sure what he meant by that, but a pleased smile curved her lips anyway. "Then I was doing it right?"

"Oh yeah," he murmured, and bent his head for a kiss. "You were doing just fine."

Then Brady slid along her length, trailing his lips and tongue down her body. Across her breasts, down her abdomen to—

"Brady?"

"Easy, Patience," he whispered and slid farther down, letting his fingers caress her skin as his mouth claimed her body in a way she never would have imagined.

She gasped aloud and reached blindly for him. But he wouldn't be stopped. His tongue swept across her most intimate flesh, delving into her secrets, caressing her until her body nearly wept with renewed need. Again and again, he tasted her, insistent as he pushed her higher, higher.

Patience's breathing staggered. Her heart pounded. Her hips lifted and fell in time with the rhythm he set and when she thought she might explode, he shifted again, this time moving to cover her body with his.

He knelt between her legs and as she watched him through eyes hazed with unspent passion, he entered her, making himself a part of her.

"Oh, Brady," she whispered, wincing just a little as her body stretched to accommodate his. She felt him filling her, becoming one with her, and she knew that this was the magic as it was intended. For man and woman to become one person. One whole made up of two parts. Their bodies joined, she felt their souls entwine and knew they would never really be separate again.

"Ah, Patience," he murmured, his voice low and husky with hunger.

He moved within her, sending sparks of awareness scuttling throughout her body. She knew now what awaited her. And Patience raced to meet that glorious sensation.

Brady lay atop her, bracing himself with his hands at either side of her head. She wrapped her arms around him, glorying in the feel of his body, so closely attuned with her own. His hips rocked against hers, setting the tempo that she quickly followed.

In moments, the ancient dance became all. It became everything. Time stopped. Hearts paused. Even the storm outside eased.

Brady stared down at her and Patience met his hungry gaze with her own. She felt herself drawn into the dark blue of his eyes and wanted nothing more than to drown in their depths. He touched her face, her neck, he bent to kiss her, and with his mouth claiming hers, she felt the first tiny explosion deep within.

Lifting her hips into the feeling, she reached for it, welcoming the spiral of sensation that would pull her down into a whirlwind of mind-numbing pleasure. He moved again and her body splintered. She felt it break apart, sizzle in the air, and come together again all in the space of a few heartbeats. And when she was spent, she held him tightly and cradled him when he took his own fall.

"Well, now!" Treasure said as she came down the stairs.

Lily woke up, blinked the sleep from her eyes, and instantly remembered where she was.

At some point last night, she and Sam had sat down on the floor, braced their backs against the wall, and fallen asleep. Now, when it was too late, when Treasure had already found them together, she tried to move away from him. But the sheriff wouldn't allow that. He kept his arm tight around her shoulder and held her right where she was.

"Looks like I missed a party of some kind last night," Treasure said as she took the last step and entered the store.

"Nothing happened," Lily sputtered, and wanted to kick herself. Her life now was so new. So fragile. Had she ruined everything by disgracing herself in Treasure's eyes?

Wouldn't that be perfect? she thought. For the first time in years, she'd spent an entire night with a man and done nothing more than talk to him. Well, a kiss or two, yes. But Sam had treated her with the same respect he would have shown a "good" woman. And that meant more to Lily than anything.

Still, if Treasure didn't believe her . . . if she looked at her as she and every other woman in town had up until a couple of weeks ago . . . Lily didn't know if she could stand it.

"Treasure," she said, when she was sure her voice

wouldn't break, "the sheriff and I—we were just talking and—"

"Hell, honey, I know that," the woman said, easing her fears instantly. "But on the other hand, you are fraternizing with the enemy." She glanced at the sheriff pointedly.

He sighed dramatically and stood up, holding one hand out to Lily to help her to her feet. Then he looked at the storekeeper. "How much longer do you figure the women in this town are going to be at war with their men?"

Treasure's gaze slid toward the window. "If not for that storm, it might've gone on for days yet," she said. "But what with how cold it was last night, I figure most of 'em are cuddled up right now, just trying to keep warm." Then she looked at Lily and smiled. "That what you two were trying to do?"

Lily actually blushed and it surprised her. She hadn't thought herself still capable of embarrassment. But then, she hadn't thought she'd be able to feel the thrill of excitement in a simple kiss either. And Sam had taught her how wrong she'd been about that. But now wasn't the time to be thinking about it. "We were waiting up. Hoping that Brady would get back to town with Patience."

Treasure's smile slipped. "I guess he didn't, then?"

"Not that I know of," Sam told her. "But we fell asleep too. So I'll just go over to the saloon and check."

"If they're not there—" Lily started.

He looked at her. "I'll go after them."

"At least it's stopped snowing," Treasure said, walking out from behind the counter to cross the room to the window. Tilting her head to one side, then the other, she looked out at a crisp, cold morning. Dawn was just streaking the sky with splashes of color and there wasn't a stormcloud in sight. "With any luck, the storm blew itself out last night."

"That'll be some help," Sam said as he shrugged into his sheepskin jacket. "But if I have to go out after them, the drifts will make it hard riding."

"I'll be going with you," Lily said and he stopped to look at her.

"I just said, it'd be hard riding."

"Patience might need me," she argued.

"Don't be foolish," Sam said.

Before Lily could say a word in her own defense, Treasure said, "That ain't foolish. It's thoughtful." She spared Lily a smile before glaring at Sam again. "We'll have food and supplies packed when you're ready to go."

The sheriff looked from one to the other and accepted defeat. "Women," he muttered and threw open the front door, stepping into a cold that was a sight warmer than what he was leaving.

Davey'd already checked the whole blasted saloon by the time the sheriff showed up looking for Brady and Patience. The boy had hardly slept, jerking awake at every noise, listening for the sound of Brady's voice, or the quick click of Patience's heels against the floor.

But there'd been nothing and Davey's stomach

was so tied up in knots, he felt sick. Clutching his magic ring tightly, he jumped to his feet when the sheriff opened the door and stepped inside.

Instantly, his gaze locked on Davey. "They didn't come back?"

The brief spurt of excitement he'd felt at seeing the big man disappeared into the twisting knots in his belly. He'd hoped—

"No, sir," he muttered and looked down at the floor. Kicking the scuffed-up toe of his shoe against the wood planks, he tried to hide the worry crawling inside him. But it was getting harder to not think about Patience and Brady maybe lying stiff and frozen in a snowbank somewhere.

"Damn it," the sheriff said and slapped his hat against his thigh. He pushed one hand through his hair, shrugged deeper into his jacket, and huffed out a breath of pure frustration.

Ordinarily, Sam wouldn't be concerned. After all, Brady Shaw was a man who could take care of himself. But that had been one hell of a storm and there was Patience to consider too. Besides that, if he didn't go out after them, Lily, Treasure, and every other female in Fortune would be after his head.

Grumbling to himself, he looked at the boy standing alone in the middle of a deserted saloon and noticed for the first time the tension in those narrow shoulders and the worry in his eyes. Poor kid. Scraping out a living by doing odd jobs for folks generally too busy to pay much attention to him.

And now, the two people he'd attached himself to were missing. But not, he told himself, for long.

Chapter Seventeen

There were just way too many things to think about for sleep.

Although, Brady told himself, with a wry glance at Patience, curled up on the bed, *she* didn't seem to be having any trouble. He on the other hand had been up all night. His brain raced from one thought to the next and he found no peace with any of them. But then that wasn't surprising. Since the day Patience had blown into town, he'd been walking the fine edge of lunacy.

And now he'd slipped over.

He slapped both hands on the mantel and leaned forward, staring down into the fire. Propping one bare foot against the hearth, he tried to figure out what to do now, but he just wasn't having any luck. He was buck naked, and the heat from the flames seared his skin but did nothing to ease the chill that wracked his bones.

He'd dug himself quite a hole last night and he wasn't sure there was a way out. Hell, he wasn't entirely sure he *wanted* a way out. And that scared the hell out of him.

"Brady?"

Swiveling his head, he looked at her and felt a stir

of desire. She pushed herself into a sitting position on the bed, clutching the blanket to her chest like a shield. Her long black hair fell wild and free around her bare shoulders. Her eyes sparkled and her lips were still full and swollen from his kisses. She reached up and pushed her hair back from her face and he followed the motion with a hungry gaze.

What was it about this woman? How could she set off fires inside him with a simple gesture?

"Is it morning?" she asked.

Jesus. Even her voice did things to him he'd rather not think about. And if he wasn't careful, his body would be proving it, real soon.

"Not yet," he muttered. "Almost dawn, though, and the storm's over." He pushed away from the mantel and walked toward her.

She studied him for a long minute before saying, "You don't seem very pleased about that."

"It's not the storm I'm thinking about at the moment, Patience."

"Oh." She gave him a smile that lit up his insides like a Fourth of July barbecue. "Then what?"

"Last night—"

"Was wonderful," she finished for him.

"And the wrong thing to do," he said flatly. As soon as the words left his mouth, he saw the change in her. That smile dimmed to less than half its brilliance and the eyes that had been sparkling only an instant before were now shooting golden arrows into his hide.

All right, he hadn't said it in the best possible way. But damn it, he'd been thinking all night and hadn't come up with anything better.

"How can you say that to me?" she demanded, scooting to the edge of the bed and swinging her bare legs over. Once her feet hit the floor, she stood up, snatched the blanket tighter around her body, tossed her hair back over her shoulder, and shot him a glare that should have burned him to a crisp. "After what we— After I—you—"

Obviously she was in such a rush to chastise him, she couldn't get all the words out. But that was fine with him, since he'd been waiting all night to say what had to be said.

"Damn it, Patience, you were a virgin," Brady countered with a hostile glare of his own.

Patience just looked at him. "Well, pestilence, Brady," she said. "If that's what's bothering you, I'm not one anymore."

He just stared at her. Of course, Patience Goodfellow wouldn't react as any normal woman in these circumstances would. Any other female would be weeping and wailing over her lost "virtue." Not Patience, though. Damned if she didn't look proud.

"That's the problem," he told her. For God's sake. He shouldn't have to explain this to her. As a woman, she had to know what folks would say about an unmarried woman who went to bed with a man.

She smiled at him, blast it.

Well, if she didn't understand, then he'd just have to find a way to protect her not only from what the townspeople of Fortune might say, but from herself. His brain racing, he muttered, "No one has to know what happened here last night."

"I want everyone to know."

"Patience . . ." He nearly growled out her name. He was trying to do the right thing here and she wasn't making it easy. "You don't know what you're saying. This'll ruin your reputation."

"Bother a reputation, Brady," she said. "I don't care what anyone—except for you, of course—thinks of me."

He rubbed his eyes, hoping to stem the headache that had started pounding to beat the band. But it didn't help. Nothing was going to help.

"Do you think badly of me, Brady?"

He dropped his hand and looked at her. "Of course not. But that's not the point."

"That's the only point," she said, and gave him another of those soul-warming smiles that he didn't deserve.

He sighed. Defeat hung in the air around him and he wasn't even surprised. How could he be? She'd been defeating him regularly ever since showing up in Fortune claiming to be the love of his life.

"As soon as we're married—"

"Whoa." He held both hands up, palms out. "No, ma'am," he told her flatly. "We are not getting married."

"But I thought that you—"

"Oh, I wanted you, Patience," he assured her, then as his gaze slid down her blanket-clad form, he added, "I still do. But that doesn't change anything."

"It changes everything."

"No." While she was sleeping, he'd thought about this all night. And no matter which way his brain turned it, it looked the same.

He scraped one hand across his face, and if he'd believed in God, he'd have prayed for patience. But since he didn't, he'd have to make do with the Patience he had.

"I can't marry you."

"But for pity's sake, why not?" she demanded.

"For the same reasons I've been saying no all along." He let his gaze slide from hers before he continued. It was finally time to tell her exactly why nothing between them was possible. Maybe then she'd let go of her delusions and let him return to a world where loneliness meant, if not peace, then at least quiet. "You're a lady, Patience. And I'm a killer."

Silence dropped into the cabin like a stone falling into a well. Ripples of reaction spread out across the room and he waited for her inevitable reproach. He didn't have to wait long.

"Pestilence and nonsense."

His gaze swung back to her instantly. Her golden eyes were sparking fire at him and the set of her stubborn chin told him that, naturally, she wasn't going to react as he'd thought she would.

"You're no killer, Brady Shaw."

He snorted. "The men I've planted would argue with you on that one."

She tossed one corner of that blanket over her shoulder, making it look as if she were wearing one of those togas the Roman fellas used to wear. And it looked too damn good on her.

Then she walked toward him, stopping just in front of him. Meeting his gaze with her own, she said firmly, "You're not a killer, Brady. You've killed men, yes, but not wantonly."

Unbelievable. "They're still just as dead, Patience."

She grabbed his hand, holding it tight between her own. Warmth radiated from her touch down into the darkest, coldest corners of his soul and he yearned for that heat. But he didn't deserve it. Still, he didn't pull away from her either.

"Brady," she said, "we all make choices. You. Me. The men who sought you out for no other reason than to build a reputation by killing you, they made their choices too."

Her touch anchored him as a sea of faces swam up in his mind. He could still see them all. Some young. Some old. All foolish. And all very dead.

His heart felt like a stone in his chest. Thick. Hard. Cold.

"And you stopped being a gunfighter a few years ago, didn't you?" she prodded, her voice soft.

"Yeah, but the killing didn't stop. What about the man who used to own my place?" And once again, the memory of the night he'd won the saloon rushed back at him, underscoring the kind of man he was. Proving to him that he didn't have the right to be in the same room with Patience, let alone in her life.

"Don't be foolish," she whispered. "That wasn't your fault."

"It sure as hell was," he said, remembering. "I could have folded on that last hand of cards. I saw the desperation in the man's eyes. Knew he didn't have the hand to back his betting the saloon." Brady looked at her, wanting her to see him for who he was.

To see that he wasn't some dime-novel hero. "But I didn't. I wanted that saloon. Wanted to be able to hang my hat up. Wanted a place of my own."

"All men want that."

"All men don't win their homes in a card game."

"Does that matter?"

"It did to that man." He remembered clearly the look on his opponent's face when Brady'd shown him the winning hand. "He called me a cheat. Drew a pistol, and in a couple of fast seconds, he was dead and I owned the place."

Hell, he could still smell the stink of gunpowder, hear the wild scraping of chairs as men hustled to get out of the way, feel the slap of his gun barrel meeting his palm, see the light dimming in the other man's eyes.

"But you didn't cheat," Patience reminded him.

"No, but—"

"And the other man," she said, squeezing his hand harder, as if trying to draw him back from wherever he'd gone. "He was holding his gun under the table. Pointed at you. If you hadn't heard him draw the hammer back—"

Shock slammed home. "How did you know that? How did you—" She hadn't been there. He knew that as well as he knew his own name.

"I just . . . *know,*" she said, letting his hand go to rub her forehead. "I can't explain it, the memory is just there."

A chill of awareness snaked along his spine. He knew damn well she hadn't been there. "You can't have a memory of that night, Patience."

"But I do," she said, looking up at him again, and he saw earnestness and desperation coloring her pale gold eyes. "I was with you that night. As I was on so many other nights."

Impossible.

"I don't understand it all myself," she was saying and he wrenched his concentration back to her. "But I was there with you on that riverboat when you were a child. I was there with you during the war."

The chill strengthened, but at the same time, a bone-deep knowledge took hold of him too. His little voice had been with him all those times. He'd counted on it. Trusted it when he trusted no one or nothing else.

"And I was with you when you came to Fortune."

He swallowed hard.

"It's as if I've always been with you," she said.

It didn't make a lick of sense, but damned if he didn't believe her. He sure as hell couldn't explain it, though. From the moment he'd met her, he'd felt as if he'd known her forever. There was a connection between them that he'd tried to deny. Tried to ignore.

But it wasn't going away. The thread stretched between them wasn't breaking. It was getting stronger. Hadn't that been proven last night? When he was inside her, he'd felt what she felt. Known what she knew.

And he couldn't explain that either.

"We're meant for each other, Brady. Can't you see that?"

"Trust me when I say I think you were meant for something far better than what I can give you."

"Oh, Brady." She shook her head and gave him a smile more meant for a child who'd said something foolish.

"Patience, you don't know what you're saying."

"I know I love you. And you love me."

His back teeth ground together. "I don't." Oh, he felt something for her. But it couldn't be love. Hell, he didn't even believe in the kind of love she was talking about.

Patience shook her head, completely ignoring his denial. "I sensed your love last night, Brady," she said simply. "You can't hide it from me now. Not after last night. You felt it too, didn't you?" she asked, laying one hand on his chest. The touch of her skin on his set another fire in his blood that rushed through his veins and left him trembling.

"I felt—it doesn't matter." Hell, he didn't even know how to explain all he'd felt last night. It wasn't only his own pleasure that had rocked him to his soul. It was being able to feel everything she was feeling. It was as if they'd shared one mind. One heart. It had never happened to him before and it was damned disconcerting no matter how you looked at it.

But she didn't need to hear that. She already had wedding bells ringing in her ears. All she needed to really set her off would be to hear that he'd felt exactly what she had.

So instead, he changed the subject abruptly and asked her about the other strange thing he'd experienced. "I heard something last night, Patience," he said. "A voice."

Something flashed in her eyes and he couldn't be sure, but Brady thought it might have been fear. And that cut him to the quick.

"A voice?" she whispered, her gaze dropping, shifting to anywhere in the cabin but at him.

Why, all of a sudden, had her bravado deserted her? Maybe he should let it go, but it was too late to stop now. "That voice. It said just one word. *Remember.*"

She stepped back and turned away from him. With her hand gone from his chest, the last bit of warmth inside him dried up and withered away. He read the tension in her bare shoulders and the stiffness in her spine. And watching her instant withdrawal tore at him.

Brady took her upper arm in a firm but gentle grip and turned her around to face him. "You heard it too, didn't you?"

"It's real, then," she said softly.

She still wouldn't look at him and that bothered him more than he cared to admit, even to himself.

"Oh, it was real," Brady said, tilting her chin up with the tips of his fingers. He stared down into those golden eyes of hers and saw relief shimmering there along with a confusion that he completely understood. "I don't know where the hell it was coming from, but it was real enough."

"Thank heaven," she muttered. Pulling in a deep breath, she blew it out again in a rush and told him, "That's why I didn't want you here yesterday. I'd been hearing that voice and I thought I was losing my mind."

"Don't blame you."

"I thought maybe it was the loneliness out here," she continued, then shook her head. "But then I heard it again even with you here."

"Whose voice is it?"

"I don't know," she said.

"Where's it coming from?"

"I don't *know*."

Her temper was rising and damned if he didn't like that better than the hangdog look she'd had before. "Well, then, what are you supposed to remember?"

"If I knew that, I'd have already remembered, wouldn't I?" Impatiently, she pushed her hair back out of her face and glared at him. "Besides, I don't want to remember whatever it is that voice is prodding me to recall."

"Why not?"

She hesitated slightly, and he wondered what she wasn't saying.

"Because I know everything I need to know already," she snapped. "I know I love you. I know we belong together. And I know that if I'm hearing voices, I'm most likely as crazy as you once told me I was."

Guilt shimmered through him. She wasn't loco. Not in the traditional sense, anyway. Hardheaded, yes. Single-minded, sure. But out of her head insane? No.

He pulled her tight against him, and even through the blanket, he felt the warmth of her skin driving into his body and he welcomed it. Wrapping his arms around her, he let his gaze move over her features, remembering every kiss they'd shared. Every touch. And he wanted more. Mistake or not, he wanted to feel her flesh against his again. He wanted, *needed* to know the wonder that he'd found within her one more time. Before he let her go, as he knew he would have to.

And as those thoughts pounded through his mind, he shook his head and whispered, "Patience, if you're crazy, so am I." He shifted one hand to touch the side of her face, smoothing her hair back, loving the way she turned into his caress. "So let's be crazy together one more time."

She stared up at him for a long moment, and then whispered, "Oh yes, Brady. Again." And she lifted her arms to wrap around his neck. The blanket fell to the floor at their feet and instantly flesh met flesh, sparking new fires, new need.

He kissed her, and with their mouths joined, walked her backward to the edge of the bed. Then together, they sank onto the narrow, thin mattress.

The fire crackled on the hearth, the first rays of sunshine poured through the windows, and the world was silent.

Brady broke the kiss long enough to trail his lips and tongue along the curve of her jaw and down the length of her neck. He paused at the base of her throat and tasted her pulsebeat, feeling its strength hammering through him. Once again, he felt the quickening of her own desire. He felt her response to his touch and it fed his own.

This was magic. There was no explanation for this and he suddenly realized he didn't need one anymore. Being with her, holding her, loving her, was all that mattered. For however long it lasted, he would enjoy the gift that was Patience.

And if the coming years were more empty because of the loss of her, at least he'd have the memories of this one moment in time.

Patience tipped her head back, allowing him more access to her throat. To feel his lips on her skin, his breath puffing warm against her flesh, was a blessing and she accepted it as such.

This was what she'd come to Fortune for. This man. This moment. This time together. Her mind whirled with delight and her body practically hummed with his attentions. His hands swept up and down her length and every spot he touched cried out for more.

Right or wrong, crazy or sane, it didn't matter. All that counted was Brady. And the fact that, whether he could admit it or not, he loved her. As much as she loved him.

She felt that truth in his every touch. So she gave him all she was and all she hoped to be.

His lips found her nipple and pleasure shot from the roots of her hair to the tips of her toes. Delight shivered through her and she clung to him, holding his head to her breast, wanting more. Needing more.

It was as if she'd waited centuries for this man. And she didn't intend to waste a moment of her time with him.

Sighing softly, she closed her eyes and etched this feeling on her mind. Mentally, she wiped away the more troubling memories she'd encountered in the last few days and replaced them with this. This image of her and Brady wrapped together, with the glint of sunlight splintering on the window glass.

And then he shifted, covering her body with his, and she tensed in expectation. She moved to accommodate him, and when his body entered hers, she sighed again at the completeness of it. This joining, this sharing, this loving, was worth everything to her.

His breath came short and quick. His heart pounded in time with hers. He moved within her, urging her higher, higher, until the peak she sought was almost within reach. And then she waited, holding back, straining to endure, wanting to experience this rush of power with him. To know that, together, they found the joy they were meant to discover.

His body tightened, he groaned and whispered her name and with one last stroke drove them both willingly over the edge of sanity into the madness.

Seconds ticked past and the only sound was the beating of their hearts. Until at last, Brady called on the remnants of his shattered control and rolled to one side of her.

If the life he'd lived hadn't earned him a place in hell already, then the way he'd spent the last twenty-four hours surely would. Staring blindly up at the beamed ceiling, all he could see was Patience's face. Her eyes. Her smile. He closed his eyes, but it didn't help. Her image remained in his mind, where it would, he knew, always be.

No doubt, he'd spend the rest of his miserable life being haunted by thoughts of what might have been. But he'd be damned for good if he even considered trying to make Patience his wife.

God would never stand for a sinner laying claim to a woman like her.

She smoothed her hand across his chest and each small fingertip lanced his body with the kind of warmth he used to dream about. Before he got old enough to know that dreams just don't come true.

Not for the likes of him.

He caught her hand, stilling it, and turned his head to look at her. You really are a bastard, he told himself and winced at the thought. He'd used her. Enjoyed her. Found a pleasure he'd no right to and now he was going to turn his back on her. For her own good.

"Patience, I—" He broke off, shooting a glance at the door.

"What is it?" she asked, drawing the blanket up over her bare breasts.

"Something," he said, shaking his head and sitting up, reaching instinctively for his gunbelt. He wasn't sure exactly what it was, but there'd been a sound that hadn't been there before. "I heard—"

The door crashed open.

Brady pulled his pistol free of its holster, leaped to his feet, and stood between Patience and whatever danger was coming.

Sunlight streamed into the room, bouncing off the mounds of snow and becoming bright enough to blind a man. But not so bright Brady didn't recognize Sam as the sheriff all but fell into the room. And right behind him, was Lily.

"Damn it," Brady muttered.

Sam whistled low and long and had the good manners to look away.

Lily was something else again. Her gaze slid from Patience, barely covered by the blanket, to Brady. And him she gave a look that should have killed him on the spot.

Brady's back teeth ground together, but he lowered his pistol.

"You son of a bitch," Lily said tightly. Then, holding out her hand toward Sam, she never took her gaze from Brady as she ordered the sheriff, "Give me your gun."

Chapter Eighteen

"Pestilence!" Patience pushed Brady out of her way and clambered out of the bed, dragging her blanket along with her.

"Ma'am," Sam muttered thickly and turned his back.

"Damn it, Lily," Brady shouted, reaching for the pants he'd thrown into a crumpled heap on the floor. "Close your damn eyes or at least look the other way."

"You've got nothin' I haven't seen before," she snapped, murder still in her eyes. "And I can't shoot you if I can't see you. Sam, I want that gun. Now."

"Don't you give it to her," Patience called out.

"No, ma'am," Sam assured her, still facing the wall, "I sure won't." Then to the furious blonde standing an arm's reach away, he said, "Now Lily, don't you go off half-cocked."

"Oh, I won't," she told him. "I want that gun fully cocked and ready for bear."

"Lily, you don't want to shoot Brady," Patience said, snatching at the blanket caught between the bed and the wall.

"No, I'd rather horsewhip him," the woman countered with a snarl that sounded like it came from a mother lion. "But I'll make do."

"Jesus, Lily!" Brady tugged his pants on and hopped unsteadily while trying to keep a wary eye on the woman looking daggers at him. He'd always thought of the woman as a friend. But right now, he was mighty glad Sam was keeping that gun out of her hands.

Hell, he'd faced gunfighters who looked more friendly than she did at the moment.

"Lily, you should calm down," Patience said, peeking out from behind Brady's shoulder.

"Calm down?" Her voice went as high as a cat's back. "How can I calm down?" she asked. Narrowing her gaze into knife points, she aimed them at Brady. "A man I thought better of took advantage of you."

He damn sure had, Brady thought, but wisely kept silent.

"No he didn't," Patience assured her friend, flipping her hair back from her eyes.

"Ah," the blonde said, disbelief coloring her voice. "So you didn't sleep with him."

"Oh, Jehoshaphat," Sam murmured, wiping his face with one hand.

"Of course I did," Patience answered. "But he certainly didn't take advantage of me," she added. "I wanted to make love."

"Patience . . ." Brady said it on a groan and quickly did up the buttons on his pants. Damn it, how had this happened? He felt as if he were in one of those silly stage plays where everything falls apart at once and the hapless hero gets in trouble from all sides.

"Well, it'd be silly to lie about a thing like that,

Brady," Patience told him, giving his arm a pat. "After all, we *are* naked."

"I ain't lookin'," the sheriff told no one in particular.

Brady shot him a dirty look.

"Yes, you are naked," Lily said. "And I'm guessing this means there'll be a wedding real soon."

"Yes," Patience answered.

"No," Brady said at the same time.

"That's all I needed to hear. Give me that gun," Lily said again.

"Damn it all to hell," Sam said on a groan.

With his pants on, Brady felt some better, but not a lot. He reached up and shoved both hands through his hair, hoping to keep his skull from splitting. It didn't help much.

He deserved this, he knew. It was his own fault. He never should have slept with Patience. He'd known from the get-go that she was a decent woman. And now he'd taken her virginity and shamed her in front of their friends. He'd compromised her reputation and there wasn't a damn thing he could do about it. Hell, marrying her would only make things worse for her.

Decent women just didn't marry saloonkeepers. Especially saloonkeepers who just happened to be former gunfighters.

Anger simmered down deep in his guts and quickly bubbled over. And since he couldn't very well yell at himself, he did the next-best thing.

"What the hell are you two doing out here, anyway?" he grumbled, shooting a glare at Sam's broad back.

The sheriff snatched his hat off and wrung the brim between both fists. He looked as uncomfortable as a cat in a room full of dogs. "It was that storm," he said, still looking stoically at the wall. "When you didn't bring Patience back to town yesterday, folks got worried and, well—"

"That's perfect," Brady muttered. No one had ever given a good damn about him. He could come and go as he pleased and no one had ever noticed. Now he had folks trotting through blizzards to hunt him down. He had one woman wanting to marry him and another ready to kill him. He had a friend who couldn't even look him in the eye.

Oh yeah. Life was good.

Still grumbling, he stepped in front of Patience, to take the full brunt of Lily's outraged stare. "All right. You did your duty. You found us. We're fine. You can see that," he said. "So why don't the two of you ride on back to town and we'll be along directly?"

"Not likely," Lily snapped. "If you think I'm going to be leaving you alone with Patience again, you've got another think coming."

"This is none of your business, Lily," he said.

"Brady," Patience started to say.

"And you keep out of this too. I'm handling it."

Later on, he figured he must not have been in his right mind, otherwise he would have realized that giving Patience orders was no way to get anything done.

She pushed him out of the way and stepped out

from behind him. "Keep out of this?" she echoed, clearly astonished. "I will not. This is as much my business as it is yours."

"Patience . . ."

She ignored him. Looking directly at Lily, she said softly, "I know you mean well, but I love Brady. So please don't shoot him."

Lily's shoulders drooped, the starch going right out of her. Shaking her head, she said, "You heard him, Patience. He says he's not going to marry you. That means you're ruined, now."

"Ruined?" Patience countered with a smile. "I feel wonderful."

Sam cleared his throat and took a step for the door. "I'll just wait outside. Lily?" He spared her a quick, sidelong glance.

The blonde folded her arms across her chest and shook her head firmly. "I'm not going anywhere."

"Naturally," Brady muttered, grabbing up the rest of his clothes and storming out the door. "I'll dress outside."

"You'll freeze," Patience called after him.

He shot a backward glance at Lily. "It can't be any colder than it is in here."

A couple of hours later, Treasure took one look at Patience and knew what had happened during that storm. There was just something about the look in a woman's eyes after she'd been with the man she loved.

"You went and did it, didn't you?" she asked.

Lily fumed silently and Patience gave her arm an absent pat. "Does it show?" she asked the storekeeper.

"Well, it's not like somebody painted a sign on your forehead," Treasure told her, coming around the counter to stand directly in front of her. "But yeah, it shows. There's a spark in your eyes that I figure only a man like Brady could have put there."

Lily groaned.

Patience ignored her, as she had for the entire ride back to town. It hadn't been a pleasant journey. What with the horses having to struggle through the piled-up snow. But it had been made worse by the cloud of restrained fury that had hung over all of them.

Lily was hardly speaking to Brady. Sam wasn't talking to any of them. Brady wouldn't even *look* at Patience. And she . . . well, she'd been left alone to muse silently over the incredible experience she'd had.

As far as she could see, there was no reason for anyone to be so upset. She and Brady coming together had been preordained. Anyone with half an eye could see that. Thoughtfully, though, she chewed at her bottom lip and reminded herself that Brady apparently didn't have half an eye. Since he seemed bound and determined to put what had happened behind them.

Still, since she wasn't going to allow that, there really was nothing to worry about, was there?

"It was wonderful, Treasure," Patience said, her voice as dreamy as the images swirling through her mind.

The older woman sighed in fond remembrance. "As I recall," she said, "there were times when—" She stopped herself, cleared her throat noisily, and asked, "But this isn't about me. So. When's the wedding?"

Before Patience could open her mouth, Lily spoke up.

"There isn't going to be one."

"What?" Treasure's soft smile disappeared and became a razor-sharp slash of disapproval.

"Of course there'll be a wedding." Patience tried to pour oil on the obviously troubled waters. She was, however, unsuccessful.

"Not according to Brady," Lily grumbled.

"Are you telling me that man is refusing to do the right thing by our Patience?"

"He loves me," Patience said, but neither woman was listening.

"He told me so himself, flat out," Lily snapped.

"Well, we'll just see about that, won't we?" Treasure said on a sniff of disgust.

"Oh, pestilence!" Patience muttered.

"And until we get this all straightened out, we should just keep this quiet. Don't want word spreading around that the honeymoon came before the wedding," Treasure said.

"Agreed." Lily nodded.

"I don't care if the whole world knows," Patience said and both of her friends turned sympathetic, nearly pitying looks on her. In response, she lifted her chin and looked from one to the other of them. "I didn't do anything I'm ashamed of."

And while the three of them argued the subject, none of them noticed Vonda Shales scurrying out of the shadowy back aisle and slipping out the side door, a smile on her face.

By nightfall, the town was up in arms. It seemed all that had been needed for the men and women of Fortune to stop fighting each other was for them all to find a common enemy.

Now they had one.

Him.

Brady picked up his drink and tossed the brandy down his throat as he would have a shot of medicine. He didn't even taste it, just relished the brief fire it ignited in his belly.

First time he'd been warm since he left Patience's arms.

And that thought was enough to prod him into picking up the bottle and pouring another drink. He leaned back in his chair and let his gaze slide around the crowded saloon. Fern and Addey were working the room, laughing and dancing with the customers. Joe was hopping behind the bar, busier than he'd been in days.

Somehow, word about him and Patience had spread all over town—even to the outlying ranches—and the saloon was packed with men who were too afraid to call him out, but were happy to settle for giving him dirty looks. Hell, the only reason he was safe from the females in town was because none of them wanted to be caught dead going into a saloon.

Grumbling to himself, he narrowed his gaze, pausing every once in a while on a particular face. He'd stare just long enough to make the man uncomfortable before spearing some other customer with the same icy glare.

Damn hard to have your private life talked about over beers and whiskeys by drunks who were far from perfect themselves. And damned if he appreciated knowing that he was the cause of all the talk about Patience.

She didn't deserve to be gossiped about.

But then, she hadn't deserved to be ruined either.

He took a sip, then set the glass down. One drink warms the belly, two warms the mind, and he needed what was left of his wits about him. Not that they'd done him much good in the recent past. Instantly, his mind screamed out, *How had this happened?* But that was a question he'd asked himself too often lately and he still didn't have a good answer to it.

"You look fit to tackle a grizzly," Sam said as he stepped up to the table and pulled out a chair that would put his back to the wall.

Brady gave the man a hard look as he dropped into the chair and leaned both forearms on the scarred tabletop. "If you're here to talk about Patience," he said tightly, "you can forget it."

Sam shook his head. Reaching up, he took his hat off, hooked it onto the back of the chair next to him, and signaled to Joe for a beer. Then glancing back at Brady, he said, "I figure you don't need me to tell you what you already know . . ."

"And that is?"

"That you ought to marry her."

Brady scowled, and picked up his drink.

"Nope," Sam said, then paused to say "Thanks" when Joe brought him a froth-topped mug of cold beer. He took a long drink, wiped his mouth on the back of his hand, then set the glass down, cradling it between his palms. "I came here about something else."

"What?"

"Texas Jack Bigelow."

Shit. Brady'd damn near forgotten all about the would-be bad man. But then in his own defense, it had been a busy two weeks. "What about him?"

Sam looked at his beer for a long moment, before lifting his gaze to Brady. "Got a wire from the sheriff in Las Vegas. Says Jack shot up the saloon after telling everyone that he was on his way here to kill you."

"Jack talks too much," Brady said, dismissing thoughts of the gunfighter. "Always did."

"Yeah, well, talking too much or not, he's going to be here in a few days and I figured you'd want to know."

"Thanks," Brady told him with a nod. "I appreciate it."

"So what're you going to do?"

"Do?" Brady asked. "What am I supposed to do? Leave town?"

Sam's mouth went grim and hard. "I don't want gunfights in the streets of Fortune." He shook his head. "When two men draw on each other, more often than not, it's some bystander that gets shot."

"True enough. But I'm not a gunfighter anymore."

"Your reputation stands, Brady," Sam said. "You know it and I know it. And Jack wants to be the man who killed Brady Shaw."

His gaze sweeping the hard expressions on the crowd surrounding him, Brady choked out a laugh. "Then he'd better hurry. The way folks around here are acting, seems there's a lot of people want my hide."

A reluctant smile tugged at one corner of Sam's mouth. "I did hear of a hemp party being planned," he said.

Brady shot him a look at the mention of a lynching.

"I put a stop to it," his friend said. "Reminded them all that if they failed, all they'd end up with was one pissed-off gunfighter. That cooled 'em down."

Brady's eyebrows lifted. "Thanks."

"Don't mention it," Sam said, and drained the rest of his beer in a few deep swallows. He grabbed his hat, settled it firmly on his head, then stood up. "Before I go . . ."

Brady frowned up at him. "What?"

"Just thought I'd say that folks around here are real fond of Patience, Brady. Maybe you ought to reconsider."

"Thought you weren't going to talk about her?"

Sam shrugged and smiled. "I lied."

Then he turned and threaded his way through the tables and chairs, nodding and speaking to the occasional man who called out to him. Brady watched him go and knew that his friend, along with everyone else in town, was expecting him to do the right thing by Patience.

Damn it, couldn't they see that by *not* marrying her, that's what he was trying to do?

Chapter Nineteen

The noise from the saloon drifted up the stairs and right through the closed door to Davey's room. Ordinarily, he'd like hearing the hum of voices and the out-of-tune piano playing. Usually, it felt real friendly. Made him feel like he wasn't really alone.

But tonight, it wasn't helping.

Not even the magic ring was helping.

He clutched it tight in both hands and hoped the warmth from the metal would seep into his bones. But it didn't. He was still cold, down deep inside.

"It ain't right," he muttered, looking at his own reflection in the mirror across the room from him. "Something's goin' on and nobody's tellin' me nothin'."

Ever since Brady and Patience had come back to town, things were different. Brady was walking around the saloon like he couldn't find a spot to sit. He just kept wandering, snapping at people—not Davey, but everybody else. And everybody else seemed pretty dang mad at Brady.

Which didn't make any kind of sense.

"And that's why I got to go see Patience." He swung his hair back out of his eyes and scooted off the edge of the bed. He'd already decided not to go downstairs, because he'd have to walk through the crowded saloon and maybe Brady'd tell him to stay put. And he didn't want to have to disobey Brady. So, he figured to leave without telling him.

Walking to the window, he opened it and shivered as a blast of icy air roared through, pushing at him as if even the wind were trying to keep him in his room. But Davey'd been cold before. Grabbing up his jacket, he pulled it on, then steadied his magic ring on the edge of the windowsill.

"I really need me a long ladder so's I can climb out the window."

Instantly, the metal hummed, heat growing, ring spilling out of its circular shape. His breath caught as he watched. The old brass slid over the sill and down the front of the building, taking on the form of rails and rungs until the metal ladder reached all the way to the ground.

Davey smiled and shook his head in pure admiration. As he scrambled over the sill and stepped onto the ladder, he told himself he just couldn't imagine how he'd ever lived without such a fine magic ring.

"Ought to tie that Vonda's tongue into a knot," Treasure muttered. "Imagine her spreading tales about Patience. You know, that woman's gone too far this time."

"The damage is done," Lily told her, disgusted, as she reached for the bottle of Doctor Moore's Female Tonic.

Patience watched her friends and reminded herself that this little get-together was in *her* honor. She fidgeted in her chair and tried not to think about Brady, alone in the saloon. How he must miss her.

As much as she missed him.

But Treasure and Lily refused to let her move back into the saloon. Instead, they insisted that she remain there, at the Mercantile with them, until Brady "came to his senses and offered marriage."

"I've got to say—" Treasure said and hiccuped loudly. "Pardon me," she murmured, then continued. "I'm surprised by Brady. Thought sure that man was a good one, deep down."

"Oh, he is," Patience blurted, and both of the women looked at her with sympathy, for heaven's sake.

Lily poured herself another glass of elixir and took a long drink. She shuddered violently as it slid down, then slapped one hand to the base of her throat as if trying to hold it down. When she had her breath back, she shook her head and said, "Brady's not bad, he just doesn't think of himself as the marrying kind."

Treasure snorted. "What man does?"

"Brady is the marrying kind," Patience said, remembering last night and how he'd looked at her. She'd seen love shining in his eyes. Felt it in his every touch. He *did* love her. She knew it.

They were *meant* for each other.

And he knew it too. There was an invisible cord binding them together. Why else would he have heard that voice? She frowned to herself as that one word echoed in her mind.

Remember.

Disjointed flashes of images raced through her mind as if summoned. Faces, places, all whirling through her mind at a dizzying rate. Puritans. Pirates. Indians. Nobility. Old. Young. Impossible to single out just one. And the very number of those images terrified her.

How could she possibly have known all those people? The answer was, she couldn't have. Hundreds of years and thousands of miles separated them from her. And yet . . . the faces had seemed so . . . familiar. As if she *should* know them. But how could that be? she wondered. Reaching up, she rubbed at the spot between her eyes, but it did nothing to ease the sudden pounding that settled in there.

"Don't you worry, hon," Treasure said, reaching over to give her hand a pat. "We'll bring that man to ground if we have to stand over him with shotguns."

"Shotguns?" Patience looked at the two women, each in turn, then shook her head. "I don't want to force him to marry me. I want him to *want* to."

"No man *wants* to, honey," the storekeeper told her. "Not until we tell 'em that's what they want, anyway."

Patience inhaled sharply, but didn't bother to argue. She'd been trying all evening and her friends were just too angry at Brady to listen. So instead, she stood up and announced, "I think I need some air."

"Sure, sure you do," Lily said, smiling.

"You go on ahead, honey," Treasure added. "We'll wait for you right here."

Nodding, Patience turned and headed for the stairs. She sailed down them so quickly, she ran headlong into Davey when she reached the bottom.

The boy hit the floor, dropping that metal ring of his as he fell.

"Pestilence," she said on a gasp of surprise as she helped him up. "I didn't see you in the dark."

"I come to see you," he said, dipping his head, then looking up at her again through a fall of hair.

The boy looked so small, so lost, Patience surrendered to her instincts and reached for him. He stepped into her embrace and wrapped his too thin arms around her waist and held on tightly. She felt his warm, solid little body pressed against her and love for him shimmered through her. Smoothing her palms up and down his back, she bent her head to rest it against the top of his.

"I missed you while I was gone," she said softly.

"I reckon I missed you too, Patience," he whispered, then shifted slightly to be able to look at her without letting her go. "Brady missed you too."

"He did?" Pleasure unwound inside her like a silky ribbon.

"Yes'm. He was cranky as all get-out without you around."

Well, that *was* nice to know, wasn't it? But it still didn't solve the problem facing her now. And that was making Brady admit how much he loved her. Making him see that they were destined to be wed. To create a family. A family that would include one love-starved little boy.

She ran one hand over his hair, smoothing it back from his face. "We never did get you to the barber, did we?"

"No, ma'am," he said, then added, "But I s'pose I wouldn't mind it too much."

Patience smiled at the concession he was willing to make for her sake.

"Patience," Davey said, "when're you gonna come back to Brady?"

"Soon," she said, putting every ounce of her longing into that one word. "Very soon."

"Good," the boy told her, stepping away long enough to pick up his metal ring. "'Cause he needs you. Real bad."

"I know that," she said wistfully. "And you know it. Now all we have to do is convince Brady."

By the next afternoon, Brady was convinced that nothing in his life would ever be the same again.

He sat in the tiny office behind the bar, surrounded by paperwork and towering stacks of liquor boxes. And he sat there alone.

Emptiness crowded him. Even when the saloon was filled with men giving him disgusted glances, he felt more alone than he ever had. And he knew, deep down, it was because he'd turned his back on Patience. It was the hardest thing he'd ever done—and maybe the only truly *good* action he'd ever taken. It was for her sake that he refused to marry her. Why could no one else see what this was costing him?

The door swung open, and without looking up, he muttered, "Go away, Joe. Leave me be."

"It's not Joe," Lily said softly as she stepped into

the room and closed the door behind her. "And I'm not leaving until I've had my say."

Tired to the bone, Brady tossed his pencil down onto the cluttered desktop and shifted his gaze to her. She looked so different, these days. Like any other proper young widow. Except perhaps for the light in her eyes that was a little too knowing. A little too old for the rest of her face.

He squirmed a bit under that direct gaze, but otherwise sat still. "What is it?"

"I just wanted to tell you what I think of you, is all."

Well, this won't be good, he thought. "I think I already know that, Lily. But thanks just the same."

"Oh no," she said, planting both hands on the desktop and leaning forward. "You're not going to get out of this so easily, Brady."

Anger spurted up from his guts to yank at his heart. "You think this is *easy*?"

"Must be," she snapped. "Or you'd be doing the right thing instead."

"And just what is the right thing?" he demanded, pushing to his feet so that he was looking down at her.

"Marrying Patience."

"So I marry a good woman and make her the wife of a gunfighting saloonkeeper?" he asked, incredulous. "How is that the right thing?"

"You *owe* her, Brady," she said, then her voice dropped a notch as she added, "As much as I do."

"Lily . . ."

"No." She shook her head, sending that blond hair of hers swinging about her shoulders. "She changed everything for us. Don't you see that? Don't you realize how much better everything is for us now because of her?"

Of course he did. He'd have to be a fool to not realize it. And Brady Shaw was nobody's fool.

"She gave me back my pride," Lily told him, obviously on a tear and not willing to slow down to let him get in a word. Assuming he could think of anything to say in his own defense. "She gave me a second chance to live the kind of life I should have had."

"I know, and—"

"And she gave you even more." Lily rolled right over his interruption, determined to have her say. "She gave you love, Brady. She made this damn place a home. She looked into your heart and found something there that no one else ever had. She gave you *everything*."

Her words hit him like tiny bullets, going deep, drawing blood. He swayed with their impact, remembering everything about the last couple of weeks with Patience. Her smile, her laughter, her touch. Agony trickled through his bloodstream, slow but steady. And he stood there in front of Lily, mortally wounded, unable to argue with the simple truth.

"And what have you done for her?" she asked, her upper lip curling in disgust. "You ruined her. Made her the meaty piece of gossip this whole damn territory's chewing on."

He knew that, too, and it shamed him to the core. But it was too late to change anything now—even if he wanted to. And he wasn't at all sure he would change a single moment of his time with Patience.

Jesus, he really was a bastard.

"What do you expect me to do about it now?" he ground out through the pain.

She huffed out a breath and paused long enough to draw more. "I expect you to be the man I thought you were. I expect you to marry her."

Brady kicked the leg of the desk and noticed absently that a couple of piles of papers slid off the stacks to land on the floor. "Damn it, Lily," he said on a low growl, "I can't marry her. I'm a gambler—and worse, for God's sake—and she's a lady."

Lily's eyes narrowed. "Not anymore she's not. Now she's your whore."

His head snapped back with the blow of that one ugly word. But Lily didn't use that word lightly, he knew. She'd had it hurled at her all too often over the years to use it casually herself. Brady's heart ached and twisted until he thought it might wring itself dry and let him drop dead on the spot.

No such luck.

He rubbed his face with the palms of his hands, and his voice was muffled as he said, "I don't have anything to offer her, Lily."

"You have your name," she said quietly. And without another word, she slipped from the room, closing the door and sealing him inside with his own worst enemy.

Himself.

Patience knew exactly where to find him.

When she went to look for him at the saloon and he wasn't there, she hired a carriage from the livery stable and drove out to the knoll she knew he loved.

As she drew up, she pulled the horse to a stop alongside Brady's mount and set the brake. Climbing out of the carriage, she quickly tied the reins to a low-hanging branch of a piñon tree, then started up the slope.

Lifting her hem in her hands, she moved clumsily, but determined to reach him. To find him. To tell him again that she loved him and that she knew he loved her. She wouldn't lose the future they could have together. Not to Brady's stubbornness.

At the top of the knoll, she stopped, swaying slightly in the cold wind. Her shoes slipped in a patch of snow and she very nearly tumbled back down the way she'd come, but she dug her heels in and stood her ground. There, just ten feet in front of her, was Brady. His back to her, he stood silently staring out into the distance, where the gunmetal-gray sky kissed the top of the mountains.

Without turning around, he said, "You shouldn't be here. There's another storm brewing."

"I had to come."

"Of course you did."

"Brady—"

"I've been thinking about this, Patience," he interrupted her neatly, still keeping his gaze locked on the faraway mountains. "And I've come to a decision."

"Yes?" She held her breath, hoping that at last he would admit to their love.

"You'll have to leave town."

She sucked in a gulp of frosty air and felt the chill of it reach down into the very corners of her soul. Disappointment warred with anger and the fury won.

"It's the only way," he said.

"No it's not," she countered, after swallowing hard and bracing her voice so it wouldn't break and betray the pain she felt.

"If you leave, the talk won't follow you," he said and slowly turned to look at her.

His pale blue eyes looked as cold as the wind felt. His familiar features were hard, as if carved in stone. "You'll be able to start over fresh, somewhere else."

"Where, Brady?" she asked, meeting his gaze and silently daring him to look away.

"Anywhere, Patience," he said. And though his gaze never left hers, she thought she noticed a crack in his expression. And that told her all she needed to know. He didn't want her to leave. It was tearing him apart, just suggesting it.

The foolish man was so busy trying to do the right thing, he was blind to the fact that the *only* right thing was for them to be together.

"I'm not leaving," she said simply and saw him wince.

"You have to."

"No," she said, and walked toward him, one slow step at a time. "I won't leave. You'll have to live here. Seeing me every day. Denying me, every day."

His eyes closed briefly, but not before she saw a dart of pain appear in them. She kept walking. Only a couple more steps now.

"Fine," he ground out. "I'll leave."

She laughed and he stared at her. Shaking her head, Patience asked, "How far can you run, Brady?"

"What?" One word squeezed past a throat so tight, she nearly heard it squeak.

"How far?" she asked again. "New York? London?"

"I don't know," he said, letting his head fall backward. "Somewhere . . ."

"Somewhere where you won't think of me?"

He straightened up as she stopped directly in front of him. "I'll always think of you."

"Then why run?"

"Because I can't be what you want me to be."

"Foolish man," she said, lifting one hand to cup his cheek. "You're *already* what I want you to be."

He groaned at her touch and reached for her. Fiercely, he pulled her tightly to him, buried his face in the curve of her neck, and muttered something she wanted to hear spoken louder. Over the thundering of her own heart, Patience asked, "What did you say?"

A shudder wracked his body, but he held her so tightly her breath was strangled. Then he lifted his head, looked her dead in the eye, and said what she'd been waiting a lifetime to hear.

"I said . . ." He paused to pull in a great gulp of air. "I love you."

She tingled.

From the ends of her hair to the tips of her toes, she fairly sparkled. Clinging to his shoulders, Patience smiled up at him and said, "I've waited quite a while to hear those words. Would you mind saying them again?"

He gave her a squeeze that should have snapped

her ribs. Then throwing his head back, he looked up at the sky and shouted over her delighted laughter, "I love Patience Goodfellow, God help her!"

It was a small wedding.

Davey and Lily stood up for the bride and groom and Treasure and Sam completed the guest list. But Patience didn't care.

It was as if once Brady'd surrendered to their love, he wasn't able to wait an extra minute. He'd driven them into town, gone straight for the church, and told her to wait while he rounded up the others.

Now they were here, in front of the Reverend Michaels, ready to pledge themselves to each other for always.

"And now the ring," the minister said, looking at Brady.

His eyes went wide. "A ring. Damn it—excuse me, Reverend—" He looked at Patience. "I forgot all about a ring."

"Do we have to have one?" Patience asked, not wanting to delay this wedding a moment longer.

"It is traditional," the preacher said.

"I can run back to the store," Treasure offered, already half up out of her seat.

"No, wait," Davey said quietly, holding his magic ring tightly. "You don't need to."

"What is it, Davey?" Brady asked, laying one hand on the boy's shoulder.

"You can use my hoop," he said, giving the worn brass metal a loving caress.

Brady smiled and looked down into those earnest

brown eyes. The kid owned nothing but that brass circle he carried everywhere. And here he was, offering it up to them. Deeply touched, Brady gave the boy's shoulder a slight squeeze. "That's mighty thoughtful of you, Davey, but it's just too big."

The kid grinned up at him. "It'll fit, Brady. You'll see." Then he held that circle close and whispered, "I need this to be a ring for Patience's finger."

A soft, otherworldly hum rose up in the church, carrying over the sound of the growing storm outside. Every eye in the place was on Davey and that brass circle as it quivered and changed shape.

"Holy—" Brady murmured.

"What the—" Sam sputtered.

"Well, call me a toad and spit in my eye," Treasure whispered.

"It *is* magic," Lily said.

When the brass hoop had become small enough to be a wedding ring, Davey handed it to Brady, giving it one last touch before releasing it.

The ring lay on Brady's palm and he looked from it to the boy. He couldn't explain what he'd just seen, but then that didn't surprise him. Hell, he couldn't explain half of what had gone on in Fortune for the last two weeks. All he knew for certain was that Davey had sacrificed everything he owned for love. And that truth humbled Brady and made him more determined than ever to raise the boy and give him the kind of life he should have.

Touching his shoulder again, he then turned to face Patience, who was staring at that ring as if she'd seen a ghost.

"What is it?" he asked.

"I don't know," she said, shaking her head. "I'm not sure but—"

He reached for her left hand, ready to slide the ring onto her finger, but she actually fought him, pulling her hand back. Fine time to be getting cold feet, he thought wryly. Then frowning, he tightened his grip, bent his head and whispered, "With this ring, I thee wed." And he pushed the ring onto her finger.

Patience gasped.

That humming rose up again, growing in strength and beauty, filling the tiny church like organ music piped into a closet. The circle of brass glowed against her hand, becoming golden, then white, then it glistened with a brightness that went beyond white. It shone and pulsed, giving off a light that was nearly blinding in its intensity.

Brady held on to her hand, confused, worried, not sure what was going on and somehow knowing he didn't want to know.

He looked into her eyes and saw knowledge and clarity and . . . *regret* shining there.

"Oh Brady," she said, over the heavenly music pouring down around them, "I love—"

And she vanished.

Chapter Twenty

"No!"

Brady howled and his voice seemed to echo on and on in the small church. Panic filled him and he turned in fast circles, his gaze darting over the inside of the building as if perhaps Patience were just hiding from him.

But he knew the truth. Down deep in his bones, he knew that Patience had disappeared because he'd dared to love her.

And he'd already acknowledged that God would never stand for a sinner like him loving a woman like Patience.

"What happened?" Davey shouted. "Where'd she go?"

"I don't know," Brady answered, panic turning into a hard ball of fury in his belly. "But I'm gonna find out."

"Lily?" Treasure asked from behind him and he turned to see the storekeeper rub her temples with both forefingers. "What in the heck are we doing in church?"

"Is it Sunday?" Lily asked, looking up at Sam.

"Don't think so," the sheriff said, shifting his gaze to Brady. "What's goin' on?"

"Patience disappeared," Brady snapped, giving them all an incredulous stare.

But Treasure just snorted a laugh. "Heck, Brady, you never did have any patience. Don't know how it could disappear on you."

He frowned at her. Why weren't they worried? Didn't they know? Didn't they remember?

"Not patience," he exclaimed, "*Patience*. Patience Goodfellow. My *wife*."

"Wife?" Sam said, looking at him as though his brain had slipped off its tracks. "Now what woman in her right mind would want to marry *you,* old friend?" Shaking his head, Sam took Lily's arm and led her down the center aisle toward the double doors. "Wife," he murmured on a chuckle. "Isn't that something?"

In seconds, the preacher, Treasure, Lily, and Sam had gone, leaving Brady and Davey alone in the muddy light streaming through the windows.

"They don't remember her," the boy whispered and moved a little closer to Brady.

His heart clenched in his chest. Going down on one knee, he took the boy's shoulders in a firm grip and asked, "But you do?"

He nodded. Tears spilled from his deep brown eyes and he wiped them away with his sleeve. "Where'd she go?" he whispered, and the quiver in his voice told Brady that his was not the only heart breaking.

"I don't know," he whispered, then pulling the kid close, Brady took comfort in those small arms encircling his neck. He held on to the boy tightly and stared up at the small wooden cross jutting up from the minister's pulpit. And when he spoke, he wasn't sure if he was talking to Davey—or to a God who'd never paid much attention to him. "But I'm going to find her. And bring her back where she belongs. With us."

Outside, the wind screeched and clouds scuttled across a dark sky, crashing into each other, spitting snow on an already too cold town. Brady glanced out the windows and told himself it looked like the end of the world. And in his heart, it was.

Patience found herself standing in front of her superior in what seemed the blink of an eye. One moment, she'd been pledging her love to Brady and the next, she was here. On heavenly ground.

"Have you lost your mind?" the angel asked.

"And heart, Joshua," she said.

"We've been trying to reach you for days now."

The voices, she thought and wondered now why she hadn't remembered instantly who was speaking to her and just who and what she was.

"Because," Joshua answered the unspoken question, "you didn't *want* to remember."

True, she thought.

"And that is unprecedented," the angel went on, stalking back and forth in front of her until his silvery robe snapped with every step. "No one has *ever* tried to forget heaven!"

Patience glanced down at her left hand, where her halo still held the shape of her wedding ring. She rubbed it with her fingertips and the motion drew up

Brady's image in her mind. What woman wouldn't want to forget she belonged in heaven if she'd found a different sort of heaven in the arms of the man she loved? She closed her eyes and groaned at the injustice of having to leave him.

"It is not injustice," Joshua reminded her.

Her eyes opened instantly. Lifting her chin, she said, "I do wish you would cease reading my mind. It's very rude."

"Rude?" the angel repeated, clearly astonished. "You've broken every rule in heaven and you're upset by bad manners?"

She sniffed and folded her hands together at her waist, her fingers still caressing her wedding ring. "I wasn't in heaven when I broke the rules, so it shouldn't really count."

"Oh, it counts, Patience," he told her, wagging a finger at her as if she were a recalcitrant child. "The very halls of heaven itself have been rocked by your actions."

A flicker of guilt tugged at her insides, but she fought it down. Love wasn't a crime. Not on earth and certainly not in heaven.

"Love between a guardian angel and her charge most certainly is," he said, once again plucking a thought from her mind. "And you knew it."

"All right, yes," she admitted, stepping in front of him to stop his ceaseless stalking. "I did know. But love can't be stopped. It can't be reasoned with. It can't be changed because it's inconvenient. It simply *is*."

Joshua threw his hands high, then let them fall to his sides. Shaking his head until his halo wobbled and tilted in the air above him, he said, "*Love* has nothing to do with this mess, Patience."

She glared at him, not even considering that most guardian angels would never think of contradicting Joshua. "You're wrong. Love has *everything* to do with this. I love Brady Shaw. And he loves me. We're *married*."

Joshua actually shuddered. "Don't remind me." Then turning his back on her, he marched quickly to a small gold desk and lifted the leather-bound ledger lying in the middle of it. Flipping through the vellum pages, he finally stopped and stabbed one finger at the place he'd found. "Naturally," he said, "you have been removed as Brady's guardian."

"Removed?" she said.

"Another angel has already been assigned." He slammed the book closed, hugged it to his chest, and glared at her over the edge of it. "Your fate will be decided by . . . *Him*."

"Him?" she whispered, unconsciously shifting her gaze upward.

"These are serious charges against you, Patience."

"I know," she said and couldn't bring herself to regret a thing.

Joshua scowled at her as he read that emotion clearly. "And if I were you, I would return my halo to its proper place." Having said that, he turned his back and she was alone, dismissed from his presence.

She stood in a long, winding corridor, down

which hundreds of guardian angels bustled along on their own business, paying no attention to her at all. Feeling more alone than she ever had before, Patience protectively covered the tiny halo on her ring finger. And to no one in particular, she whispered, "It *is* in its proper place."

Brady didn't know what to do. Or where to look. She was gone as if she'd never been. No one in Fortune remembered her. No one but he and Davey. He stalked down the boardwalk, unmindful of the screaming wind and the snow slapping into his face. He was alone. Anybody with sense was holed up in their homes, waiting out the cold.

But he just couldn't sit in that saloon for another minute, surrounded by memories of Patience.

Shoving his hands into the pockets of his sheepskin jacket, he shrugged deeper into its folds. He kept walking until he was at the edge of town and still he didn't stop. Jumping off the boardwalk into the snow, he walked on, though it was heavy going.

"Go back."

He stopped dead in his tracks. Cocking his head to one side, he listened, thinking that maybe there was someone out there in the snow. But the voice was coming from within him.

"Patience?" He said her name aloud and it felt good to hear it. "Is that you?"

"Yes."

It *was* her. He knew it. Felt it. His little voice was back. Only now did Brady realize that the voice he'd heard and trusted for so many years had stopped when Patience arrived in town. And now that she was gone, it was back.

An angel? he thought and surprised himself by believing it instantly. It was, as strange as it sounded, the only explanation for what had happened around here in the last couple of weeks.

"Where are you?" he demanded, needing to know how to reach her. How to bring her back to him. If she'd been here once, she could be here again. And he was willing to do whatever he had to do to find her. To hold her. To fill the emptiness she'd left in her wake.

"I love you, Brady," Patience said, reaching out one hand to him. But her touch went unfelt as her fingers moved through his arm.

"Damn it, Patience," he shouted, turning in one spot, his gaze searching the clouds overhead. "Come back to me."

"If there were any way for me to come back," she said, "I would. Know that. Feel it." She filled her mind with his image, knowing this was the last time she would see him. She was already breaking more rules by being here. But she'd had to see him one last time. Had to tell him that she loved him and would always love him.

"Patience, tell me what's happening," he shouted and she heard the desperation in his voice. "Tell me how I can get to you."

"You can't," she said, sorrow rising up within her like a tide threatening to drown her.

"There has to be a way!" he shouted, frustration ringing in his tone. "We can find it together."

"I have to go."

"No, don't," he ordered. "Don't leave me alone, Patience. I can't be alone anymore."

Tears swam in her eyes, and his image blurred, but still she couldn't look away. "You'll never be alone again, Brady. No matter what else happens, I will always be with you."

"Patience!"

Her tears fell as his pain hovered in the air around her. "I will love you forever, Brady," she said one last time as she felt herself being torn from him. "Forever and beyond."

And loneliness crashed down onto him, leaving him shaking in the cold.

ONE WEEK LATER

"You don't know what you're saying," Lily said, shaking her head.

"I know exactly what I'm saying," Sam told her and laid both hands on her shoulders.

Heat from his hands slipped down inside her, but she wouldn't give in to it. Wouldn't allow herself to hope. It was enough that she was free of the saloon, working at the Mercantile, and renting a room from Treasure. She still wasn't sure how she and the storekeeper had become friends. She couldn't remember how she and Treasure had bridged the gap that had separated them any more than she could recall how she and Sam had found each other, but she was grateful for both facts every day.

She wasn't going to be greedy and wish for more than she could have. No matter how tempting Sam's offer.

"I want you to marry me."

There. He'd said it again. And Lily's stomach jumped in response.

"No you don't."

"I love you."

She backed up a step, though every instinct she had was screaming at her to leap into his arms and never let go. He followed her, keeping pace with her.

Tears filled her eyes and heart. How long had it been since a man had said those words to her? How long had it been since she'd given up hoping to ever hear them again? Her heartbeat quickened and her mouth went dry. She folded her hands at her waist and held on tight. Nerves skittered along her spine and she glanced nervously around the room. Anywhere but at him.

"Lily," he said, his voice soothing as though trying to gain the trust of a wild thing. "Do you love me?"

Her gaze snapped to his. Oh God, she loved him more than anything. But she couldn't tell him. Couldn't allow him to go on with such foolishness. Her breath caught in her throat. "Sam," she said, swallowing hard, "don't do this."

"Don't love you?" he asked, laying one hand on her clenched fists. "Can't help it."

She huffed out a breath. "Try harder."

He actually laughed. "Who are you trying to protect me from?"

"Yourself."

"Nope," he said, shaking his head and smiling, "I think you're trying to save me from you."

"Somebody has to! Sam, you're a sheriff," she said. "And I'm a—" She choked on the word, not quite able to say it.

"Shh . . ." He scooped her hair back from her face, threading his fingers through the soft, blond mass. "That's past, Lily. Hell, do you think I don't have things in my own past I'm ashamed of? When we're old and gray, I'll tell you some stories that'll curl your hair."

She shook her head, wanting to believe, afraid to.

"You and me," he said, "we'll sit on our porch and watch the grandkids and steal kisses in the sunlight and hold each other every night."

She swallowed hard and blinked back a sheen of tears that wouldn't go away. Grandkids? He wanted to have children with her? Everything inside her ached for the wanting.

"And I will love you until the day I die," he said softly, his voice carrying deep within her heart until it echoed there, trembling with the sweetness of it.

"Sam—"

"So," he interrupted her gently, "will you marry me?"

The door swung open and slammed into the wall opposite with a crash. Sam muttered a curse and swung around to face whatever was coming, planting himself firmly between Lily and any threat.

Davey stood in the doorway, hands on his knees, chest heaving. He fought for breath, flipped his hair back out of his eyes, stared at the two of them and blurted out, "Sheriff! You gotta come. The saloon. Texas Jack's gonna kill Brady!"

Joe reached for the shotgun kept beneath the bar.

"Don't do it," Texas Jack ordered, his voice a whip slicing through the room.

The bartender froze, his worried gaze flicking to Brady where he stood at the end of the bar.

"Back off, Joe," Brady muttered.

"Boss?"

"Step away," he said, pushing away from the bar to face the gunman standing across the room from him.

Brady stared at his opponent and felt the past reach forward to grab him. He'd thought these standoffs were behind him. He'd thought that here, in Fortune, he could have a different life. Then, when Patience showed up, he'd actually thought he might have a *real* life.

But she was gone from him now, melting away as surely as the snows and damned if his past hadn't reared up to get him. Hell, he thought, staring into the flat, black gaze of the man watching him, maybe this was how it should be. Maybe he could do the world a favor by taking Jack out of it—and at the same time, leave it himself. In the space of a heartbeat or two, Texas Jack could do Brady a good turn.

He could kill him.

Because God knew, that was the only way he'd ever find Patience—or peace—again. Dying was the one chance he had of being with her.

Chair legs scraped against the floor. Men scattered, ducking for cover. But none of them left, preferring to risk danger rather than miss the coming battle.

"You've been avoiding me," Jack said, flipping the right-hand side of his jacket behind his back with a practiced sweep of his hand.

"I've been right here." Brady actually chuckled. He'd had almost no sleep all week and his eyes felt gritty, but he could still see the humor in the situation. Every young gunman he'd ever met was convinced of his own superiority. And every damn one of them ended up the same way. Six feet under.

Thoughts, memories, pieces of his past, rushed through his mind, flashing briefly, then disappearing back into the mists. Until finally, his brain settled on one thought.

Davey.

The kid had been stuck like a burr to Brady's leg all week. And he now gave silent thanks that the boy had picked today to be somewhere else. A flicker of worry spit through his veins as he wondered what would happen to the boy when he was gone. A pang of regret echoed inside him at the notion of not being around to ease the boy into manhood. But an instant later, he told himself that Sam would look out for him. And Lily would give the child the kind of motherly love Patience would have if given the chance.

"You gonna stand there forever just daydreamin'?" Jack taunted. "Or are we gonna do this?"

"Don't be in such a hurry to die, boy," Brady said and even his voice sounded tired.

"What makes you so sure I'm the one who's gonna die?"

"What makes you so sure you won't be?"

Jack snorted a laugh. "You were good once, Shaw. But you've been out of the game too long."

"It's not a game, fool," he snapped, then reminded himself that you couldn't tell a man something he had to discover for himself.

Shaking his head, he stepped out into the center of the room, pushed the right-hand side of his jacket free of the holster tied to his hip, and planted his feet in a wide stance. Instinct took over and everything else within him went still and silent.

Heartbeats of time passed.

A fly buzzed.

Someone coughed.

Then the world erupted in a flurry of smoke, the smell of gunpowder, and the flash of light blasting from the barrels of two pistols.

And everything stopped.

As if from a distance, Brady watched the scene play out. He could actually *see* two bullets pass each other in the air. His flew at Texas Jack and, on impact, slammed the gunman back against the wall as a brilliant red flower of blood blossomed on the man's starched white shirt.

But Jack's bullet had yet to hit. Brady stood his ground, watching it come. Knowing it had been aimed well and his life was almost over. From far away, he heard Davey shout, "Brady!"

Regret shot through him for chances missed and

love lost. He thought about the boy and Sam and Lily, but mostly, his mind locked onto the image of Patience. In an instant, he'd be with her again. He'd be able to touch her, hold her. And this time, it would be for eternity. With her face before him, he watched the bullet stop directly in front of him. Before he understood what was happening, the damn thing made a sharp right turn, avoiding him completely, and crashed harmlessly into the plank wall.

Patience. He staggered back as if the bullet had actually hit him. She'd saved him. Somehow, someway, she'd reached out from wherever she was to keep him safe.

"Damn it, *no,*" he murmured, wrapped in the pain he'd hoped would end.

And time started up again. A roar of sound hit him as voices and shouts echoed in and around him. He felt Davey when the boy's small body slammed into his. Absently, he hugged him, holding him tight until the boy's trembling eased. Then he looked down into tear-streaked features.

"I thought he was gonna kill you," the boy managed to say, though his lips curled and shook.

"I'm all right, Davey," he said, though inside, he felt far from all right. He'd wanted to be with Patience, but he had to accept that saving his life was her final gift to him.

And there had been a lot of gifts. Brady stood up and looked around the saloon at his friends and neighbors. Not one of them remembered Patience, but evidence of her presence was everywhere he looked. In the love Sam and Lily had found together against all odds. In Davey's features and trusting eyes. Hell, Brady thought, in his own heart, there was proof of Patience's existence. He'd been no better off than Davey.

But because of her, Brady knew, really *knew,* that love changes everything.

He ruffled the kid's hair and added, "I want you to stay here and wait for me, you hear?"

He nodded, wiped the back of his hand across his eyes, and asked, "Where you goin'?"

Brady lifted his gaze to stare across the room at the slice of daylight above the double swinging doors. "There's somebody I have to talk to." Then he looked down at the frightened boy again. "But I'll be back. I promise."

"Yessir," Davey said and reluctantly let him go.

With one last glance at him, Brady stepped around Davey and walked toward the door. He brushed past the well-wishers, left Sam and Lily staring after him as he quickened his strides.

Jumping off the boardwalk into the street, he silently challenged the dray wagons and the cowboys to run him down. But they went around him, or pulled up short, apparently unwilling to smash a fool into the dirt.

Brady hardly noticed. He stared at the church at the end of Main Street and headed right for it. His long legs ate up the distance quickly. His heart pounded, blood pumped through his body, and with every pulsebeat, his fury strengthened.

He took the five steps leading up to the double doors in two strides, grabbed one of the brass latches and threw the door open, letting it swing slowly shut behind him. His bootheels clattered loudly against the polished wood floor, but he didn't even hear it. His gaze locked on the simple cross jutting up from the pulpit, he kept walking until he came to a stop right in front of it.

"You want to punish me?" he shouted, stabbing his index finger at the cross. "Then do it quick. Just kill me and get it over with."

Nothing. No voice from the sky. No sensation of having been heard. But then, he really hadn't expected anything. All he wanted was a chance to speak his mind to a God who clearly didn't give a damn about him.

"You know," he said, shifting his gaze now to the beamed ceiling and what lay beyond. "You talk a good game. You've got Your preachers out, singing Your praises. Getting folks to bow and scrape. But what do You do for us?" He shook his head and a strangled laugh escaped his throat. "Hell, I just killed a man and You didn't even send me to hell."

Silence mocked him.

He kicked at the front pew and felt the solid smack of pain jolt all the way up his leg. Gritting his teeth, he reached up, tore off his hat and flung it into the shadowy corner. Tears stung the backs of his eyes, but he hadn't cried since that night on the riverboat what seemed a lifetime ago and he wasn't about to start now.

"You lied," he said. "All of Your preachers claim

that You think love is the greatest thing in the world. Well, I *had* love. For the first time in my whole damn, miserable life. I had love. And You *took* it!

Patience's features rose up in his mind and pain squeezed his insides until he nearly crumpled under the staggering weight of it. Reaching out blindly, he grabbed hold of the back of a pew and dug his fingers into the old, scarred wood.

"You snatched her away from me. Away from *us*." A choked-off laugh shot from his throat as he muttered, " 'Suffer the little children—' " He paused and gave the ceiling a withering stare. "You said that, didn't You? You care so much about children? What about Davey? What about taking away that kid's best chance at a mother?"

A whisper of sound pulsed briefly in the air around him and he half expected to be sizzled by a lightning bolt. But he was just too damn sick of it all to care.

His fingers tightened on the wooden pew until he wouldn't have been surprised to feel the wood snap in his grip.

"I want her back, You hear me?" he said, his voice harsh, scraping across his throat like shards of broken glass. "She belongs here with me. She loves me, damn it. And I love her." The words seemed to throb in the air around him. Just saying them aloud nearly did him in. Love. He'd found love when he'd given up hope. Found a life when he'd thought his was over. Found happiness when he'd thought that people like him weren't allowed such things.

And now it was all gone.

"Damn it!" he shouted, raising one fist and shaking it at the ceiling. "You broke Your word. You're the one who said marriage was a sacred thing. Well, Patience and me, we made a vow. Here. In Your house."

Thunder rumbled.

The little church trembled.

Brady didn't care.

"You don't scare me," he said, letting his hands fall to his sides. "You've already done your worst to me. You've taken Patience."

A sudden, howling wind screamed around the church like lost souls mourning the loss of heaven and Brady wanted to scream along with it. Instead, though, he shot one last look at the ceiling and in a flat, toneless voice, he said, "Yeah. You took her. But You can't take her out of my heart. That's something she gave *me*. Try as You might, there's some things even You can't do. That memory is mine. That love is *mine*." Brady blew out a breath. "You and me are through. I want nothing from You. And I'll be damned before I'll ever set foot in one of Your houses again."

He crossed the floor, bent down and scooped up his hat. Curling up the brim in one tight fist, he said, "Patience may be one of Your angels. But she's *my* wife. And damn it, my claim is stronger than Yours."

Above him, the ceiling creaked and groaned. The walls swayed in the harsh, unforgiving wind, and the stained-glass windows shivered.

And suddenly, everything went still.

A chill snaked along his spine.

Air left his lungs.

His vision blurred.

From directly behind him came the nearly musical clink of something small and metal falling, hitting the floor. A tiny golden ring rolled along the glistening wooden planks and landed beside his right foot.

He bent to pick it up, cradling it in the center of his palm. "Patience?"

"I'm here," she said softly.

He whirled around and nearly staggered. There she stood. Beautiful. Alive. Staring at him with wide-eyed wonder.

"You're back."

"I'm back," she agreed, looking at him as though she could never see enough of him. He looked tired, as though he hadn't slept in days. A week's worth of whisker stubble scarred his cheeks and his eyes held the echo of a pain she understood all too well. But despite everything, she thought, he looked wonderful to her.

She laughed then and the rippling joy in it sliced through him, carving away the darkness, splintering the shadowy depths within. He grabbed her, pulling her close, holding her tightly enough that if anyone tried to take her from him again, they'd have to take him as well.

"How?" he asked, running his hands up and down her back, caressing, stroking, assuring himself that she was real and his life was once more his own.

"He heard you," she said, wrapping her arms

around his neck and holding him as tightly as he did her. "You did it, Brady. You convinced Him that our love was too precious to be denied."

He moved his hands to cup her face, looking into her eyes and shaking his head. "I thought He was going to fry me with a lightning bolt."

She covered his hands with hers, turning her face to kiss his palm. "Maybe that was what persuaded Him. You risked His wrath. Risked your soul. For me. For love."

He bent his head until his forehead rested against hers and silently thanked the God he'd been cursing only moments before. "I would risk anything for you, Patience," he said, his whispered words a vow. "Heaven or hell. I love you more than my life."

A single tear rolled down her cheek and he shook his head. "No tears tonight," he told her. "Only smiles. And laughter. And loving."

"Yes, Brady."

Then it was his turn to laugh. Throwing his head back, he let the pure joy inside him rush into the stillness.

"What's so funny?" she asked, just a little defensively.

Still chuckling, he told her, "I figure that's probably the last time in my life I ever hear you say 'yes, Brady' so easily."

One corner of her mouth tilted into a reluctant smile.

"And that's just the way I want it," he said, looking into her eyes, willing her to see the depths of his love for her. Wanting her to know what having her in his life really meant to him.

"I do love you so," she said softly.

"And I you," Brady said, taking her left hand gently in his.

She looked up at him, heart in her eyes as he slowly slipped that tiny halo back onto her ring finger. Where it belonged. Then curling his hand over hers, he kissed that ring where it lay and made his vow one more time.

"I will love you forever," he said.

"And beyond," she added, lifting her face for a kiss that would seal their marriage and begin their life together.

Epilogue

THREE YEARS LATER . . .

"Patience," Brady said, mentally counting to ten. He made it to five and gave up. "Your daughter got into the paint again."

He clutched his two-year-old daughter's bright blue hand and still managed to keep her at a distance from his freshly pressed pants.

"Isn't it wonderful?" Patience asked. "I just know she's going to be a great artist one day."

"Uh-huh," Brady said, giving little Sarah a rueful glance as she wiped her free hand on his pants leg. "Either that or a vandal." But as he watched the tiny girl, she gave him that smile of hers and his insides melted into the gooey mess they'd been since the moment of her birth.

Amazing, really, he told himself as his gaze shifted to Patience, cuddling their infant son. He never would have believed that he could be so happy. It was as if he, too, had come to life on that dark night in the church when her halo had dropped at his feet.

"What are you thinking?" Patience asked, a slow smile curving her mouth as she walked to the edge of the boardwalk.

"Just that I'm a lucky man."

"I do love you so, Brady." She reached out and cupped his cheek in her palm and it was all Brady could do to keep from grabbing her up and carrying her off to their rooms above the saloon-turned-restaurant. But he could wait, he told himself. When all three kids were asleep, the night would belong to him and Patience.

And he would take the time to show her just how much he treasured her. Then smiling to himself, he acknowledged that if they kept this up, they'd have to add on rooms for all the children headed their way. Strange, he hadn't once regretted not building that house out on the knoll. The minute he'd found Patience, he'd realized that the only home he'd ever need was in her heart.

"Brady?"

"Hmm?"

"Didn't you talk to your son about racing that mare of his?"

"I did." And it hadn't been easy. The kid had led such a hard life up until three years ago that Brady tended to bend over backward to make that up to him. Still, as his father, he'd had to put his foot down. "I told Davey just yesterday—no more racing. He nearly broke his neck last week."

"Oh dear."

Brady followed her gaze and shook his head. Apparently, it was time for another talk. "Be careful," he shouted.

"I must have help," Ezekial told his superiors. "Davey Shaw is wearing me out. No guardian angel should have to work this hard."

"He's a thirteen-year-old boy," a stern voice reminded him. "You have nearly two hundred years on him."

"And it isn't enough," Ezekial murmured, shifting his gaze to follow his charge as the boy ran for the livery stable. "Now look. He's going riding again. If it wasn't for my diligence, he would have fallen from the horse when he jumped that ravine last week."

"That's your job," another voice intoned.

"Yes, but—" It was no use and he knew it. Ezekial would spend the rest of Davey Shaw's life riding herd on him. No easy task. But, he told himself, at least he was a good-hearted—if too adventurous—youngster. It might have been worse, Ezekial reminded himself. He could have been put in charge of Sam and Lily's little boy. The child was a ring-tailed terror—into everything and absolutely fearless. Or, Ezekial thought, he might have been assigned to one of Patience and Brady Shaw's other children.

He shuddered at the thought. Already, the two-year-old Sarah was more of a handful than Davey had ever been. And six-month-old Andrew looked to be the kind of spirited child who would run any guardian angel into the ground.

Ezekial glanced at Patience, standing on the

boardwalk in front of the restaurant. Brady stepped up behind her and laid one protective arm around both her and their baby and Ezekial shook his head. One would think that a former guardian angel would give birth to children with at least a modicum of decorum.

But then, Patience had never been an easy angel herself.

A boy's high-pitched shout of pure glee reached him and Ezekial groaned as Davey, astride his mare, left the livery at a fast gallop.

No, he thought. Heaven had never been so much work. Then, tipping his halo into a fighting tilt, Ezekial took off after the boy, muttering complaints as he flew.

Wish Upon a Cowboy

KATHLEEN KANE

Jonas Mackenzie isn't sure what to make of the beautiful stranger who showed up at his Wyoming ranch with marriage on her mind. While he's trying hard to ignore the sparks flying between them, Hannah Lowell is a woman on a mission with a stubborn streak as wide as his own.

Hannah hadn't been thrilled at the idea of marrying a man she didn't know . . . until she had a good look at the lean and rugged cowboy who was her destiny. But how is she going to convince a man who doesn't believe in magic, that he's got the power to save a town from a terrible fate? And that it all boils down to his belief in his legacy, his heart, and in the most powerful magic of all . . . their love.

"True to her talent, Kane keeps the conflicts lively to the end and fills the plot with many surprises."
—Publishers Weekly